A NOVEL

Finished @
3:57 AM ~
13 October,
2021

DICK TRACY

A NOVEL

← Warren
Beatty
art work
as is
shown
on the
cover!

by

Max Allan Collins

BASED ON A SCREENPLAY

BY JIM CASH & JACK EPPS, JR.

AND ✓

BO GOLDMAN & WARREN BEATTY

AND

THE COMIC STRIP CREATED

BY CHESTER GOULD

BANTAM BOOKS

NEW YORK • TORONTO • LONDON • SYDNEY • AUCKLAND

EDITOR'S NOTE
*The following novel was freely adapted from the screenplay to
the film Dick Tracy and draws on the rich sixty-year history of the
great detective. While true to the story of the film, there are scenes
and characters that do not appear
in the finished motion picture.*

DICK TRACY

A Bantam Book / June 1990

ISBN 0-553-28528-9

Published simultaneously in the United States and Canada

---

*Bantam Books are published by Bantam Books, a division of Bantam Doubleday
Dell Publishing Group, Inc. Its trademark consisting of the words "Bantam Books"
and the portrayal of a rooster, is Registered in U.S. Patent and Trademark Office
and in other countries, Marca Registrada. Bantam Books, 666 Fifth Avenue, New
York, New York 10103.*

PRINTED IN THE UNITED STATES OF AMERICA

0 9 8 7 6 5 4 3 2 1

A TIP OF THE FEDORA

I would like to thank my agent Dominick Abel, for his patience and persistence; Elyce Small Goldstein, director of licensing, Tribune Media Services; Matt Masterson, my friend and the world's top TRACY fan, who provided research material and support; actor Ed O'Ross, "Itchy" in the film version of this story, who lent support and help; Robyn Tynan of Disney Publications; Barrie Osborne, Executive Producer of the film, for providing valuable guidance; George Bamber of Mulholland Productions for his intelligent and thorough suggestions; Mike Argirion, editor of Tribune Media Services, for helping put this project in motion; Robert S. Reed, president of Tribune Media Services, who (with my former editor Don Michel) selected me as the writer of the "Dick Tracy" strip back in 1977; Lou Aronica, Robert Simpson and Colleen O'Shea of Bantam Books; Paul Thomas, for background information regarding vintage recording devices; my lovely, talented wife, Barbara Collins, for helping prepare a detailed synopsis of the screenplay; and my ornery seven-year-old son Nathan, who provided inspiration for a certain character in these pages.

"The Kid"!

M.A.C.

To the memory of Chester Gould.

Thank you, Chet . . .
from the eight year-old kid
you encouraged.

— 1 —

Once upon a hard time, in a cold gray city on a cold gray lake, a nameless urchin, the pockets of his frayed jacket filled with other people's watches and wallets, ducked into an alley, avoiding the cop on the beat.

The boy scooted behind a cluster of garbage cans, startling a mangy cat who was nestled there nibbling at a fish head. The cat, as gray as the overcast afternoon, and looking only slightly less scruffy than the boy himself, reared back and snarled, its fur standing up like porcupine needles.

Scrawny as it was, the cat looked to be a vicious beast, but the kid wasn't scared; almost routinely, he slapped it with one of the leather billfolds and the cat yowled and scurried down the alley, its claws clicking on the bricks.

The gray cat might have seemed an omen of bad luck to the kid, only it wasn't exactly black, and besides, the kid didn't believe in any kind of luck, good or bad. To him life was a matter of survival, pure and simple—well, more like impure and not so simple. He was as much an animal, a scavenger, as the cat he'd spooked.

He was eight years old, but he didn't know that; he was the illegitimate child of a chorus girl who'd left him behind at her rooming house, but he didn't know that, either. He knew only a life of stealing and scrounging at the behest of a tramp called Steve, who had no last name that the kid knew of, but still had one more name than the kid. In fact, that was as close to a name as the kid had: the Kid. And the Kid could not remember any life

1

before this one, this life as the chattel of his burly, unshaven Fagin.

The boy huddled against the brick wall of the building, hoping the beat cop—there was a pair of them, actually—would not check the alley. He was big for an eight-year-old, though sewer-rat skinny, his hair a reddish mop sticking out from under an oversized cap copped from a railroad worker; his threadbare black jacket had once belonged to an adult—its elbows were carelessly patched, as were the knees of his raggedy blue denims. Within his shoes, which were too large for him, were pieces of cardboard, covering the holes in the soles.

Winter was coming, and he and Steve would soon hop the rails to a warmer clime—or at least so the Kid hoped. That was the best part of living with Steve—seeing the world; the Kid had been in small towns, he'd spent time on farms, he'd seen the West, he'd been to New York, too. This here town was okay—plenty of open-air markets to cop fruit and vegetables off stands, some nice parks to sleep in, railroad dicks less mean than some places; but it was no place to spend the winter, the wind riding in off the lake like a witch on her broom, chilling your bones.

Convinced the beat cops had moved along on their way, the Kid sighed with satisfaction as he spread his spoils out before him on the table that was the alley's brick floor. Three wallets and two watches. Steve ought to be pleased. The watches—one a fancy wrist number on a leather band, the other a gold-plated pocket watch—would together bring in three or four bucks from that pawnshop fence Steve had been using.

But when the Kid dug into the wallets, he came up near empty: one buck in one, two bucks in the other, and nothing at all in the third. Usually a five-spot would show up in one out of three. The Kid sighed again, this time in weariness and frustration. Steve would beat the tar out of him, sure.

Of course Steve beat the tar out of him on general principles, even after a good day; but a disappointing haul like this would get the Kid a whale of a licking. A bad haul was out of the question: the Kid wouldn't go back to Steve, *couldn't* go back to Steve, with little or nothing. Not unless he wanted to lose a tooth or two, or go to sleep for three days, like that one time.

A loud rumble made the Kid jump. It sounded like a freight roaring into the trainyard, or maybe the noise the ground might make cracking apart in one of those earthquakes they say happened out West sometimes.

But it was only the sky.

Thunder, threatening rain. Yesterday he'd got caught out in it; it came down straight, and it came down hard, and had seemed to the Kid a fusillade fired from thousands of angels with tommy guns, aimed right at him. Today he wasn't about to get caught out in it.

On this cold gray dying afternoon, as what there was of the sun began slipping below the horizon like another sneak thief, the Kid gathered the money and the watches, stuffed them in his pockets, and dumped the wallets in the nearest trash can; and he moved down the alley, till he found the recession of a doorway where he could get out of the line of watery fire the rumbling sky was promising.

At least it wasn't cold enough, yet, for snow, the Kid thought, and he pulled the lapels of the oversize tattered coat up around his face and leaned back against the door.

And it gave way.

Just a bit; but it had been unlocked and just barely shut, or barely not shut, and the Kid almost started to believe in luck. Because he suddenly had a dry, relatively warm place to be.

Slipping inside, shutting the door quietly, he found himself in a garage. Various trucks and automobiles were parked in neat rows, over across from him, and off to the left, along the Seventh Street side, were double garage-doors. To the right was a service area where the hood of a car was up, the engine being worked on, only not right now. Tools were scattered around, but it was after hours. A glassed-in office area was in the corner adjacent to the service area. Nobody was working here.

But five men were playing.

Playing cards, poker, their chairs pulled up to a bright yellow table. On a fruit crate nearby was a radio with a plug plugged into a couple of extension cords trailing off somewhere; from the radio came a hillbilly band, making a racket.

A pretty crummy backdrop, the Kid thought, for five guys who were dressed up so natty. It seemed odd to him, for a second, the expensive wide-lapelled suits with the colored silk shirts and bright ties and fifty-buck fedoras—till he saw the men's faces, and realized who it was that dressed so fancy at crazy hours, at ill-suited places.

Hoodlums.

On the table—amid the clutter of cards, paper money, ashtrays, beer, and whiskey bottles—were several revolvers and an automatic. This would not seem a game worth cheating in.

The Kid, still in the shadows, remained unnoticed by the five hoods seated in the center of the big high-ceilinged garage, under the room's only lit lamp, a hanging shade that sent a cone of light down on them like a spotlight presenting the star attractions of the afternoon.

And the Kid meant to stay unnoticed—and to stay warm, and dry; he ducked behind a stack of boxes. He nudged a box and bottles clanked, and an oil can clunked to the floor.

Several grim faces at the table turned his way. From his vantage point, ducked down as he was, he didn't see this. But then, on his belly like a snake, he peeked around the corner of the boxes, fronted by a row of fifty-gallon metal drums, and did see two of the men rise, each of them filling a hand with a revolver.

But another of the men at the table, an odd duck with a large round face and tiny features, said, "Sit down, Shoulders! It's nothin'."

"I heard something," the one called Shoulders said. The guy had a thin, pockmarked face and shoulders so wide he might've had a plank under his bright green suit-coat.

Only that was no plank: it was really shoulders. And the man called Shoulders looked dangerous as green-rainbowed meat; and right now he was moving across the cement floor toward the Kid's dark nook.

The Kid gritted his teeth, balled his little fists, rose up on his haunches, though still not up above the boxes.

"Little Face is right, Shoulders," called out the other one who'd risen. He was a big guy smoking a cigar; his mustard-color suitcoat was off and his dark green shirt was cut by suspenders. "It's just thunder—gonna rain, maybe."

"Look, Stooge," Shoulders said, "I *heard* something *drop*."

"It's the sound of your money droppin' into my pocket," another of the guys at the table said. This one was a muscular-looking horror with a heavily ridged forehead. He wore a suit that was redder than blood and a shirt as black as death and a tie that was redder than the suit. "Come on back here and play cards."

"You ain't my mother, Brow," Shoulders said crankily, as he prowled.

The revolver clunked on the yellow table as Stooge sat back down and said, "Who didn't ante up?"

5

"Careful with that rod of yours, Stooge," another one said. Under his derby was a round, ratty face, cigarette dangling in his lips, bobbling as he spoke. He had slick black hair and a whiskery mustache; wore a purple suit and matching shirt and tie. "It'll go off, tossin' it around like that. It ain't no toy."

"You're such a nervous little girl," Stooge said, studying his cards. "I almost hate to take your money. I hate to make a little girl cry."

"Just be careful! When I die, I want it on purpose, not by accident. What was that?"

The Kid heard it, too—something rustling in the darkness.

The Rodent stood; his nose and mouth twitched. His eyes moved back and forth.

Then that mangy gray cat—how did *he* get in here?—stepped into the pool of light.

"I *told* you I heard somethin'," Shoulders said, vindicated.

"Hiya fella," Rodent said to the cat.

With frightening quickness, Rodent grabbed the animal and flung it by its tail into a wall of drums. The cat screeched and skittered away into the dark to lick its wounds.

"You're a card, Rodent," Stooge said.

"Speaking of cards," Brow said, "who dealt this mess?"

Several hands went by uneventfully, and the Kid—hoods or not, grateful to be in where it was warm and dry—settled himself on the cement floor and curled up and allowed himself to fall into a state approaching sleep.

He never let himself go quite under, though, and snatches of conversation would come his way: "Don't breathe that clam-sauce breath of yours on me, Shoulders!" "Shut up and deal, Rodent!" "Are we gonna hit

Caprice or not?" "The boss ain't said yet—just play cards."

"Uh oh!" the one called Stooge said, and he said it loud enough to startle the Kid.

Alert now, the Kid again peeked around the edge of the stacked boxes.

"What's wrong with you?" Shoulders asked, in a casually disgusted tone.

"I drew aces and eights," Stooge said, cards tumbling from his fingers.

"The dead man's hand!" Rodent squealed.

"Are you girls kidding?" Shoulders said. "You throw down a hand like that? You coulda won with that hand!"

"He did the right thing!" Rodent said. "It's the dead man's hand, I tell you!"

"Rodent," Little Face said, cards held daintily in his two hands, a big smile on his little face, "this ain't Deadwood, and you are not Wild Bill Hickok."

"Bad luck," Rodent said, standing, shivering, cigarette tumbling from his lips, "bad luck!"

A loud rumble made the Kid jump.

But this time it wasn't the sky.

One of those double garage-doors along Seventh Street burst open, like a jack-in-the-box, only it was nothing so harmless as a grinning toy clown, even if the grille of the black sedan that had splintered its way into the garage did seem to be grinning—a wide, ghastly silver grin.

Frozen with fear, but fascinated, the Kid peered over the tops of the boxes and drums as the sedan screeched in, coming to a sideways stop. A man leaned out the open door and stood on the running board, a tommy gun in his hand, but he was no angel and the rain he poured on the room was a lead rain.

The Kid ducked back down, his mind filled with the face of the man spraying those tommy-gun slugs; it was a horrible face, a face that branded itself into the Kid's consciousness: hooded eyes, pug nose, Cupid's-bow mouth, heart-shaped, pimpled face, and a head as flat as an anvil.

"Flattop!" somebody shouted.

It was Little Face, who had been dealing when the cardplaying quintet had been so rudely and violently interrupted; Little Face threw the cards into the air and scattered them all about, and he and the other four scattered the same way, heading for cover, grabbing their guns off the table as they went.

But Rodent didn't make it very far.

Flattop traced an angular line of fire across his back, which sent Rodent twitching to the cement. Then Rodent calmed down once and for all.

Flattop, imperturbable in his violet sport coat and bright blue tie under his long, dark topcoat, smiled faintly, and fanned the tommy gun around the room, chewing up metal and glass.

Stooge tumbled from behind a delivery truck.

Flattop paused in his machine-gunning to laugh, reached inside the black sedan where somebody was handing him out another tommy gun, like a caddy handing the proper wood to a golfer. Changing magazines was too much time and trouble.

The Kid, huddled against the wall behind the drums, wondered why nobody else had returned fire. That Flattop guy was standing out in the open, like he was unafraid, like he thought nobody could hurt him.

Of course, those guys had revolvers and automatics, and Flattop was blasting away with a Chicago typewriter, against which handguns were like party favors, and anyway, if they fired at him, they'd give their positions away. The Kid nodded. They're smart. They're waiting for him to get close. Then they'll shoot.

The air cracked, as somebody did; Flattop whirled and

wrote something obscene with his "typewriter," and Shoulders tumbled from the running board of the parked auto he was firing behind.

"That leaves two," Flattop yelled above the din of the tommy gun, which he was spraying around the room; one of the wooden chairs fairly flew off the floor and danced in the air and seemed to explode into fragments. The bullets kissed and kissed and kissed the metal of trucks and autos, leaving puckers behind, windshields shattering here, spiderwebbing there. The radio exploded and cut off the hillbilly band. The glass of the corner office area turned to shards and fell noisily to the cement and made even smaller pieces of themselves. Bottles in the stacked boxes burst and broke and bled whiskey and gin.

Flattop was empty again; gray smoke curled out of the Thompson barrel. He had the empty gun in one hand and was reaching back to his unseen assistant in the sedan for another loaded one, when Brow came screaming out of somewhere, firing his revolver.

Several bullets stitched the sedan door just behind him, but Flattop merely looked casually Brow's way, as if the flying slugs were gnats, a nuisance requiring swatting. With a fresh tommy gun in hand, Flattop tore off a volley and the Brow went down, limbs askew, like a dime store paper skeleton doing its dance.

"That leaves you, Little Face," Flattop said.

There was silence.

"Come on out, Little Face," Flattop said. His voice was sweet. Melodic. His hooded eyes gave him a lazy look.

Little Face stepped out from behind a parked truck.

His tiny features were squinched in irritation.

"What's wrong with you, Flattop?" Little Face said. "You coulda killed me!"

"It's a dangerous business we're in," Flattop said, blandly.

"I *left* the side door open for you!" Little Face's tiny teeth were clenched. "Jeez, what's the idea of coming in like gangbusters? Every cop in town'll be here in two minutes."

The Kid was edging toward the door; it was so close. . . .

"I don't think so," Flattop was saying. "We paid off the beat cops with a sap. And there's a thunderstorm coming. Also, this neighborhood minds its own business."

"That's your opinion. I must say I don't much like your style."

Flattop shrugged; the tommy gun moved with his shoulders. "No hard feelings. Anyway, I appreciate the tipoff, Little Face. And I appreciate you leaving the side door open. I just like to do things my own way."

The Kid was by the door, sitting by that door, but he couldn't reach the knob unless he stood up.

"Well, fine," Little Face said to Flattop, gesturing dismissively, about to turn, "but let's both take our separate powders. You tell Big Boy he can pay me off later—there's no time, now."

"We'll make time," Flattop said, and he fired a burst from the tommy gun.

Little Face hung in the air for a long moment, enormous surprise taking the tiny features; and then fell flat on his little face.

"Lezgidoutaher," a voice from the sedan said.

"Not yet, Mumbles," Flattop said. "Not yet. Gimme a hand, Itchy—if you can spare one. Get their wallets."

There were two men in the black sedan; the driver was the mush-mouthed one, a sulky hood in an amber-colored cashmere topcoat. The other, who now climbed out of the car, scratching his neck impulsively, was a blond, purse-lipped hoodlum with Coke-bottle glasses.

The Kid's hand reached up and touched the cold metal knob.

Like an angel of death in his dark topcoat, Itchy was going from corpse to corpse, removing wallets and other identification, while Flattop surveyed the scene with a demented-cherub expression, and the boy turned the knob.

He turned the knob and opened the door and let in the sound of thunder.

It froze the boy for just a fraction of a second.

Flattop looked sharply over and brought the tommy gun up and fired.

But the weapon was empty. There was only a tiny, impotent clicking, and the Kid was out the door, in the alley, in the street, running into a damp, darkening night and a damp, dark world that was his, where the likes of Flattop would never find him.

Flattop pursued the little brat into the alley, but the boy was gone by the time he got out there.

"Kidsawya," Mumbles said, slouching behind the wheel of the black sedan.

"I *know* he saw me. That's why I chased him into the alley, you moron!"

"Dincatchem," Mumbles said.

"No kiddin'."

"Gidagulukatim?"

"No, I didn't get a good look at him!"

Itchy was already back in the sedan. "Shake a leg, Flattop! For cryin' out loud! We gotta get goin'!"

"Ishysishy," Mumbles said, with a childish grin.

"So what if Itchy's itchy," Flattop said irritably. "We ain't quite done, yet. Get me that last tommy."

Mumbles handed Flattop the final Thompson submachine gun and the flat-headed gunman beamed beatifically, seeming at once maniacal and relaxed, as cordite singed the air, and the tommy gun echoed and rang in the big room.

2

The fat lady was singing, but the opera wasn't nearly over.

Dick Tracy slumped in his plush, padded seat, unable to resist the urge to doze. A gently reproving look from the slender beauty beside him—one Tess Trueheart—made him straighten temporarily, but a long morning at headquarters, catching up with weeks of paperwork he'd put off, conspired with the boredom of culture with a capital C, to make the plainclothes detective's eyelids grow heavy.

Among all these tuxedos and gowns, his severe black suit with red and black tie stood out; but on his salary, Tracy couldn't really spare the tuxedo rental. The public, and Tess, would have to accept him as he was: a working cop on a budget.

After all, Tracy was not here to please himself. He was here to make three people happy. First and most important was Tess herself; attending this charity matinee performance of something called *Die Schlumpf* at the Civic Opera House, amidst assorted faces straight off the society page, was a rare treat for a working girl. How could he deny his sweetheart the thrill of viewing the city's cultural event of the moment?

These seats, incidentally, had been provided them by another of the persons he wanted to make happy with his presence: Diet Smith.

Smith was a wealthy industrialist who had taken a big interest in the local police after Tracy cleared the millionaire of a murder frame-up. Since then Smith had set his regiments of researchers and inventors to work on various gadgets, the latest and potentially most applicable of which was a two-way wrist radio—a portable police-band radio no bigger than a wristwatch. In fact, it *was* a wristwatch, keeping perfect time in addition to its sending/receiving capacities.

Tracy was wearing one of the handful of experimental models right now. As Chief of Detectives, he had distributed the wristwatchlike devices to the half-dozen members of the Major Crimes squad he personally headed up. Nobody was quite used to them yet, and there was some grousing, but Tracy saw the two-ways as heralding a future where policework would be more scientific, more technologically advanced.

Diet Smith was a true ally in the war on crime, and Tracy meant to keep the rotund multimillionaire happy. And when Smith made a gift of his seats to the premiere performance of an opera directed by actor Vitamin Flintheart, there was no way Tracy could graciously decline.

Beyond that, there was Flintheart himself, who had been helpful to Tracy in several cases that had veered into the theatrical world. The pompous old ham had a big heart, and Tracy had come to be very fond of him; Flintheart had organized a group of actors who regularly made the rounds of hospitals, orphanages, and soup kitchens, giving free shows.

Tall, dignified, and utterly self-absorbed, actor Vitamin Flintheart (the nickname came from a propensity toward chugging health tonics and popping vitamin pills in pursuit of a youth long since fled) was not merely directing the opera. He had taken on one of the leading roles. Even now he was joining in with the heavyset soprano whose steel breastplates and Norse horn helmet matched Vitamin's own, though admittedly each cut his or her own distinct figure. With his flowing silver-white hair and mustache darkened for the stage, Flintheart—

famed for his striking profile, drinking problem, and squandered talent—made a less than convincingly youthful Viking.

But the actor had a melodious, soothing voice, which lulled the detective to sleep—until the formidable soprano would reach for an earsplitting high C, her voice all but shaking the paint off the Opera House walls, and jarring Tracy awake.

"Dick," Tess whispered. "Please try to stay awake."

She wasn't at all cross about it; but at least a little embarrassed.

"I was resting my eyes, dear," he whispered back.

"You were snoring," she said, and smiled in her crinkly, endearing way, cornflower blue eyes sparkling. She wore a handsome dark green dress and matching hat—modest but stylish, and definitely attractive.

"Sorry," he said, smiling back at her.

Her eyes narrowed. "Vitamin certainly has knobby knees, for a Viking."

"Vitamin has knobby knees anyway you look at it," Tracy said.

Boredom soon settled in again. Tracy's eyes moved above and to the right, where the Mayor and his wife, and the District Attorney and a bejeweled society-girl date, shared box seats. The Mayor was a heavyset, balding West Side politico who wheeled-and-dealed his way into office, building ethnic coalitions around the city; he and his matronly wife were dressed to the teeth, but going the cultural route was obviously purely a political move on their part. The Mayor had his eye on the statehouse.

D.A. Fletcher was His Honor's heir apparent. Handsome, mustached, graying at the temples, Fletcher was smooth with the public and the press, and one of the best courtroom prosecutors Tracy had ever seen. But the detective was uncomfortable with the D.A.'s social climbing and political aspirations. Fletcher was the kind of

D.A. who would bounce any case he didn't feel he had a lock on winning and who would not prosecute anybody if the wrong toes were getting stepped on.

Tracy and Fletcher enjoyed a limited truce, whereas the Mayor was consistently fawning over his young Chief of Detectives. His Honor was grooming Tracy for the Chief of Police slot—Chief Brandon, who'd hired Tracy, was nearing retirement—but Tracy wasn't eager for this advancement.

This morning, plowing through all that deskwork was a reminder to him that even his role as Chief of Detectives was more bureaucratic than he'd like. He hadn't gotten into this line of work to sit behind a desk. He liked field work; he liked chasing down crooks and clues, just like Sherlock Holmes in the stories he'd read as a kid.

Funny. Growing up in a little town in the Midwest, his father a local attorney whose speciality was wills and contracts, not criminal cases, Tracy had never even day-dreamed of being a detective, despite his interest in Nick Carter dime novels and Sir Arthur Conan Doyle's tales of the Great Detective. He'd gone to the big city with a nest egg (provided partly by his father and partly through his own summer-job savings) to attend business college. Which he had, and he'd graduated with honors.

Being a cop had never been part of the plan.

But shortly after he graduated, he'd gone to call on Tess, his college sweetheart, hoping to gather courage to propose. Had he done so, and had she said yes, it would have made him the happiest young man in the country, or anyway the city. Of course, he'd gone to the Trueheart home (Tess's folks had become like second parents to him) on many a night, with proposing in mind; but he'd never quite found the words. . . .

That particular evening, however, had been different. Not because Tracy had finally summoned his courage to pop the question; he hadn't. But because, while Tracy and Tess were in the upstairs parlor courting, Mr. Trueheart had been robbed in his first-floor delicatessen.

Two armed thieves demanded Emil Trueheart open his safe—in which he kept his life savings, having lost over five hundred dollars in small bank failures not so long ago—and Mr. Trueheart refused, and fought back.

The two thieves shot the old man; two slugs in the chest.

Tracy, hearing the gunfire, had rushed downstairs and got the butt of an automatic on the back of his skull for his trouble.

In a melodramatic moment that Vitamin Flintheart might well have relished, a tearful Tracy swore vengeance over the corpse of his sweetheart's father. But even in the colder, more rational light of day, when all the melodrama was drained out of him, Tracy had been determined to find those two thieving murderers.

He had gone to Chief Brandon, who attached him temporarily to the plainclothes squad; and after he tracked the two thieves down—in fact shot them dead when they were kind enough to draw down on him—he found himself invited by Brandon permanently aboard.

The two thieves had been low-level hoodlums whose allegiance was to Alphonse Capricio, A.K.A. Al "Big Boy" Caprice, one of the city's most powerful gangsters. Tracy could hardly leave the force until he'd brought down the Big Boy himself—otherwise, he wouldn't really have kept the promise he made over Mr. Trueheart's bullet-racked body.

That was several years ago, and Big Boy still had not been brought to justice; like so many big-shot gangsters, Caprice was well-insulated, with scores of underlings doing his illicit bidding. In that same short time, however, Tracy had been put in charge of the city's detective squads, and had formed the select Major Crimes squad, bringing dozens of criminals—mobsters, murderers, outlaws—to meet their just desserts—and sometimes their maker. Now Dick Tracy's profile was at least as famous as that ham actor's down on stage—in this burg, anyway.

The attention embarrassed Tracy—the editorial cartoonists exaggerating his shovel jaw and hooked nose into something absurd, the national newspaper syndicates hounding him to let them assign a "ghost" to write up his "casebook," Hollywood making noises about doing a movie biography—and it had, to a degree, hampered his effectiveness on the job. The time when Dick Tracy could go undercover, for example, was long since past.

And now his success was threatening to take him out of the action and put him in bureaucratic mothballs altogether. It was a dilemma, all right; the increased money—to a man who hoped one day to get married, buy a house, fill it with kids—was a serious consideration.

It could also be argued that, from the command-post position of Police Chief, he might be able to direct an all-out war on crime, and in the bigger picture accomplish much more than he was able to out in the streets. Maybe that would be what it would take to bring down the Big Boys of organized crime.

Still, the successes of a commanding general could never compare to the foot-soldier thrills of engaging in individual skirmishes.

"Calling Dick Tracy," a scratchy, loud voice said. "Calling Dick Tracy!"

The voice was coming from his wrist.

It startled Tracy momentarily, and then he bent over in his seat, as if tying his shoes, but cocking the side of his head to his raised wrist, even as he adjusted the volume lower on the two-way gizmo, from which the rather high-pitched voice of his partner, Detective Pat Patton, had crackled.

"What is it, Pat?" he whispered.

Tess was sinking into her seat. The eyes of the packed Opera House were on them—on the main floor, and in the balconies alike, the theater was a sea of faces turned their way. Not a patron was paying any heed, at this moment, to Vitamin Flintheart's Wagnerian excesses.

"We've got five dead hoods over at the Seventh Street garage," Pat's voice said breathlessly over the staticky two-way. "I never saw anything so vicious, Tracy."

"Have you I.D.'d the stiffs?"

"That's just it—we can't even tell who they are, or were. They've been shot to pieces."

The Opera House, seeing only an apparently vacant seat where Tracy had ducked down, had returned their attention, perhaps reluctantly, to Vitamin's musicale. Both the D.A. and the Mayor were hanging over their box seat, however, straining to listen to this little drama, as it came over Tracy's wrist; Tess, too. Any thought of embarrassment had flown from her mind—her eyes reflected only concern.

"Don't let anybody touch a thing, Pat. I'm on my way."

Sitting up straight, he gave Tess's hand a quick squeeze and said, "I'm sorry."

She smiled just a little. "No, you're not. Don't *you* get shot to pieces."

"I think the shooting's over for tonight. Anyway, I'll try to make it back for Vitamin's big death scene."

"Take your time," she told him wryly, as he rose. "Vitamin will no doubt take his."

he corpses littering the cement floor of the garage on Seventh Street hadn't taken *their* time dying. It had been sudden and it had been brutal.

The gawkers had found their way here; uniformed men had roped off the area where the garage door had been, prior to the killers' car bursting through it. Chief Brandon, on the sidelines, was explaining to the forensic team that he wanted Tracy's opinion before letting them take over. The rain had not yet come, but the thunder continued to provide its occasional punctuation. Dusk was settling on the city like fog.

Tracy, his yellow camel's hair topcoat hanging open, his yellow snapbrim fedora pushed back on his head, stood with hands on hips as he stared grimly down at a bullet-torn body. He nodded and Pat Patton covered the corpse back up.

Patton stood, sighed, tucked his hands in the pockets of his emerald topcoat, his Kelly-green derby pulled down almost to the eyebrows of his round, open face, which was as white as the underbelly of a fish. Of a dead fish.

"I thought we'd seen it *all* by now, Dick," Pat said. He shook his head. "This takes the cake. These babies are obliterated."

"Somebody used a tommy gun like a buzz saw," Tracy said. He gestured. "Look at all the spent shells. They're everywhere."

Shell casings were scattered about the vast cement floor like golden confetti.

"'Cept for the crime-scene shutterbug and the M.E., we haven't let any of the boys in," Patton said, nodding toward the Chief, "'cause of your standing orders to diagram the crime scene, and mark the location of every scrap of evidence and every spent shell, 'fore anything's touched or moved. But Tracy, these babies are gonna get ripe before we get that done."

"Then hold your breath," Tracy advised. "And pick up every one of those shells with your tweezers, and put 'em in individual evidence envelopes, noting their location."

"We're gonna run out of envelopes."

"Then send out for more."

Patton made a face, shrugged. "Dick, it's obviously a Thompson submachine gun. Forty-five caliber slugs with the characteristic breech-face marks, firing-pin marks, and shell bulge."

"I agree. That's a nice analysis, Pat."

Patton grinned. "So—all we need is one or two samples."

Tracy shook his head, no. "Pick up every slug."

Patton's grin fell.

"We're going to check for prints and run ballistics, too," Tracy said. He knelt over by the parked delivery trucks. "The victims seem to have returned fire, little good though it did 'em." He pointed forcefully at Patton. "We want those individual weapons identified. And any prints sorted out."

Tracy walked over to the central area where it looked like it had snowed spent shells. Black tiremarks streaked the gray floor. "The car that broke through those garage doors left its own sort of fingerprints; have Casey get closeups of those skidmarks."

Patton nodded and hustled off to get evidence envelopes and tweezers from the squad car.

The newest member of the Major Crimes squad, rumpled-faced, freckled Sam Catchem, was at the periphery,

20

where lab technicians, various detectives, morgue attendants, and Casey, the crime-scene photographer, waited with the onlookers, behind the roped area by the ruptured doors. Tracy moved methodically around the room, lifting the sheets off corpses one by one and studying the victims.

Pat Patton began gathering the spent shells and recording them in his field notes, while Chief Brandon moved away from the forensic team to join his ace detective. Brandon was a husky man with a rock jaw, a ski nose, and black-marble eyes. He moved through the garage like a tank.

"Watch your step, Chief," Catchem said wryly, as the Chief didn't seem to notice Patton in his path, crouching over the slugs with his tweezers like a little kid searching for four-leaf clovers.

Brandon nodded at Patton, and did indeed watch his step; it amused Tracy to see the big fullback of a man trying to dance daintily around the evidence.

"Five dead men," the Chief said grimly, "and we don't even know who the hell they are."

Catchem approached lazily, a cigarette drooping from his full lips, hands in the pockets of his rust-color topcoat. "Whoever did it took their I.D.," he said, "but didn't take a dime."

"When you're through with that cigarette, Sam," Tracy said not unkindly, "don't toss it in here. . . . I don't want the evidence compromised."

Tracy was studying a burly corpse whose red suit was matched by a bloody face; the most distinguishable remaining feature was a heavily ridged forehead.

The Chief laughed humorlessly. "How in heaven's name are we supposed to identify *that*? Are all these birds the same? Riddled with slugs and stripped of I.D.?"

Tracy nodded. "Unless, when they're stripped at the morgue, some laundry marks turn up."

"It's going to be impossible to make 'em."

"This one's street moniker is the Brow," Tracy said casually. "East Coast boy. Red Hooks Gang graduate. List of aliases that would fill a phone book."

"How in . . ."

Tracy stood. "Note the prominently ridged forehead."

The Chief, visibly impressed, removed his white cap with its shining gold badge and scratched his head, ruffling his snow-white hair. "Can you make any of the others?"

Tracy walked to another corpse and nodded to Catchem to remove the sheet. "This is a Detroit Purple Gang torpedo they call the Rodent."

"*Called* the Rodent," Catchem corrected with a smirk.

The Chief's eyes were wide and a little glazed. "He looks like just another one of these shot-up stiffs to me."

"That long nose and weak chin, even after the tommy-gun damage, are the key identifying features." Tracy bent down and turned over one of the body's palms, so that the knuckles faced up. "Those nails are chewed to the quick. Rodent was a nervous little rat."

Tracy strode over to another corpse and Catchem kept up, flipping the sheet off the next body Tracy was calling the Chief's attention to.

This one was a thin but wide-shouldered thug in a dark green suit and a green and tan tie that bore a violent abstract design.

"You can see why the boys called this fella Shoulders," Tracy said matter-of-factly. "West Coast free-lance torpedo."

The Chief seemed frankly amazed. "How do you . . ."

"You know, Chief," Tracy said with gentle sarcasm, those circulars the other P.D.'s and the F.B.I. send around aren't just to help decorate our bulletin boards."

The detective moved along to the next body. He glanced at Catchem, who took the silent cue and pulled back the sheet like a magician pulling a tablecloth out from under a fully set table, a table that remained motionless. Like the body that had just been revealed.

"This fella was something of a dude," Tracy said, "even if he did die in his suspenders, with his coat off."

Catchem's face—which seemed somehow mournful and amused at the same time—revealed his frank but unsurprised admiration for the ranking officer's detecting abilities.

"Those are rubies in this pinkie ring," Tracy said, kneeling as if being knighted, taking the corpse's right hand in his own. "But underneath it all, he was just another stooge. . . ."

Tracy began unbuttoning the dead man's silk shirt.

"Tracy," the Chief said, "what are you . . ."

Tracy didn't respond; the answer to the Chief's question was on the exposed chest: a battleship—that is, a tattoo of a battleship, punctured here and there with entry wounds, but staying afloat on tattooed waves, nonetheless.

Tracy stood. "I'd rather not bother undressing him further, but you can take my word for it: he's got 'Mother' in a heart-shaped tattoo on his left arm, and 'Home Sweet Home' with some entwined flowers, on the other."

"Who *is* this stooge?" Chief Brandon asked, mystified.

"Stooge Viller." Tracy said.

Finally Tracy ended up where he began—with the first corpse he'd uncovered.

"Lift it, Sam," Tracy directed.

Catchem did.

"Surely you recognize *this* thief, Chief."

"He does look familiar, Tracy," the Chief said with heavy sarcasm. "He reminds me of four other fellas I saw of late, all of 'em doing their Swiss cheese impersonation."

"Look at the ears."

The Chief leaned over the body and squinted at it, specifically at either side of the big head. "Well, I'll be . . . look at all that scar tissue."

"Little Face Finny," Tracy said. "Last time we encountered him he was heading up a stickup gang. We had him on the lam, and he hid in a cold storage locker and half froze to death."

"Ye gods," the Chief said, shivering, "I remember— the doctor almost had to amputate the man's ears."

"Finny almost lost his hands, too—you can see some scarring there, as well, and on his face and neck. The jury felt so sorry for him, they let him off easy. But when he got out, he headed east."

Tracy nodded to Catchem and the torso was covered up.

The Chief was back to scratching his head. "What brought him to the city, Tracy? I'd think tangling with you again would've been the last thing he'd want to do."

"Tangling with somebody was the last thing he did, all right. But what brought *any* of them here?"

"I don't know." The Chief shook his head. "Somebody imported these rods. *Why?* It's not like there's a shortage of guns in this fair city of ours."

"This fair city of ours," Tracy said, "is divided up into so many little fiefdoms, among seven or eight of the most vicious gangsters in this country." He began ticking them off on his fingers. "Pruneface, Johnny Ramm, Texie Garcia, Ribs Mocca, Spud Spaldoni, Lips Manlis . . ."

"And Big Boy himself," the Chief added.

Tracy nodded gravely. "Lucky for us Big Boy's never been able to form a coalition between those groups . . . instead, they squabble amongst themselves, and skirmishes flare up, and they do us a favor now and again, and kill each other, a little."

"So far we've been luckier than a lot of towns," Brandon said. "No civilian casualties."

"That's because there's never been an all-out war. But with Prohibition over, the revenue is drying up. The legitimate liquor industry is geared back up and serving its public. The bootleg mobs are confined to serving the dry counties here and there, and new sources of income are sorely needed. The local mobs are ripe for weeding out and consolidation."

Brandon's face was tight with thought. "You think somebody—Lips Manlis, maybe, or Big Boy, or Pruneface—is planning to be the city's one and only crime boss?"

"Yes, I do," Tracy said flatly. "Moreover, I think somebody else *knows* about it and is planning a counter-attack."

"How do you figure that, Tracy?"

He shrugged, gestured around himself to the sheet-covered corpses. "Why would you stick around after a noisy, risky execution in the middle of town, taking billfolds off corpses? Why risk a shoot-out with the cops, or exposing yourself to eyewitnesses, to do that?"

Brandon didn't have a clue; he said as much.

"I don't know about takin' the I.D.s outa wallets," Catchem admitted, "but as for this butchery . . . maybe the shooter just *likes* firin' tommy guns. Looks to me like a crazy man did this, hired gun or not."

"What do you think, Pat?" Tracy called out, to his loyal assistant, who was standing rubbing the small of his back, tired from all that bending over, putting shells in evidence envelopes. Tracy knew Pat had been listening; Patton was not brilliant, but he was alert, and he was not stupid.

"Maybe whoever had this done didn't want us to know

somebody had imported these gunmen," Patton said. "Maybe they wanted us to think these unidentified stiffs were local. Because imported talent would mean a major gang war was in the making, and then we'd really crack down."

"That's part of it," Tracy said. "But a massacre like this isn't the move of somebody afraid of us cracking down. There's more to it than that. Yes, the man behind this wanted to keep us, at least momentarily, from realizing these gunmen were out-of-town talent; but he also wanted to keep us from finding out *who* imported these boys."

"But, Tracy," Catchem said, "we *don't* know who imported 'em. How could we know that?"

"Pat—Little Face Finny, back in his stickup gang days, was in whose camp?"

"Oh," Patton said, slowly, "I get it. Lips Manlis!"

Tracy nodded again. "I think if we can track the ownership of this garage back through the dummy corporations and holding companies and such, we'll find the smooth and oh-so-ugly proprietor of the Club Ritz."

"That'll take time," Patton said gloomily.

"I know," Tracy said. "Time is exactly what good policework takes, Pat."

"We ought to go over to the Club Ritz," Patton said, "and just roust that greasy little bum!"

"Not a bad idea at that," Catchem said.

Tracy was almost amused by his partner's naive enthusiasm. He put a hand on Patton's shoulder. "We don't play it that way, Pat. We go by the book. Remember? When we get Manlis, and when we get whoever is *after* Manlis, we'll put them both in jail."

"They belong in the *ground*," Catchem said.

"If they shoot first," Tracy said calmly, "they will be."

"Somebody may beat us to Lips Manlis," Brandon said, surveying the roomful of corpses.

"At the very least," Tracy said, "somebody's sending a message to Lips."

"And to us," Pat said.

"And to us," Tracy agreed.

The four cops exchanged glances; they were as silent as their sheet-covered companions.

A Plymouth or is it supposed to be a Chevrolet?

ASW III

12 Oct., 2021

* These side-mounted, fully exposed headlights were used on many sedans in the '30's & '40's 27 !!

— 4 —

In a dressing room filled with flowers, its bulb-outlined makeup mirror adorned with congratulatory telegrams, Vitamin Flintheart, who was on the wagon, lifted a champagne glass filled with soda water to toast Tracy and Tess. The couple's own glasses brimmed with real bubbly from a bottle currently residing in an upended Viking helmet packed with cracked ice.

"Even the Great Flintheart," the Great Flintheart humbly said, above the clink of the glasses, "never quite becomes accustomed to a standing ovation."

Tracy sipped his champagne, thinking that Vitamin may have misread the eagerness of some of the Opera House patrons to rise and stretch at the conclusion of an interminable performance.

"Richard," Vitamin said, putting his arm around the detective, "I am delighted you returned from the scene of that carnage in the nick of time, so that you might savor my death scene."

"A lot of people died this afternoon, Vitamin," Tracy said, "but none more grandly than you."

Flintheart beamed and bowed elaborately, making a *salaam* gesture. "Richard Tracy, graciousness is thy middle name."

Tess giggled. It was partly the champagne; but mostly Vitamin, who was the only man on earth who called Tracy "Richard."

Flintheart stroked his mustache, which, like his hair, had postperformance been returned to its natural shining white. "You must allow me to take you lovebirds to dinner. A veritable feast awaits the cast and crew at the Dorf Arms."

"Vitamin," Tracy said, shaking his head gently no, "I promised Tess a quiet after-theater dinner."

"Ah! No doubt you've selected a suitably secluded, romantic spot for your lovely lass."

Tracy was getting embarrassed. "Thanks for the offer, anyway, Vitamin. We'll leave you to bask in the kudos you'll no doubt collect."

"Can I have my limousine driver drop you anywhere?"

"No, thank you, Vitamin. The restaurant's close by; we'll hoof it."

"Well, at least let me walk you out, then, you two," Flintheart said, gathering himself into a silver-fox coat, slinging a silk scarf about his neck, cocking his black hat sideways on his head. "Vitamin Flintheart can always use a police escort."

Tracy helped Tess into her black woolen coat; she slipped one hand into a dyed-black rabbit muff—a few small animals had died for Tess's garment, whereas half a forestful had died for Vitamin's—and the couple followed the old ham through the backstage area, where he bestowed his gratitude to everyone he met, from costars to stagehands.

As the trio reached the front of the theater, a gaggle of reporters awaited beyond the doors, pencils poised over notebooks, flashbulbs popping in blinding little bursts.

Flintheart, raising a hand to protect his eyes, said to Tracy, "You see, my boy—you see what I must put up with, with this cursed fame of mine? I'd best duck out the stage door. . . ."

"Tracy!" they shouted. "Dick Tracy! Tracy!"

"What's the story, Tracy?" said one of the eager faces in front.

"Yeah," another yelled, "who pulled off the Seventh Street Garage Massacre?"

"Well, Bart," Tracy said calmly, as he and Tess slowly but steadily shouldered their way through the clamoring group, Vitamin having disappeared, "I see you haven't wasted any time giving it a name."

"Who was killed, Tracy?" another one said.

"We haven't confirmed the identifications yet, fellas. You'll just have to wait on that one."

Tracy and Tess were to the street now, the crew of newshounds sticking with them like gum on a shoe.

"You think this was Big Boy's work, Tracy?" yelled skinny, intense Larry Charet of the *Trib*.

"If it is, we'll find out. Excuse me, fellas . . ."

"Any comment," Charet persisted, "on the rumor you're in line for the Police Chief slot, when Brandon retires?"

"My only comment is I hope Brandon *doesn't* retire."

"Well, we're not far away from the mayoral race," said Bart Bush of the *News*; he was a sleepy-eyed, easygoing reporter who never missed a detail. "Some people think you could have *that* job, if you wanted it."

"No offense meant to His Honor the Mayor, but I wouldn't want to take a demotion. I already got the most important job in town: I'm a cop."

Tracy protectvely slipped his arm around Tess's shoulder as the pressboys crowded around; a flashbulb popped. "If that shot's any good, McNally," Tess called cheerily, "I want a copy!"

Tracy moved away from the boys, who finally backed off, just as a rather morose Vitamin rolled by in his limo; the actor smiled sadly and lifted a gloved hand in a half-hearted wave as he passed.

"Poor Vitamin," Tess said. "Those reporters let him down."

"He'll get his ego reinflated at that big cast party,"

Tracy said good-naturedly, as Tess slipped her arm in his.

They strolled slowly down a quiet, nearly deserted street close to the theatrical district. Shops were closing, though several cozy restaurants caught Tess's attention; she seemed to be wondering which one her beau had picked out. Twilight had settled on the city. The evening was cold, but not bitterly so. The sky had cleared.

She nestled against him, just a little, as they walked. "You know," she said, "you *would* make a swell Chief of Police."

He sighed. "It does pay darn near twice as much."

"Chief Brandon says you're the only man he'd trust to take over. That's why he hasn't retired before now."

He shook his head. "I'm uncomfortable behind a desk, Tess. I'm already doing more administrative work than I like."

They were crossing with the light.

"Besides, if I let 'em kick me upstairs," he said, "who would nail Big Boy?"

"Dick . . . there *are* other detectives on the force."

His eyes tightened as if that thought had never occurred to him. "I suppose somebody else *could* get something on Big Boy. But . . ."

It was something they never spoke about; but Tracy felt his pledge to Tess's late father would not be complete till he put Caprice away.

She squeezed his arm as they walked. "It's just that I'd feel more secure knowing you weren't out risking your life every night. I know you *love* it, but I worry. I'm human. And so are you, Dick. So much death around you . . . you might catch a dose of it yourself."

"Not me," he said confidently. Then he tried to make a joke out of it: "The bad guys do the dying; not the good guys."

"But do the bad guys know that?"

He laughed silently. "Hey, as far as this Chief job is concerned—I'll keep an open mind . . . if you will. But let's drop it for tonight."

"Sure," she said, and hugged his arm as they walked. He liked it, but he didn't hug back. Showing affection didn't always come easy to him.

He just looked at her and smiled shyly. He felt a warmth toward her unlike anything he felt for anyone else on the planet.

"The night's really cleared up," he noted.

"Maybe tomorrow we can finally get around to that ride in the country. Might be a nice day for it. Don't you think?"

"Sure."

"Say," she said, as the shopping district began to drop away and the outskirts of an industrial district were looming ahead, "where are we going, anyway? Somewhere 'romantic,' and 'secluded,' you said."

"That was Vitamin who said that. But 'secluded' is right."

Mike's Diner was a chrome-trimmed storefront on a corner near the trainyards. Greasy-spoons didn't come classier.

"Mike's *again?*" Tess asked, though, detective that he was, Tracy suspected she'd known it all along.

"They serve a mean bowl of chili here," Tracy said, escorting his dressed-up date toward the glow of the diner's door.

"How mean?" Tess asked.

"I've seen it eaten without crackers," Tracy said, straight-faced.

It was not the first time they'd had this exchange.

As Tracy held the door open for Tess, a small figure came quickly out and bumped into Tracy.

"Gee, mister," the kid said, moving away from Tracy, "I'm sorry . . ."

He was a red-haired street waif with an oversized cap, a frayed black jacket, and patched denims. A cute, bright-eyed kid, who at the moment had Tracy's two-way wrist radio in his hands. An antenna wire from the wrist radio extended up Tracy's cuff, so the "watch" was still connected to the plainclothes detective.

"That's not a wristwatch," Tracy said with a mildly scolding smile.

The kid dropped the wrist radio, which hung limply from Tracy's wrist by the wire clipped up Tracy's shirt sleeve, and he bolted. Or tried to bolt. The long arm of the law—specifically, the long arm of Dick Tracy—settled a firm hand on his shoulder, gripping him, stopping him.

"Bad luck, kid," Tracy said, shaking his head. "The first thing a good dip learns is don't pick a cop for a mark. You just tried to lift a two-way police-band radio off the wrist of a city detective."

"Let go of me, you stinkin'—!"

Tracy frowned and squeezed the boy's shoulder. "Watch your language, junior! There's a lady present."

Tess seemed distressed by this; her eyes were wide and sympathetic as she said, "Dick—please! He doesn't look like he's had a decent meal in weeks."

"He'll get a meal at Juvenile Hall. A night or two there will be most instructive, I think."

The kid sneered. "Go to blazes, flatfoot!"

"Listen, you little—"

"Dick!" Tess said, moving nearer Tracy. "Please! Let him go. He's got a hard enough life . . ."

Tracy glanced at Tess, and her look melted him, and he was about to let the kid off with a lecture when a heavyset figure filled the door and bellowed, "My watch is gone! That brat must have *stolen* it!"

The big man's face was as red as a tomato and so was his suit; he wore a bowler hat and a napkin was tucked in under his double chin.

The kid took advantage of the moment to shove Tracy in the stomach, pushing him into Tess. The couple didn't quite lose their balance, catching themselves on the sleek surface of the diner, but Tracy did lose the boy.

Who was a small, fleeing figure, heading toward the railroad yards, disappearing into the dark night.

"That little son of a . . ." Tracy started, and caught himself.

"There's a lady present," Tess reminded him, with a pretty little smirk.

"Gun," Tracy said, embarrassed. "Get us a nice booth, honey." He was rebuckling the two-way as he took off after the boy, yellow coat flapping as he ran.

The kid was fast, but Tracy was fast, too, and the footsteps of both echoed through the night, the kid's making small slaps, Tracy's making ominous louder ones. Sometimes there was a splash as feet punched puddles, the aftermath of yesterday's rainstorm. The streets were as black and slick as patent leather.

The train tracks were half a block away when a freight roared along, its beam cutting through the darkness like a giant's flashlight, the shrill of its whistle piercing the air, the blatt of its horn shaking the ground, the bells and the clanging and the rattling of the tracks filling the world, and—

—and the kid ran right in front of the train!

Tracy threw on his own brakes, the brakes of his heels, and barely missed bumping into the crossing guardrail, its red lights flashing; just beyond, the train whooshed joltingly by, scattering sparks. Shaking his head, Tracy grinned at the passing train. This kid was long on guts; short on brains, maybe—but long on guts.

When the caboose rushed past, Tracy didn't wait for the guardrail to raise; he ducked under and ran into the dimly lit yard. A railroad yardman spotted him and said, "Hey, you!"

Tracy slowed and flashed his badge and the yardman, carrying a kerosene lantern, said, "What's up?"

"Chasing a little pickpocket," Tracy said. "Just a kid."

The yardman pointed to the right. "I spotted a kid running down that way. I was going after him when I seen you."

Tracy nodded and ran where the yardman had pointed.

He didn't see the urchin at first and was looking frantically left to right; but then, there the kid was: scrambling up the iron ladder of a boxcar. As Tracy took pursuit, the kid was running along the boxcar's roof, and jumping to the next one, and the next.

Tracy climbed one of the iron ladders and joined in.

"Give it up, son!" he called out.

Without looking back, the kid called, "You gotta catch me first, copper!"

Tracy pursued the brat from one boxcar to another, the leaps shaking the detective from his ankles to his ears. Once, he nearly lost his balance and went tumbling to the cinders.

But he didn't.

And he followed the boy the length of this thankfully motionless train, where the kid stopped short as he found himself atop the caboose.

"Give it up, son," Tracy said, and the kid turned, poised at the edge of the caboose's roof, his back to air.

And the kid gave the detective an elaborate, and apparently heartfelt, Bronx cheer.

And jumped from the car.

Expecting to hear the howl of an injured child, but hearing nothing at all, Tracy moved to the edge, peered down and, expecting at this point to see the youth in a crumpled pile, saw nothing.

Just the darkness of the trainyard.

* * *

The Kid slowed as he entered the Hooverville on the other side of the trainyard. Fires glowed, as the otherwise homeless men, women, children, dogs, and cats huddled for warmth. The "houses" of this city within the city were made of this and that—walls of discarded boards, corrugated metal, packing crates; tar paper for roofs. The ground mixed cinders from the 'yards with straw and chicken feathers. Nobody nodded at the Kid as he moved through; the boy wasn't a permanent resident. He and Steve had moved into a shack after Steve pulled a shiv on its previous owner.

The boy ducked into the shanty, where Steve lay on a "bed" that consisted of several boards atop steel drums; Steve had a mostly empty bottle of whiskey in his two hands. The tramp was a burly brute, bald, his jowly face so gray with stubble it looked dirty, which of course it was, and so scarred he might have been a fighter, which he also was, just never in a ring. He had black beady eyes and a nose he'd broken almost as often as the law. His coat was a tattered black-and-white checkered affair that had been fashionable, a decade ago; his pants were patched like the boy's.

"Where the hell have you been, boyo?" Steve asked gruffly, sitting up. He took a long swig, and then tossed the empty whiskey bottle to the hard-packed earthen floor where it rolled.

"I been working, where d'ya think?" The Kid sat at a soapbox table, turned up the glow of the room's only lamp, a kerosene lantern stolen off a railroad yardman. The light revealed the remains of a chicken dinner scattered on the table; Steve's mouth still looked greasy. There was nothing in the way they lived that reflected the money Steve made off the Kid's stealing—other than the whiskey bottles littered here and there. Most of the Hooverville residents were lucky to get rubbing alcohol.

36

Steve pulled up an orange crate and sat at the table; the crate creaked under his weight. "Where's the take? What'd ya get?"

"I got hungry is what I got. You said you'd save me some chicken. All I see's bones."

Steve slapped the Kid, and the Kid fell off his own orange-crate chair.

"Let's see the loot, you little mongrel."

"Okay, okay." He picked himself up, wiped the blood from his mouth, and got out the watches he'd got—the fancy gold-plated pocket watch, and the wristwatch on the leather band, plus the fat guy from the diner's silver pocket watch. Steve fingered these appreciatively.

"Not bad, not bad. Any cash?"

"I lifted three wallets, but these guys was as broke as us, maybe broker." He put the three bucks on the table.

Steve scowled; his eyes were black pools of distrust surrounded by bloodshot white. "If you're holdin' out on me . . ."

"I'm not, Steve! Honest! I wouldn'ta come back so empty-handed, except . . ."

The tiny eyes narrowed. "Except what?"

"Nothin'."

The Kid didn't figure he better tell Steve about the shooting at the garage; he didn't know why, exactly— he'd just learned that telling Steve as little as possible was the best way to get hit as little as possible.

"You was out of breath when you come in. You was runnin', weren't you? Why? Who from?"

The boy made a face; how he hated to admit this to Steve. But he better. "I took a watch off a guy, outside that diner, and he turned out to be a copper."

"A copper!"

"How was I supposed know? He was wearin' plainclothes! He chased me awhile, into the 'yards, but I shook him."

Steve backhanded the boy; this time the Kid didn't get up so fast. He didn't get up at all, just cowered, and tasted the blood in his mouth, and tried not to cry.

"If you led a plainclothes dick here, you little vermin, I'll give you the beating of your life."

"There's an old expression," somebody said.

The Kid turned toward the space that served as a doorway; a shadow stood there—it had spoken.

It spoke again: "Pick on somebody your own size."

The shadow moved into the room and it wore a bright yellow coat and a matching fedora. It was the square-jawed plainclothes cop who the Kid had hoped he'd lost, but now was glad had found him.

Steve stood and, with a strange grace for such a big man, picked up one of the orange crates and smashed it over the cop.

The cop was not fazed; he swung a hard right into Steve's stomach and doubled the tramp over, then crossed with a left that connected with Steve's stubbly jaw.

Steve went down hard, and the plainclothes cop loomed over him with fists half-raised. The tramp appeared to be knocked out.

"Careful," the Kid said. To the plainclothes cop.

The plainclothes cop glanced at the Kid and smiled and that was when Steve made his move; the tramp came up with a board in his hand, a board with a nail that glinted in the lantern-light.

Only the plainclothes cop sidestepped and sent Steve crashing into the wall of the shack, knocking a hole in the packing-crate wall, shaking the flimsy structure. As Steve lumbered back at him, the board-with-nail still in hand, the plainclothes cop kicked it out of the tramp's grasp.

Steve growled and dove at the cop, and the cop went down with the big smelly tramp on him like a rabid attack dog. Steve's hands went to the cop's throat, but the cop must've plowed Steve in the belly real good, because Steve went rolling off him, doubled in pain.

"Come on, kid," the plainclothes cop said, and reached out a hand.

But Steve, despite his pain, got to his big feet and tried one more time, charging the cop like a car trying to run somebody over.

They stood slugging it out, until a flurry of yellow-sleeved punches sent Steve flying into another wall and suddenly the whole shack came down on them.

The Kid found himself being pulled out from under the tar paper and boards and such by the plainclothes cop, who said, "Give me a second with your pal. Don't go anywhere now, junior, or I'll chase you down again."

The Kid felt pretty shook up, but he still managed, "Go suck an egg, mister!"

The cop seemed to find that funny. "The name is Tracy. Detective Tracy."

"Oh. I think I heard of you. You're Dick Tracy, ain't you?"

"That's right. Now, let's have the loot. You got a watch to return."

"Why should I?" the Kid asked, but he gathered the stuff, just the same.

Tracy was kneeling over the now genuinely unconscious Steve, who was half-under pieces of the demolished shack; he was cuffing Steve's hands, in back.

"Is this guy your old man?" he asked the Kid.

"Him? Not on your life!"

Nobody in the Hooverville was paying any attention to this, strange as the sight of the interloper might be. In fact, many of them had disappeared into their shanties; nobody liked having a cop around, and despite the plainclothes, it was obvious that's what Tracy was.

"Now," Tracy said, smiling, taking the watches from

the boy, slipping them in his topcoat pocket, "we'll be on our way."

"What about Steve?"

"Is that his name? I'll find the nearest patrol car and have him hauled in."

"You taking me to Juvenile Detention?"

"You bet, junior. But not right away."

"Not right away?"

Tracy lifted the half-conscious tramp to his feet. The trio began walking through the Hooverville, toward the trainyards—though the lumbering Steve was being half-dragged as the cop and kid moved briskly along.

"First we're going back to that diner and get you a decent meal."

"Jeez, mister. That's decent of ya."

"I'm doing it for myself, really."

"Yourself?"

"You saw that good-looking lady I was with."

"Yeah." The Kid whistled. "Nice shape on that dame."

Tracy looked at him with wide eyes. "How *old* are you?"

"I don't know. How old are you?"

"Never mind," Tracy said. He scolded the boy gently with a wag of his forefinger. "Look, she's not a 'dame'— she's a very proper and respectable young lady. But . . ." And Tracy grinned, suddenly, like a kid. " . . . if I don't take you back to that diner and give you a meal, that very proper and respectable young lady just might get tough with *me*."

"I know the feelin'," the Kid admitted.

5

Breathless Mahoney, in a midnight-blue gown that left nothing to the imagination, was singing a torch number her piano player had written for her: "I Always Get My Man." She stood defiant, insolent in her beauty, in the midst of the black-marble dance floor of the Club Ritz, whose elegant chrome-and-glass showroom was filled to capacity; the bandstand behind her was empty, the orchestra on break but for the piano player, if anyone noticed or cared. One shapely leg exposed thanks to a slit in her painted-on gown, the young woman seemed half Harlow, half harlot—heaven in a hell of a package.

There was a studied casualness about her beauty: her white-blonde hair a mass of curls, some of which nearly cascaded over one eye; her eyebrows dark, rather thick, unplucked; her eyes liquid blue and sleepy; mouth red-rouged and swollen. Her breathy singing and her passive sensuality projected a strange air of boredom—a boredom that was a challenge to the men of the world to wake her up.

Lips Manlis, despite all his money, his power, even his capacity for violence, had never quite woken her. He'd been with her for over a year; it made for an elegant sort of misery—she made no attempt to feign ardor, much less passion.

He figured she was playing him for a sap, but he was hooked. She was driving him bughouse, and for the life of him, he didn't know why he put up with it. After all, there were twenty dames in the chorus line, any one of

41

whom would go with him at the nod of his bucket head. For years, frails had worked off their tails making him feel like a man, convincing him that they were crazy about him.

But Breathless didn't even bother.

Maybe that was the fascination in itself. Manlis had been a power in the city for over ten years; worked his way up, a West Side kid who went from pushcart sneak-thief to stickup man to truck hijacker. He'd gotten in on the ground floor of Prohibition and in a matter of a couple years controlled the central city and several suburbs. For a long time that had been enough for him. But since Repeal, things had been getting tight. The pie was getting smaller, but there were still just as many pieces getting sliced out of it.

Time to make a move. That was why he'd imported the expensive shooters from all over the country; and with his old pal Little Face heading 'em up, they'd make a deadly assassination squad, and Big Boy and the others wouldn't know who, let alone what, hit 'em.

Maybe when he was sitting on top of the whole town, maybe then Breathless would moan with delight at his touch. Maybe then.

He was a squat, dark, hairy man with the large, almost malformed lips that had given him his nickname. The black tuxedo, with rose in the lapel, was meant to give him a dapper man-of-the-world look, but didn't—particularly since he had a napkin tucked in his collar like a bib. He was faintly aware of all this, but nobody dared make him feel his deception was anything less than fully successful.

Except, of course, the sullenly arrogant Breathless Mahoney.

She was lucky, Lips thought, that God gave her skin like cream and breasts like peaches. Lips frequently thought of women in terms of food. He loved food. He was, at the moment, slurping the third of twenty-four oysters that had been served him on the half-shell.

The Club Ritz—a private club, the most successful night spot in town, with a bustling casino room—was only moderately busy tonight. Still, the take would be well into the thousands. Manlis could have been content to loll in the income of this one property. But somewhere in him was the need to prove himself. Somewhere in him still lived the little West Side kid they called "Liver Lips" Manlis, who wanted to be respected by men, and loved by women.

The bodyguard who approached—who also wore a black tux, as did all of Manlis's help, even those with cauliflowered ears and automatics bulging under their arms, like this fellow—seemed ill at ease. Caught in mid-oyster, Lips knew the news was bad.

"Give it to me straight, Joey," Lips said

Joey bent over to whisper in his boss's ear. Out on the obsidian dance floor, Breathless was singing about a man, but didn't seem very interested.

"They bumped off everybody," Joey said.

"What do you mean—'everybody'?"

"I mean, *everybody*. Little Face included."

"Damn." Little Face had been a good friend for a long, long time; they went back years in the stickup game. Lips ate another oyster. "So who did it?"

"Nobody knows. Not the cops, not nobody."

"Smells like Big Boy."

"I don't know, boss. It was real mean. The boys was shot up so's their own mamas couldn't recognize 'em."

"Maybe Pruneface, then," Lips mused. "He likes to pitch in on his own dirty work, that trigger-happy lunatic.

"Sorry to bear ya bad tidings, boss."

Lips was thinking. "Nobody knows we're the ones

who brought those boys to town. We just gotta lay back for a few days, let the dust settle, and try again."

"Sure, boss."

He waggled a finger at the bodyguard. "But beef up the security. I don't want nobody getting within a mile of me, or my girl."

"You got it, boss."

"You're a good boy, Joey. Go fetch Breathless, before she starts another number."

Breathless spoke a word to, and smiled faintly at, her piano player, a brunette pretty boy with Oriental eyes who tickled the keys regularly at the Club Ritz. His name, at least his stage name, was "88 Keys." Keys looked at her with open admiration as she walked across the empty dance floor, as slow as a summer afternoon, but hotter. Every man in the room watched her with longing; every woman with envy. She shimmered, and shimmied, and she didn't even try, or anyway seemed not to. Nor did she seem to care.

Lips didn't get up; but he did gesture to a chair. "Sit, baby, sit."

She sat. "Cig me," she said.

"Sure, baby." He snapped open a gold cigarette case and held it open in front of her and let her select one. She did.

"Match me," she said, holding the cigarette between two fingers.

He lit it for her with a decorative silver lighter shaped like a nude woman. The flame came out of the silver woman's head. Lips found it classy.

Breathless inhaled, blew a smoke ring, tossed her head of curls. The gesture fully revealed her previously half-hidden eye; it proved just as blue, and just as uninterested, as the other.

"Magnificent, my dear," Lips said between oyster slurps, "as always."

"I'm so happy you like it."

"I love it. You're singing great."

"What about that talent scout from a record label you promised me?" she asked. "When's he coming around?"

"Soon. Soon. But baby, you don't belong on records, you don't belong on the radio, you belong in the movies where they can see you, see that shape of yours. Watching you walk over here, why sugar, it was like watching Jell-O quiver on a plate."

"You say the loveliest things," she said, sucking smoke, not looking at him.

"You should be nice to me, baby."

"You should close your mouth when you chew."

He frowned; then he slurped the fourteenth oyster. "Sometimes you don't seem to know which side of the bread the butter's on, baby."

"I'm sure *you* do."

"There's a gang war brewing in this burg, and you're gonna know, soon enough, that you're lucky to be in *my* camp. In fact, I don't want you going nowhere without two bodyguards, plus a chauffeur with a gun."

"I'm safe enough when 88 takes me around."

"If I didn't know that guy was one of them 'arty' types, I'd swear you two . . ."

"I'm always true to you darling, in my fashion."

He snorted; spoke through a mouth of half-chewed oyster. "Save the song lyrics for the customers, baby."

A bell began to ring shrilly.

"It's a raid!" Lips said, half standing, spewing pieces of oyster as he spoke.

"No kidding," Breathless said, blowing another smoke ring, crossing her legs and studying her own well-turned ankle.

Customers were scurrying for exits, but Lips half stood and said, loudly, "Be calm, ladies and gents! Be calm—take your seats, no reason to panic."

"Then why did you?" Breathless asked, with jaded contempt.

His thick lips in a wide, tight smile, Lips gestured with his arms open, waving them calmingly; he looked like an enchanted prince who hadn't quite made the transformation back from a frog.

Several bodyguards moved in behind Lips, their tuxedos open for easy access to their shoulder-holstered weapons, while Lips and Breathless, who was having him light her up a new cigarette, sat quietly, unconcerned, as the trio of uniformed policemen burst in.

"Gentlemen," Lips said grandly, and he slurped an oyster. As he rolled it around luxuriously in his mouth, he said, "Buy you a drink? It's legal now, you know. It was in all the papers."

The three uniformed cops were big, tough, no-nonsense Irishmen. The one in front said, "You're under arrest, Manlis."

"What charge?" He swallowed the oyster; it slid down his throat like a kid on a sled.

"Owning and operating a gambling establishment."

Manlis smiled slyly. "Can't we make some kind of . . . financial arrangement, gents?"

"No."

He frowned. "Let's see your warrant, then."

It was slapped on the table in front of him like a winning poker hand.

He looked it over. It was legit, all right. Judge Debirb's signature was on it.

"On your feet, Manlis. You, too, girlie."

"Me?" Breathless said, wide-eyed. Suddenly interested.

"You. You can grab your fur on the way out."

She looked irritably at Manlis, silently demanding he do something.

Manlis shrugged. "Your name's on the warrant, too, baby."

Her nostrils flared, her lips curled in a sneer as the three cops hustled them out and down to the street, where an unmarked car waited.

Pat Patton yawned. It had been a long day and as evening turned to night, it wasn't looking to get any shorter. He had spent all morning and afternoon at HQ catching up on paperwork, which he finally wrapped up only to be called to that garage shooting, where Tracy made him pick up hundreds of shell casings and make field notes till his notebook had more writing in it than a Russian novel.

Now, at Tracy's orders, he was staking out the Club Ritz. Lips Manlis not only managed this club, the crown jewel of his various enterprises, legal and ill; the liver-lipped ganglord lived there as well, in an apartment on the second floor. Tracy was convinced it had been Manlis who brought in Little Face and the others; and it only made sense that in the wake of the garage massacre, either Manlis would be hit again, or would himself strike back.

So here, in an unmarked car, nestled in the backseat to make the car look unoccupied at first glance, was Patton, arms folded, feet straight out on the seat, as he tried to resist taking a nice long nap. It had been quiet so far. It would probably stay quiet. Only the gaudy neon of the sign over the door of the otherwise relatively nondescript brick building kept him awake; its flickery glow pulsed in his face.

Patton did not resent being, in effect, Dick Tracy's flunky. He liked Tracy as a man and admired him as a detective. They had a lot in common, Patton and Tracy; both were small-town kids who came to the big city. Like Tracy, Pat had grown up reading Nick Carter and Sherlock Holmes. Some kids dreamed of being cowboys or firemen; for Pat Patton, the dream was always to be a cop.

That is, specifically, a detective, and now he was one. And while he'd hoped to be Sherlock Holmes when he grew up, he could settle for being Watson to an American Holmes. Which Tracy surely was.

Pat had almost nodded off when he noticed three uniformed cops piling out of a black sedan that had pulled up in front of that canopy across the way. What were three uniformed men doing in an unmarked car?

He sat up and got a fairly good look at them, but didn't recognize any of 'em. Of course, it was a big department; but still, he knew most of the men at least by sight, if not name. And if this were a raid, why only three cops?

And what were *any* cops doing, pulling a raid tonight, after that massacre? *He* was the cop on the job, after all.

He fiddled with the two-way radio on his wrist and called Tracy.

"Yes, Pat," Tracy's voice said scratchily out of the tiny cloth-covered speaker.

"I'm staking out Manlis's club, like you said. I just saw three uniforms go in."

"Anybody we know?"

"No, that's just the thing. And Dick, they showed up in an unmarked car."

"Well, that's the rule on a raid, isn't it? Otherwise you'd tip off the doorman."

"Yeah, but the rule's also the first wave is in plainclothes. And only one car?"

"Maybe more will be along.

Tracy sounded distracted to Pat.

"Dick, did you hear anything about a raid comin' down on Manlis tonight?"

"It's a big department," Tracy confirmed. "Maybe it's an operation we're unaware of. Keep an eye on it. Keep me informed."

"Where are you?"

"Mike's Diner. Tess and I are entertaining a guest."

Pat signed off and continued to keep watch. Minutes later, the three cops exited the club, with Lips Manlis and a platinum blonde in tow. The cops stuffed the ugly gangster, with his napkin still tucked in his collar, and the beautiful babe, who was bundling herself into a dark mink coat, into the backseat of the unmarked car; which then tore away from the curb, burning rubber.

Patton climbed in his front seat, started the engine, pulled a U-turn, and tailed the car, calling Tracy on his two-way as he drove. His eyes reflecting back at him in the windshield glass were as bright and round and shiny as brass buttons.

Ahead, the sedan's taillights burned red holes in the night.

6

Lips, not being particularly a gentleman, had gotten in the black sedan first; Breathless, gathering her dark fur around creamy shoulders, followed. They were not yet seated before they realized they shared the backseat with a flat-headed hood with a tommy gun cradled in his arms. His cupid's mouth smiled ever so slightly; he wore a black topcoat and a silk scarf.

"Flattop!" Manlis said.

"Is that bad?" Breathless asked.

"Depends on who you ask," Flattop said.

The car squealed away into the night.

Five long silent minutes later, it pulled into the loading area of Manlis's own riverfront dockside warehouse. The three "cops" piled out, while in back Flattop nudged Manlis with the tommy. Manlis got the point and nodded to Breathless and, the door opened for them graciously by one of the cops, she got out, showing off plenty of leg. Manlis followed, thinking how Breathless never failed to try and make a good impression on the men around her. If he had gams like hers, he'd be trying to trade 'em for a break himself.

But the only the break he was going to get, he'd have to make himself.

So he did.

He elbowed the "cop" at his right, and the guy doubled over, gun pointing downward, and Lips headed toward the wall of crates, looking for cover. But he'd eaten too many oysters tonight, and too much of a lot else over the years, to move very fast. He knew, even as he tried it, he was waddling; tears of humiliation came to his eyes as he heard, instead of gunfire, the sound of male laughter.

Someone stepped out from behind the stacked crates and stuck a leg out and, awkward as the kid they used to taunt and call "Liver Lips," Manlis tumbled to the cement, falling flat on his froggy face.

He tried to gather himself, tried to assemble his dignity; his tuxedo was streaked with dirt and grease, his lapel rose was bruised, torn, its shape gone forever. Before him were the legs of the man who had tripped him. The shoes were brightly shining wing tips; Manlis saw his own frightened, ugly face look back at him in their reflection.

"Aw. You got your pretty tux dirty, Lips."

Manlis looked up at what seemed to be a tall, imposing figure; actually, it was mostly the perspective. Al "Big Boy" Caprice was not tall; he wasn't even very wide. But he wore power like some people wear a gaudy suit. Like the gaudy money-green suit he was wearing, in fact. A glimpse of the bright green suit meshed with the gangster's vibrant green topcoat with its lamb collar. Big Boy's green fedora was a little too small for him, fitting his head like a crown; his big hands were stuffed into kid gloves.

"Big Boy," Lips said, trying not to sound groveling as he groveled. "Ain't we pals?"

"No pals in this business, Lips. You taught me that."

"Can't . . . can't we work this out?"

Big Boy's eyes were large and dark and buggy in a face that might have been handsome, had each feature not been slightly distorted, the brow not so low, the cheekbones not so angular, the cleft chin not so extended. Pencil-thin mustache above full lips or not, Caprice would never be mistaken for Clark Gable.

The big head was wagging from side to side, the brutish face a mask of mock-regret. "I don't think so, Lips. You

didn't bring Little Face, Shoulders, and them other torpedoes to town to start no ballet troupe."

"That was just for protection, Big Boy. Things are getting tougher."

Big Boy nodded sympathetically, as if seeing Lips's
point. "Let me help ya up," Big Boy said.

And he did. He generously brushed off Lips's suit.
Over by the car, Breathless stood, uncharacteristically
alert, with Flattop, Itchy, and the three cops providing
an audience. For her, and for Big Boy and Lips.

"Big Boy . . . Al . . . we go way back. I can see that
while the world is our oyster, our oyster is gettin' smaller.
I can see that. I would settle for a smaller share."

Big Boy was reaching into his topcoat pocket; Lips recoiled, expecting a gun, but instead the gangster removed
only a handful of walnuts. He cracked one in his massive
fist. "See, that's the problem. You don't see that our
world, our oyster if you will, is gettin' bigger. Not smaller. You don't see that, 'cause you're the past, Lips. I'm
the future."

"Just let me keep my club. My life, and my club."

Big Boy, chewing a walnut, slipped an arm around
Manlis's shoulder. "Well, let's talk about your club, first.
I'd like to buy your club."

"Buy my . . . my club?"

"It's the classiest joint in town. I really like it. I like it
so much I took the liberty of drawing up a paper that
states you're transferring title to me."

"For . . . for how much?"

Big Boy chewed a walnut thoughtfully. "A dollar."

"A dollar?"

"A dollar. Quite a deal, Lips. Here." Big Boy withdrew
a folded paper from the vest of his money-green suit
under his blue topcoat. "Pen!" he called, and snapped his
fingers, and Itchy smoothly provided one. Neither Itchy

nor Flattop were brandishing their guns, Lips noted with faint relief—on the other hand, the "cops" had their tommy guns trained on him.

Big Boy handed Lips the pen.

"Sign," Big Boy said.

"This is not fair."

"Life ain't fair. Didn't you learn that on the West Side, Liver Lips?"

"Up yours, pal!" He threw the paper at Big Boy.

"No pals in this business, Lips, remember? But, hey— you don't like the price? I'll up the ante. A dollar . . . and your life."

Manlis licked his lips; it took a while. Then he said, "I could leave? I could start over someplace?"

"Sure. You got money. You got plenty big of a stake to start up again. Just not in my town."

"I'm not the only one in your way."

"You're not in my way anymore, Lips. And you're just the first of them that's gonna get out of my way. Sign."

Manlis swallowed. Big Boy turned his back to Manlis, to give him a surface to sign against. Manlis did, though he thought about embedding the tip of the fountain pen in Big Boy's fat neck.

Big Boy turned and took the signed paper. "Good boy," he said. "You know, Lips, I'm even gonna throw something else in on the bargain."

"Big Boy . . . just let me go. I'll get out of town. Just let me get outta here."

Big Boy put a hand on Manlis's shoulder and the smile under the little mustache was as wide as it was insincere. "That's what I'm talkin' about. I'm gonna provide ya your means of transportation. You like rail, or air, or water? You know me, I like water. You can't beat the ocean. Or even the river."

The sound of an engine starting up in the recesses of the warehouse reverberated and Manlis turned to see a cement truck come rumbling down a platform, its huge mixer churning.

"You're going first class, Lips," Big Boy said, working his voice up above the grinding of the cement mixer, patting Manlis's shoulder. "But before you go, let's get you presentable . . . you're dirty, Lips! You need a bath."

Lips knew what that meant and it chilled him. "Not the bath, Big Boy! Not the bath . . ."

And Flattop and Itchy and the others moved toward him; they were on him, and though he struggled, though he squirmed, Lips felt himself lifted, carried, and set down upright inside something, something wooden, like a coffin. A crate—a wooden crate . . .

The truck rumbled into position and halted; the mixer tipped—and as Lips knew it would, cement began to splatter down on him, more a shower than a bath, really. The cement was thick, pouring out like ice cream; it was cold like ice cream.

His mind flashed on hot afternoons on the West Side; kids splashing in the spray of a fire hydrant. You scream, I scream, we all scream for ice cream.

Lips Manlis began to scream.

Breathless was watching; something close to pity was in her eyes. Finally he'd evoked an emotion other than contempt in her. He laughed, and screamed, and the men above smiled down on him.

Pat had followed the "cops" in the blue sedan to the warehouse, and along the way filled Tracy in.

"Radio for some *real* cops to check out the Club Ritz," Tracy said. "You stick with that car and let me know where you land. And then I'll be right there."

Well, they'd landed and Patton circled around back of the dockside warehouse; it was in a largely unlit industrial district near the riverfront and he had to move carefully and slowly, so as not to disturb any rubbish cans or send any cats yowling into the night.

Wrist radio to his lips, he whispered his location to Sam Catchem.

"We'll be right there," Catchem's voice said. "Don't make a move till you got backup, boy."

"Don't worry," Patton said.

But Patton's curiosity got the better of him. He found a window he could get in and he was raising it carefully, hoping Tracy would be pleased with his initiative, not irritated with him, and the world caved in on him.

His derby had been crushed, and to a lesser degree so had his skull; but Patton didn't know that. He lay crumpled by the trash cans, no more conscious than the cans were.

Itchy and Flattop were nailing the lid on the wooden crate. The sound of it was like gunshots.

"You're sure that thing's airtight?" Big Boy said. "If the water gets in, that cement won't set, and then Lips'll come floating back up to haunt us."

"Sure I'm sure, boss," Itchy said, digging his fingernails into the back of his neck. "The water ain't gettin' in, and Lips ain't gettin' out!"

Itchy's weasellike laugh echoed in the massive warehouse.

The sound of it made Breathless shudder; she was cowering over by the car, trying to disappear into the dark fur she was swaddled in. She didn't look so brave, or so cocky, or so bored, now.

Big Boy walked over to her. "Wonderin' why you're here?"

She nodded; tried to keep her chin up and managed, but tremblingly.

"Everything that Manlis owned is mine now," Big Boy said. "Understood? Everything."

She smiled slowly. Then she nodded. "Understood."

He pawed the fur she was wearing. "What is this, some kind of dyed dog?" He pulled it off her shoulders contemptuously. "My women wear mink, or they wear nothin'."

"As it happens," she said sultrily, her confidence back, "I look good either way."

Big Boy smiled. He liked that. He dropped a few walnut shells into his topcoat pocket and offered her his arm regally and she took it.

They were heading for Big Boy's sedan when from the dark recesses of the warehouse, Mumbles appeared. The sleepy-looking blond hoodlum approached Big Boy deferentially.

"Trazpalwzsnooppinrowdoutther," Mumbles said.

"*What* did he say?" Itchy asked.

"Did you take care of him?" Big Boy asked Mumbles, ignoring Itchy's question.

Mumbles nodded.

"Kill him?" Big Boy asked.

Mumbles shook his head no.

Mumbles murmured a few more words of explanation, which no one but Big Boy understood.

Then there was silence.

Big Boy crushed a walnut in one huge fist; the sound cracked in the room, and the shells fell to the floor as Big Boy popped the nuts in his mouth and began to chew fiercely. He glanced down at the shells, considering picking them up, when he noticed a spatter of cement on his shoe. He pointed to it absently and Mumbles said, "Surboss," knelt and wiped the shoe off with his handkerchief.

Meanwhile, Flattop and Itchy were in the process of wrapping the cement-packed crate in heavy chains.

Big Boy patted Mumbles on the head, as if the little hoodlum were a much-loved pooch, then again began moving toward his own parked sedan. He turned to Itchy. "Take a look around outside, 'fore we fade."

Itchy nodded dutifully and walked into the darkness of the warehouse.

Big Boy put a paternal hand on Flattop's shoulder. "You and Itchy can come back in the launch in a day or so," he told the gunman, "and hook onto those chains and take Lips underwater water-skiin'. Then give him a burial at sea."

"Why not do it now?" one of the fake cops asked.

"All of this activity's gonna flush Tracy outta his rathole," Big Boy said. "His dim-bulb assistant's outside right now, sleeping with the garbage. Best, tonight, we all go about our own business."

Another of the fake cops, who seemed confused by all this, pointed a thumb at the wood-and-cement coffin, which by now was wrapped up in more chains than Houdini doing a death-defying stunt. "What are you gonna do with *him* in the meantime?"

"Keep him in cold storage," Big Boy said matter-of-factly.

Flattop laughed at that, and his laugh was like high-pitched obnoxious tommy-gun fire. The fake cops exchanged uneasy, bewildered glances.

"You boys from outta town don't quite know how I do things," Big Boy said understandingly. "Let's just say I don't like people who cross me. Like Lips, there. You cross me, the floor can drop right out under ya. It's a good object lesson for you new fellas."

Big Boy withdrew another walnut, cracked it, and looked toward Mumbles, who was standing by a support beam. The gangster nodded at the sulky blond hoodlum, who released a concealed lever and a trapdoor beneath the wooden crate opened and dropped the late Lips Manlis, cement coffin and all, twenty feet into the dark river, where it was deep enough to conceal the cargo, but not so deep that it couldn't be retrieved.

The splash jumped up through the open trapdoor, and the fake cops jumped back as the water dampened the floor, diluting some of the wet-cement spillage.

"Clean up and get out," Big Boy told the stunned fake cops, who were taking all this in with popping eyes. "Then cover up that trapdoor with crates."

Itchy reappeared like a ghost materializing. "Coast is clear now, boss," he said, tucking his silenced revolver back under his dark topcoat somewhere. "I, uh . . . ran into a beat cop who was lookin' a little too interested."

Big Boy's eyebrows knit. "Yeah?"

Itchy paled suddenly. "Had to plug 'im, boss."

Big Boy's face darkened and he drew back his hand as if to slap the man; but then he only patted Itchy on the face, almost affectionately.

"You mean well," he said benevolently. "But killin' cops ain't smart."

Itchy gestured nervously. "The body's out of sight. Stowed it behind some barrels out back."

"There's a dead *cop* out there?" one of the fake cops said, eyes wide. His two brothers in blue were similarly wide-eyed.

"Yeah, a dead cop," Itchy sneered, as if to say, *Wanna make somethin' of it?*

"When you're done in here," Big Boy told the uniformed trio, "throw the late John Law over the side of the dock. Nevermind the cement overcoat. Shake a leg."

Another of the "cops" said, "What if his body floats up on shore someplace?"

"Then," Big Boy said, tossing more walnuts into his

mouth, "it'll give that flatfoot Tracy something to think about."

And Big Boy's laughter echoed through the warehouse as he moved with Breathless toward his dark sedan, with Flattop, Mumbles, and Itchy trailing after him, the grotesque courtiers of a grotesque king.

7

They were sitting in the booth Tess had saved, Tracy and Tess on one side, and the Kid—after reluctantly washing his face and hands in the john, at Tracy's insistence—on the other. The trio had the place to themselves—just them and the good-natured, heavyset counterman/manager/chef, Mike, who was at work behind the shiny counter.

Tracy was amused and touched by the way the Kid was polishing off Mike's Blue Plate Special. Amused because the boy's table manners were right out of Genghis Khan's Book of Etiquette; and touched to see the pitiful eagerness the hungry child brought to the task.

He could tell Tess felt the same way. She'd started to comment on the Kid's uncouth approach—and Tracy couldn't blame her: he'd never seen anybody eat mashed potatoes with his hands before—but she'd softened. She seemed sad, barely poking at her own Blue Plate Special. Tracy wasn't doing much better with his chili.

"What do you call this stuff?" the Kid asked.

"Meat loaf," Tracy said.

"It's kinda like fancy hamburger, ain't it?"

"Isn't it," Tess corrected gently.

The boy nodded at her, as if she were merely agreeing with him. He took a big swig of milk and thereafter wore a moist white mustache.

"You got a name, junior?" Tracy asked. The detective was breaking up crackers to drop in his chili; with what was going on across from him, it was a lapse he figured Tess would grant him.

"Don't have one, 'xactly," he said, unconcerned. He was carving up his meat loaf with his fork and spearing pieces one at at a time, more or less following Tess's example.

"So what do they call you?" Tracy asked.

"'Kid,'" he said, shrugging. "Just 'Kid.'"

"What's the name your mother and father gave you?"

The Kid snorted a laugh. "What mother and father?"

"Do you mean you have no mother or father?" Tess asked, ever gentle.

"If I did," he said, "I never knew 'em."

"I'm sorry," she said. "Did they pass away?"

"More like passed through," he said, and gulped some more milk. "I don't remember ever being with nobody but Steve."

"Why didn't you leave that brute?" Tess asked.

"I tried a few times," he said. "But he catched me and beat me silly. Besides, bad as Steve was, I usually had some kinda roof over me, and food now and then."

"But he *beat* you," Tess said, incredulously.

"Sure," the boy said. "But nobody *else* ever did. With Steve around, I was safe. And Steve hardly ever walloped me real bad, 'cause without me, where was his next meal comin' from? A kid riding the rails *needs* somebody lookin' after him."

Tracy was studying the boy. "You feel bad about Steve going to jail?"

"No, sir. Not really. It was gettin' worse lately. Steve was drinking heavy and that's when he'd really whup me. So Steve can rot in blazes, far as I'm concerned. Excuse me, ma'am. Shouldn'ta cursed."

Tess only smiled, in a melancholy way.

"What happens at this Juvenile Detention hall?" the boy asked.

"You'll get square meals," Tracy said, "and a bed and a roof and clean clothes and you'll be in out of the cold."

"*Jail*, you mean."

"Not exactly," Tracy said. "I'll see what I can do for you. I'll call the Welfare Department. The local orphanage isn't a bad place."

"Orphanage!"

"Settle down, son. In the meantime, I'll see if I can get you in a nice foster home. I'll pull some strings."

"Well, I like travelin' around."

Tracy shook his head, no. "You need friends your age, and you need school."

"School!"

"Sorry, pal. It's the law."

"Jeez. I was better off with Steve the Tramp." He shook his head and went back to wolfing his meat loaf.

A few moments later, Tracy's two-way spoke; it was Pat—he'd seen three uniformed cops go into the Club Ritz where Tracy had him staking out the place. Pat seemed suspicious, and it did sound a little kinky. Tracy told Pat to keep an eye on the situation, call for backup, and keep him posted.

"Jeez," the boy said, looking at the two-way with big eyes, "that thing really *is* a radio."

"Beats two tin cans and a string." Tracy grinned.

The boy polished off his plate before either Tracy or Tess were half finished.

"Thanks, mister," he said to Tracy. His manners extended that far, anyway. The boy's eyes shifted from Tracy's chili and then back to Tess's Blue Plate Special, like a dog waiting for scraps.

"You still hungry?" Tracy said, amazed, lifting a spoon of chili.

"No, but the more I eat now, the less hungry I'll be later."

Tracy had a feeling the boy knew hunger intimately.

"How about some ice cream?" Tess asked.

"I had that once!" the Kid said.

"Ever hear the old expression," Tracy asked. "You scream, I scream, we all scream for ice cream?"

"No," the Kid said, "but I'll scream, if you want me to. If that'll do the trick."

"Not necessary," Tracy said. He called over to the counterman, saying, "Mike, fix this kid up with a couple of scoops of . . . what do you want, junior? They got vanilla and strawberry and chocolate."

"Gee," the boy said, pretending to ponder. "I can't make up my mind. Maybe I oughta try a scoop of each one of them."

Tracy smiled and nodded to Mike, who fixed the boy up.

Tracy was just starting a piece of apple pie when the Kid was scraping his spoon on the bottom of what had been a humongous bowl of ice cream. Despite this manful effort to get every last melted drop of his dessert, the boy finally looked full. Tess was sipping coffee.

"Are you guys married?" the Kid asked them.

"No," Tess said, and looked down at her own piece of pie.

Tracy cleared his throat and looked at the boy sharply.

"What's the matter, Tracy?" the Kid asked. "Did I touch a sore spot or somethin'?"

"First of all, it's Mr. Tracy, or Detective Tracy—got that?"

"Yeah, yeah. Mr. Tracy. Detective Tracy."

"Second of all, mind your own business," Tracy advised, shifting in his seat.

Tess smiled faintly.

So did the Kid. His face wore memories of the food he'd just eaten—various shades of ice cream mingling with brown gravy smudges. His face looked like an abstract painting.

Tracy was about to introduce him to the world of napkins when Sam Catchem's voice jumped out of the two-way.

"Tracy, something's up down at the Southside Warehouse, on the riverfront. Better get down there."

"What's going on?"

"To tell you the truth, Tracy, we don't exactly know. Pat called in and asked us to send some backup, 'cause he saw some suspicious lookin' cops take Lips Manlis inside that warehouse. . . . "

"I know all about that. I told him to call it in."

"Well that's fine, and he did, and we're on our way over now—but when I try to check back in with Pat, I can't raise him."

"He may not be able to respond without giving away his surveillance position."

"Yeah, sure, but then we had a call from a uniform cop patrolling the area, who also saw suspicious vehicles heading into that warehouse, and now we can't raise *him*, either."

"I'm on my way," Tracy said hurriedly, and slid out of the booth, tossing some dollar bills and coins on the table; both the Kid and Tess were looking at him wide-eyed.

"Got to go," Tracy said.

"What about the eating machine?" Tess asked, nodding pointedly toward the boy.

"Next stop," the boy said with glum sarcasm, "Juvenile Hall."

"It's awfully late for that," Tess said. Her eyes beseeched Tracy to give the boy a reprieve.

"Take him to my place, then," Tracy said impatiently. He put a key on the table. "I'll arrange something with the orphanage tomorrow." He was half out the door. "I'll radio for a squad car to pick you two up."

Tess blew him a kiss and Tracy blew her one back. The

Kid made a face at such mush, even as he eyed the money Tracy left.

"Touch that," Tess said without looking at the boy, "and I'll break your arm."

The boy made a disgusted face, but withdrew his hand.

"I don't like dames," he said.

"Good," Tess said. "Neither do I."

But Tracy was already out the door, where he walked quickly to his car, which he'd left at Mike's earlier that day in anticipation of his dinner date with Tess. He wasn't wearing a gun—normally, even off-duty he wore his shoulder holster—but it hadn't seemed necessary for a trip to the Civic Opera House earlier this evening, a century ago.

He drove with one hand and reached over to pop the glove box with the other, grabbing the spare .38 within and slipping the gun into his topcoat pocket. Something at the back of his neck was tingling. Had Pat stumbled onto something big? If so, Tracy only hoped his zealous little partner would have sense enough to wait for the cavalry.

The industrial area along the riverfront was a maze of narrow streets, with the occasional pools of street-lamp light mere drops in a dark ocean. But Pat's directions had been good, and Tracy saw the squad car parked in the alleyway where Pat said it would be, and pulled over himself, and walked toward the Front Street warehouses, one of which would bear the number Pat had given him. He had the gun in his hand in his topcoat pocket. The rain had never come tonight, but yesterday's wetness remained.

Shortly, he found the massive redbrick warehouse; a few lights were on inside, but he could hear nothing, even when he pressed his ear to the cloudy glass windows along the Front Street side of the building. He went around back and found a window ajar.

And found Pat.

The pudgy detective was sprawled amidst some garbage cans, and next to him, with a dent significantly reminiscent of Patton's head, was the garbage-can lid he'd been smacked with.

Tracy cradled his partner in his arms like a big baby, and the man began to groan, and come slowly awake.

"Tracy . . . oh!" Patton touched his head. He wasn't bleeding, but he had a bump on his head like a doorknob.

"Are you okay, Pat?

Tracy helped him slowly, tentatively, to his feet.

"The best you can say is I'm alive."

Tracy was still steadying him. "I don't suppose you know who hit you."

Patton shook his head; the motion hurt him and he winced.

Tracy let go of his partner and then watched him, to see if he'd fall again; but Patton seemed steady on his feet. Steady enough, anyway.

"Did they take your gun?"

Patton checked. "No," he said.

"Okay. Stay put. And really stay put this time. Sam and some boys should show any minute."

Tracy climbed in the window and moved through a dim—but not pitch-dark—warehouse where wooden crates and boxes were stacked high, like fortress battlements. He tripped on something, caught himself without making any noise. A train track embedded in the cement floor had caught his toe. Railroad tracks, in fact, seemed to wind here and there, throughout the warehouse.

That made a sort of sense. There was probably a freight elevator in back, with tracks on its bed, that lowered to an underground railway tunnel. The system of underground railway tunnels—fifty miles of them, on which diminutive battery-driven trains carried freight, coal, and cinders beneath the central city—had been a boon for bootleggers. Due to corrupt city officials, some of those tunnels, not long ago, had been used to ship hooch from the riverfront to warehouses like these to speakeasies like Lips Manlis's joint.

Taking care not to trip over the rails, Tracy wound his way through the towering crates, the .38 out of his top-coat pocket and tightly in hand now; he was listening quietly, hearing nothing.

Then he heard it: the echo of voices.

Tracy froze.

He moved closer to the sound, and the blurred words became distinct enough to make out.

"I didn't come to this burg to be a lousy janitor," some-body said.

"Just finish up so we can get out," another voice said.

Tracy moved toward the voices. Quickly but carefully, quietly.

"The boss sure does mean business," a third voice said, "don't he?"

The voices were louder now; cavernous though the warehouse was, Tracy was closing the distance.

"Personally," the first voice said, "I think the boss has got a screw loose."

The voices were just around the corner now.

"That's it," one of them said. "Let's get out of here before the cops show."

"*Raise 'em!*"

Tracy yelled the words as he stepped out into the open where three men dressed as cops were standing in a loose circle near some stacked crates and boxes, not doing any-thing apparently. But nearby were several mops in buck-ets, the sight of which deflected Tracy's attention just long enough for the phony cops to go for their guns, which were hipholstered in true cop fashion.

A bullet whizzed through Tracy's hat and sent it flying and he moved right toward the fake cops instead of taking cover, he charged right at them, firing his .38. Bullets zinged and sang around him, but the bad guys were unnerved—they could shoot, but they couldn't aim, back-pedaling, as he bore down on them.

There were six bullets in Tracy's .38, and Tracy parceled out two per hood, bullets going in straight as arrows but spiraling out the back.

And all three of the "cops" were as lifeless as the cement floor by the time they hit it—two face down, one face up.

Tracy stood over them, his eyes wide and burning from the cordite, his breathing heavy, near panting, his gun trailing smoke.

Then he began looking around. The buckets of soapy water interested him.

But not as much as the walnut shells.

8

Tracy was just finishing up a quick, expert diagram of the crime scene when he heard the sirens of arriving squad cars. Something blue winked up at him from the floor, and he knelt, found a sapphire earring, which he studied briefly, then dropped in his pocket.

A phalanx of uniformed men descended, with Sam Catchem leading the way.

Catchem stood with his hands in his topcoat pockets and stared down at the three corpses in cop uniforms. He wore a red fedora and a loud tie and his perpetual smirk.

"You been a busy boy, Tracy," Catchem said. "These the first cops you ever shot?"

"Recognize them?" Tracy said, joining him.

Catchem was a veteran of several police forces; he'd never lit in one spot longer than a year or two, with the Boston Police Department his most recent stop. Tracy had recently interviewed and hired Catchem for the Major Crimes squad, taking a chance on him, because the man had racked up citations for bravery and cracked major cases from L.A. to Brooklyn.

"Philly talent," Catchem said. "Brothers. The Crouch boys."

"I didn't know you were ever on the Philly force."

"Wasn't. That was when I was in the delicatessen business." He fished some smokes out of his pocket.

Tracy grabbed his arm. "No," he said. "No smoking in here till we deal with the evidence properly."

"There was a crime committed here?" Catchem asked curiously. "Killing the Crouch boys is a public service."

Chief Brandon arrived with a second wave of men. He was turning in a slow circle, looking around at the warehouse's mostly empty floor, with the expression of a tenant who had come home to find his apartment burgled. "What happened in here?"

"Lips Manlis came in," Tracy said, "but he didn't come out. Isn't that right, Pat?"

Patton was bringing up the rear, working on his derby, trying to restore its shape. "Far as I know," Patton admitted. "I slept through part of it."

"Officer Lefty Moriarty was patrolling the area," Catchem said, "and called in about the unmarked car, but that's the last we heard of him."

"Have a couple men check the periphery," Tracy said to Patton, "outside the building."

Patton nodded and did.

Moriarty was a reliable veteran cop whose beat included this waterfront area. Tracy knew him only slightly, but the man's reputation was solid.

"As for the unmarked car both Pat and Officer Moriarty saw," Tracy said, "you'll find it parked behind that wall of crates. I already checked it—no plates, no registration. You can be sure it's hot."

"Who all was *in* here?" Brandon demanded. "Besides these phony cops you drilled? What *happened* here?"

"There's a recently-in-use cement truck parked up top of that platform over there," Tracy said, pointing. Brandon and Catchem took that in, but obviously didn't grasp the significance.

Tracy walked and gestured toward the mops in buckets of water, off around the corner of the stacked crates. "We'll have the lab check that dirty water—but from the smell and texture of it, I'd say the remains of Lips Manlis were recently encased in quick-drying cement."

Now Catchem, Patton and Brandon got it, and exchanged nods and knowing looks.

"Lips always did want to be a pillar of the community," Catchem said. "So the Crouch boys were cleaning up, while somebody else dumped Lips in the drink?"

"Most likely," Tracy said. "Plenty of access to the dock from this warehouse. Neither Pat nor Moriarty would have seen that." Tracy shook his head. "It's too bad those phony cops all went down."

Catchem snorted. "Why?"

"Because," Tracy said, quietly arch, "corpses don't respond all that well to interrogation. And because I want the one who hired them—the one who ordered the rubout."

"You don't *know* for sure Manlis is dead," Brandon pointed out.

"Then," Tracy said, "we better *find* Lips Manlis, fast."

"We'll put an A.P.B. out on him," Patton said.

"Write that A.P.B. on a slip of paper," Catchem said wryly, "tie it to a rock and throw it in the river, why don't ya, and let Lips know we're lookin' for him."

"But *who* was responsible?" Brandon asked, frustration tingeing his voice. "It could be any one of the major gang figures." Brandon counted them off on his fingers. "Pruneface, Johnny Ramm, Mocca, Spaldoni, even Texie Garcia . . . with this gang war brewing. . . ."

"I *know* who was responsible," Tracy said.

Brandon looked at his ace detective with a wide-eyed, frozen expression.

"Well, c'mon, Tracy—spill!" Catchem said.

Tracy curled his finger at Catchem, Patton, and Brandon, and they followed as Tracy walked a few paces and knelt. He pointed to the walnut shells. "See those?"

"So somebody was eating walnuts," Catchem said, unimpressed. "So what?"

"So crushing walnuts and wolfing them down," Tracy

said, "is one of Big Boy Caprice's least offensive, but most distinctive, habits."

"That's right," Patton said, nodding eagerly. "I hear some doctor told 'im it was good for his liver."

"So would be givin' up booze," Catchem said.

"Walnuts," Brandon muttered, and sighed and, shaking his head, went off to meet the morgue boys who had arrived for the stiffs.

Tracy, still kneeling, said to Catchem and Patton, "Get an evidence envelope and tweezers and pick up those walnut shells carefully. We're going to see if we can't find the fingerprints of a certain Al 'Big Boy' Caprice."

Catchem shrugged. "Getting prints off a surface like that is probably a long shot."

Tracy smiled faintly. "Sam, you look like a man who's bet on his share of long shots."

"Sure," Catchem said, "but ask me if any of 'em ever come in."

"I'll take care of it, Dick," Patton said. "What's another evidence envelope after all those slugs back at the warehouse?"

Patton went off after the envelope, and Tracy stood, reached into his pocket, and withdrew the blue sapphire earring. He dangled it before Catchem's bemused face like bait.

"Is this expensive, you think?" Tracy asked him.

"On our pay, it is," Catchem said, eyes narrowing in on the jewel. "I don't figure you could spring for a pair of those for Tess. On the other hand, for people with good jobs, like your average hoodlum, it's affordable."

"Something a gangster's moll might wear, then."

"Yeah, or a movie star or a high-ticket lady of the night."

"Okay, then. Tell me: what was a *woman* doing here?"

Catchem shrugged. "Maybe pulling a trigger. It's happened before."

"There's a hair caught on there," Tracy said, demonstrating by turning the earring in the light.

"So there is," Catchem said. "Well, detective that I am, I can report that the human ear is often in the general proximity of a head of hair."

"In this case," Tracy said thoughtfully, "a platinum blonde head of hair."

Patton was back with his evidence envelope.

"Still got your tweezers?" Tracy asked him.

Patton nodded, reached in his pocket, and gave the tweezers to Tracy, who carefully plucked the silver hair from the earring and held the tweezers out for Pat, who opened the small manila envelope for Tracy to drop in the platinum strand.

"Now what?" Patton asked.

"Now you get another evidence envelope for the walnut shells," Tracy said.

"I figured you'd come up with something else," Patton said, good-naturedly smug. "So I brought a couple."

Tracy dropped the blue sapphire earring in a spare envelope Patton provided and handed the envelope with the hair in it to his bright-eyed partner, saying, "Give that to the lab boys, and the walnut shells, too." He handed the packet with the earring to Catchem, saying, "Take that back to the office—maybe we can find its owner."

"I didn't figure you were gonna suggest I take it home to the wife."

"What good would one sapphire earring do her?" Patton asked him.

"It's one more than she's got now," Catchem said.

Brandon, who'd been talking to the two uniformed men that Pat had sent out to check the periphery, was rejoining the Major Crimes squad detectives, wearing an expression longer than this evening had been.

"What's wrong, Chief?" Tracy asked hollowly. The

depth of the news was apparent in Brandon's features before even a word could be spoken.

"We've found Officer Moriarty," Brandon said. "Out behind some barrels. Shot dead."

"Damn!" Tracy said. His eyes were burning. "That tears it. He's killed a cop now. Big Boy's killed a cop now. . . ."

"If you'll excuse me, gentlemen," Brandon said somberly, "there's a widow to whom a few words need to said in bereavement. . . ."

And the big bear of man lumbered off.

"You can bet Big Boy didn't pull the trigger," Catchem said with a sneer.

That made Tracy stop and think; he drew a breath, gathered his composure.

"Gentlemen," Tracy said, all business once again, "you saw the imported talent that got shot up at the Seventh Street garage earlier tonight."

His assistants nodded.

"Well, now some boys from Philly show up in cop suits and apparently help fit Lips Manlis for a cement overcoat."

They nodded.

"So," Tracy continued, "who else in town has been bringing in out-of-town guests?"

Catchem shrugged. "Big Boy's got three heavy-hitters on his team."

"Yeah?"

"Includin' that character from the Cookson Hills, Flattop."

Tracy's eyes tightened in thought. "Flattop Jones. I thought he was running with outlaws, robbing banks, pulling payroll robberies. . . ."

"Yeah," Catchem said. "He's new to the city. They think he's Robin Hood back in the hills, but robbing hood is more like it. He did a year in an Ohio county jail;

no warrants out on him. They say he's meaner than diarrhea."

"Who are the other two?"

"'Itchy' Oliver, and a guy they call Mumbles, who's got half a dozen aliases. East Coast babies. They both got records, but no outstanding warrants. Arrests on charges rangin' from armed robbery to confidence rackets. If I had to lay odds, I'd give ten to one those three made the garage hit. Tommy gun is Flattop's style."

"Sam," Tracy said, "I respect your opinion."

"Hey, well that's nice."

"I respect it so much, I want you and Pat to bring those three in. Flattop, Itchy, and Mumbles."

"Flattop, Itchy, and Mumbles?"

Tracy nodded. "Flattop, Itchy, and Mumbles."

Catchem rolled his eyes. "Sounds like the law firm for the circus, don't it?"

"You know where to find 'em?"

"Sure," Patton said. "We got addresses on all of 'em."

Catchem laughed humorlessly. "Fancy Gold Coast apartments the likes of which we'll never see. They'll be snug in their king-size beds about now."

"Wake 'em up. I want to talk to 'em."

"When?"

"Now. Tonight. A tour of the HQ holding cells will give 'em a taste of their future."

Catchem's eyes were narrow and doubtful. "On what charge, Tracy? We ain't got any warrants on 'em!"

Tracy smirked. "Bring 'em in on suspicion of being ugly."

Catchem's eyes widened and the doubt disappeared. He nodded and shrugged at Patton who nodded and shrugged back.

"I can live with that," Catchem said seriously, and he and Patton set out to do it.

9

At Central Police Headquarters downtown, with midnight approaching, Tracy strode up the limestone steps, yellow topcoat flashing, past the white globes labeled POLICE and inside. Once up the stairs, he cut through a sprawling squad room where plainclothes detectives moved in and out among a dozen scuffed-up desks; overstuffed file cabinets lined the walls like so many suspects in a lineup. Cathedral windows threw the shadows of their panes on the green-painted walls and bare wood floors. His own office was a smoked-glass-and-wood affair at the end of a hall of similar offices; on the door it said, simply, DICK TRACY.

He went to the closet to hang up his coat; as for his hat, it was ventilated beyond further use. Tracy's assistant Pat Patton continually kidded him about going through "so gosh-darn many hats." On one wall of Patton's office down the hall, tacked like trophies, were half a dozen of Tracy's old hats, each of them riddled with at least one bullet hole, and tagged with a date and description, *i.e.*, "Boris Arson shoot-out, March 3, 1933." Smiling at the thought of this Patton-ed whimsy, he placed the latest of the drilled fedoras on a shelf in the closet, saving it for his friend. It was the least he could do for the man, whose own derby had seen hazardous duty tonight.

In the meantime, he put on another of the yellow snap-brims; he'd feel naked without one.

Tracy took his place at his desk, which faced the door. Right now that desk was relatively clean, due to the long morning he'd spent handling paperwork; still, it was cluttered with files, mug shots, half-written reports, and law books, overseen by a heavy black phone and a green-shaded banker's lamp. A framed picture of Tess was the sole personal touch.

The crime-scene photos from the garage massacre were waiting for him on his desk; they were still damp. He silently thanked Casey for staying through the evening, getting these done; but he saw nothing in the photos that his eyes hadn't told him on the scene.

He got up and went to a file cabinet and removed a can of chili from a lower drawer (it was not filed under "C," which he realized was careless of him) and opened the small can and placed it on the hot plate by the window. It didn't compare to Mike's chili, but it would suffice.

He was stirring it, bleakly pondering what Officer Moriarty's family must going through right now, when Sam Catchem came in, smiling, saying, "I got three ugly, mad-as-hades hoodlums who'd like a word with you. They're having a long, hard, frustrating night."

"Well, we all have that much in common, don't we?"

"Don't we though. After I rousted 'em outta their digs, they started asking for their phone calls, and I explained that 'departmental policy' didn't allow 'em a phone call till after they'd been booked."

"And of course you never got around to booking them."

Catchem's grin was lopsided. "Darnedest thing. I thought Pat was gonna handle that, and here he thought I was gonna. Well. Screwups do happen, don't they? Pat's taken 'em down to the holding tank, so they can keep the drunks company."

Tracy chuckled and turned away from the hot plate, where the chili was starting to bubble. "Bring 'em on up, Sam. I want to apologize for the inconvenience."

Soon Catchem and Patton were hustling the three hoods into the office. They were a well-dressed trio, at least in terms of money spent, with no sign of casual dress or getting ready for bed, which you might reasonably expect, as they'd been picked up at home relatively late at night. These boys, Tracy knew, were dressed for work.

Which meant they'd been working.

Tonight.

Itchy, who was living up to his name by compulsively scratching under one arm, seemed angriest; he stepped forward, while Flattop insolently laid back, with arms folded, and Mumbles tried to fade into the woodwork.

"We get to make one phone call each!" Itchy said. He began scratching the side of his neck. "That's the law, copper!"

"Maybe they *are* a law firm," Catchem offered.

Tracy shrugged at Catchem. Then he sat on the edge of his desk and said casually, "You guys been denied a phone call?"

"Yeah!" Itchy said.

Flattop nodded.

"Salaa," Mumbles said.

"*What* did he say?" Catchem asked.

"He said it was the law, Sam," Tracy said. "See, the thing is, you guys aren't under arrest. You're in protective custody."

"Protective custody?" Itchy said. He scratched his buttocks. "What are you trying to pull?"

"There was a death threat against the three of you," Tracy said.

"Dethret?" Mumbles said.

"Yes, a death threat," Tracy said.

Catchem and Patton sneaked confused looks at each other; even they didn't know what Tracy was talking about.

"Who made this death threat?" Itchy wanted to know. He was scratching his head.

Tracy shrugged. "I don't know. It was anonymous. Could've been any gangster in town. Big gang war brewing, I understand." Tracy's smile was pleasant and false. "Hell—it could've even been me."

That made Itchy twitch.

"You talk tough," Flattop said with a tiny, derisive smile. "But talk is cheap."

"I consider that an expert opinion," Tracy said sunnily, "coming from a cheap hood like you."

Itchy wasn't scratching now; his hands were fists and he was shaking them in the air. "We want our phone call."

With sudden savagery, Tracy grabbed the phone off his desk and yanked it out of the wall. He threw it at Itchy, who caught it clumsily. The eyes behind the Coke-bottle lenses blinked and the lips pursed nervously and then, with an unconvincing show of defiance, Itchy hurled the dead phone to the floor, where it jangled and clunked.

"Sam," Tracy said, "make a not of that—they waived their phone calls."

"It's their privilege," Catchem said with a shrug.

"Have a seat, boys," Tracy said, and Catchem roughly sat them down.

"Wastbowtraz?" Mumbles asked, shifting in his seat.

"It's about Lips Manlis, Mumbles."

The three hoods said nothing; they were motionless, except for Itchy, who was digging at one eyebrow.

Finally, Flattop said, "Who's Lips Manlis?"

"Oh," Tracy said, "I forgot. You're new in town."

"That's right. I never heard of the bum."

"You ever hear of Lefty Moriarty? Any of you? Officer Lefty Moriarty, who was killed down near the Southside Warehouse tonight?"

The hoods said nothing, remaining motionless, but for Itchy scratching his Adam's apple.

"Cops get a little testy, you know." Tracy said blandly, "when one of their own gets it. What about Big Boy Caprice? Any of you ever hear of him?"

The hoods said nothing. A sneering smile had formed on Flattop's cupid lips.

Tracy moved back to the hot plate and turned the heat down, stirred the chili. "You fellas work for Caprice, don't you?"

Flattop rose and moved forward. "Are you gonna charge us with something, flatfoot?"

Tracy took a spoonful of chili; he brought it up near his lips, but the steaming stuff changed his mind. "You can talk," he said, his back to them "or go back into protective custody for a while. I'm sure there are a few dozen holding tanks in town for you to tour before we ever get around to booking you on anything."

Flattop moved over to Tracy, who turned away from the steaming chili, the spoon still in hand. With a thick finger, Flattop thumped Tracy in the chest. Three times. Hard. He left the finger against Tracy's chest, like a pointing gun, when he spoke through tiny teeth clenched in his wide, chubby-cheeked face.

"We got *rights* coming to us, flatfoot. Book us, or shake us loose, or *you'll* be the one cooling your heels in stir. If you live that long."

Tracy gently turned the spoon sideways and the steaming hot chili slid onto Flattop's hand.

Flattop yowled, recoiled in pain, then instinctively threw a fist toward Tracy.

Tracy ducked out of the way, Flattop's punch slipping harmlessly past, and the detective came back with a roundhouse right, landing in Flattop's rather soft belly, doubling him over.

Flattop went down on his knees, as if praying to Tracy;

the hood held his belly with both hands and his face distorted like a child's before crying.

"He *said* he had rights coming to him," Catchem said to Tracy, shrugging. "Well, you gave him one."

"Take the bad man away, Sam," Tracy said. "He scares me."

"Come on, pal," Catchem said. "Come along, before you get a *left*, too."

"Take 'em all way," Tracy said disgustedly, and sat at the desk, while Patton and Catchem herded them out.

Soon Catchem came back in and said, "I've got each of 'em in his own interrogation room. But they're right. We can't get away with holdin' 'em much longer."

Tracy thought about it. "You spent more time with 'em than me. Who's the weakest?"

"Mumbles, I'd say. Flattop would spit in his mother's eye on her deathbed. Itchy's nervous only in the epidermis; I think you'd have to burn the bottom of his feet to get him to talk."

"I've got matches."

Catchem's expression was one of concern. "Tracy— take it easy. The D.A. ain't gonna put up with this."

Patton peeked around the corner. "Dick—I *know* how you feel about Big Boy. But you're the one who always says we gotta stick to the law. . . ."

Tracy grimaced.

"Don't get me wrong," Catchem said as he was going out. "I'm no stickler for detail when it comes to making a life of misery for the hoodlums of the world."

Mumbles was in interrogation room B, seated against the wall under the beam of a blinding spotlight. Other than a few chairs, the room was furnished only with a red table on which sat a ceramic gray-blue polar bear, perched on its hind legs, looking as cool as the room was not; a strangely decorative touch for such a spare, severe cubicle. By way of contrast, the sleepy-eyed hood was sweating, his blond hair messed and matted and moist; he was sitting in his lavender shirt and tie, and boxer shorts and shoes and socks. Catchem had collected the hoodlum's trousers, as a little humiliation was as good a place as any to start an interrogation. In the darkness, against a plaster wall, a uniformed man watched. On entering, Tracy sent the uniformed man out; then it was just him and Mumbles.

"Turnofflice," Mumbles said irritably.

"If I turned off the lights, Mumbles," Tracy said, pulling a chair over and resting one foot on it, leaning an arm on his knee, "then it'd be dark. And we need to throw some light on the subject."

"Thirdree," Mumbles said. "Wanmylawr."

"You're right," Tracy said pleasantly. "I *am* giving you the third degree. And if I were you, I'd want my lawyer, too."

"Aintawkn."

"Oh, you'll talk."

"Swattyuthnk."

"It's exactly what I think." He took his foot off the chair and went over to Mumbles and grabbed him and shook him till his teeth rattled.

"Lips Manlis is missing," Tracy said, and grabbed Mumbles by the shirt. "I want to know what happened to him."

"Dunno! Dunno!"

"A cop is dead, Mumbles. A career cop with a family."

"Idindunuthin!"

"As long as you didn't pull the trigger, then I don't care about you. Get it? I don't even care if you're the one that sapped Pat Patton."

Mumbles blinked. Tracy had hit a little too close to home. "I want Big Boy," Tracy said. "I know he was there. Did he do it personally?"

Mumbles's eyes went suddenly wide.

"You wonder how I know?" Tracy asked. "I have evidence, Mumbles. I may even have an eyewitness. How's your alibi for last night?"

"Sayrtyt."

"Air tight? For both the garage, and the warehouse?"

Mumbles swallowed. He nodded. Sweat ran down his face from his hair in a steady stream.

"We're building a case, Mumbles. We're building it slow, and careful. And you're going to be part of it. It's up to you which side of the courtroom you sit on."

"Ainnosqeeelr."

"That's very noble. I'm sure you're not a squealer. Though you may squeal, some, when they turn on the juice.

"Jooz?"

"The electric chair juice, Mumbles. Big Boy will be sitting in his fancy office, and you'll be frying in the hot squat."

"S'hot." He squirmed. "Turnofflice."

"No, I think we'll leave the lights on."

Sam Catchem came in.

Tracy was pacing around Mumbles's chair. "Tell me about Lips Manlis, Mumbles."

"Dunnonuthn."

"You know plenty. You give me Big Boy, and I'll give you a pass. You'll be our star witness, Mumbles. You'll be a hero."

"Smwatter."

"What'd he say?" Catchem asked.

"He wants some water," Tracy said. "That does sound refreshing. Get me a couple glasses with some ice, would you, Sam?"

"Sure."

Catchem slipped back out, and Tracy returned his attention to Mumbles.

"Where's Lips Manlis?" Tracy asked.

"Dunnonuthn."

"Where's Lips Manlis?"

"Dunnonuthun!"

"Where's Lips Manlis?"

Mumbles folded his arms, sucked in air, and jutted his chin out defiantly; his shirt was soaked with sweat. He crossed his bare, bony legs.

And Tracy noticed something.

"That's interesting," Tracy said.

"Wusstrstin?"

Tracy yanked the right shoe off Mumbles's crossed leg and held it up so the hood could see the dirty sole of it. The dirt was gray, powdery.

"Cement," Tracy said. "Cement. Maybe I already have Lips Manlis's murderer in custody."

"Yrcrazee! Yrscrueeyrnutz!"

"I'm not crazy. I'm not screwy. Nor am I nuts. But you, my friend, are in way over your head."

Catchem came back in, carrying, waiterlike, a tray with several ice-filled glasses. Tracy directed him to set it on the table near the ceramic polar bear and Catchem did. Then he handed Catchem the shoe.

"Take this to the lab right away," Tracy said. "Confirm that the substance on the sole is cement, would you?"

"Sure." Catchem grinned. "Be right back."

Tracy swiveled the ceramic polar bear slightly and revealed a spigot and filled the glasses. Mumbles's eyes widened as he realized how close to the water he'd been all along.

Mumbles reached for a glass; Tracy slapped his hand away. Catchem caught this from the corner of his eye as he was going out.

"This water isn't for you, Mumbles," Tracy said. "It's for me. I'm working up a thirst, questioning you."

Tracy poured a large glassful of water, ice cubes clinking in the glass. Mumbles, his face wetter than a man taking a shower, looked yearningly at the glass as Tracy slowly drained it.

"Ah," Tracy said. "That's refreshing."

Mumbles, caught in the beam of the spotlight like an animal in the headlights of a car, looked frantically at Tracy. And then the hoodlum hung his head. "Awrytawrytawrytalredyahltawk."

"Hold that thought," Tracy said, and he called in the plainclothes policewoman stenographer, Mrs. Green, from the hall.

Mumbles was giving his statement when Catchem returned.

"BigBoydidit," Mumbles said.

"Did what, Mumbles?" Tracy asked, handing him a glass of ice water.

Mumbles gulped it. Then he exploded: "BigBoydiditItelyuhedidit! HekildLpsMlis!"

"Where? When?"

"Warehousetonighcementoverct. Isawtall."

"Okay, Mrs. Green," Tracy said to the stenographer, "you heard him. That's his testimony."

"*What* did he say?" the stenog asked.

"He said he was at the warehouse tonight," Tracy said. "They gave Manlis a cement overcoat. Mumbles said he saw it all." Tracy nodded to the stenographer. "Thank you very much, Mrs. Green. You may go now."

The confused woman did, and Catchem nodded for Tracy to step out in the hall. Tracy found Pat Patton waiting there, looking eager but apprehensive.

"That was cement on his shoe, all right," Patton said.

"Good," Tracy said. "See if the lab boys can match it to the cement in the back of that truck at the warehouse."

"And to the dirty water in those mop buckets," Patton added.

"Right," Tracy said, nodding. "Good man, Pat."

Catchem pointed toward the interrogation booth. "What do we do with Mumbles now?"

Tracy shrugged. "Give him his pants and shake him loose with his pals. We'll keep that statement of his tucked in our back pocket, for now."

"That was coercion, Tracy," Catchem said, "and you know it. Inadmissible. And illegal."

Tracy bristled. "As illegal as killing Manlis? As illegal as killing Officer Moriarty? As illegal as shooting my girl's *father*?"

Catchem smiled soothingly, cigarette drooping from his lips. He put a hand on Tracy's shoulder. "Hey— Dick. Pal of mine. I'm on your side. But if we keep playin' fast and loose with the law, the bad guys are gonna walk on a technicality."

"Not if we shoot first," Tracy said, "and investigate afterward."

"Good point," Catchem admitted. "Unfortunately, right now Pat has some more news—bad news, in this case."

"Oh?"

Patton nodded glumly. "We checked that cement truck for prints; wiped clean."

Tracy frowned. "What about the walnuts?"

Patton said, "Lab boys are still working on those."

Tracy sighed. "Well, we got enough to make the arrest. The fingerprints on the walnuts'll clinch it, tomorrow."

Catchem's eyes tightened with doubt. "We're picking up Big Boy already? Shouldn't we have a little more be-fore—"

"Sam, we're picking him up *now*. Tonight."

"It's a gamble," Patton said.

"Worth taking," Tracy said.

"And here I thought gambling was illegal," Catchem said.

 Keys was handsome in an insolent, almost pretty manner: his eyes were slanted, dark hair slicked back, cigarette drooping seductively down like an extension of his upper lip.

Skilled fingers glided over the ivories with an effortlessness that belied years of practice. Classical training as a youth, before his father's business went under; playing honky-tonks and bordello parlors as a kid and a young man. He'd played recitals, and he'd played jam sessions, and spent a season with the Spike Dyke Orchestra.

There'd been an agent, not so long ago, who had him marked for stardom; was getting ready to put a stage band together for 88 to lead. That went south when the agent caught his best girl in 88's arms.

Dames had always been 88's blessing and his curse. He couldn't resist them, and they couldn't resist him; the only difference was, his attraction was strictly physical, and eventually wore off—the girls always took it more seriously. Saw something in him they wanted to tame. He was a bad boy and good girls liked that.

He'd have never got stuck here, in this rut, in this glorified joint, backing up this two-bit torch singer Breathless Mahoney, if something unlikely hadn't occurred: he'd fallen for her.

And Breathless liked him, too, or at least so it seemed; she showed him little of the arrogance or the willfulness she'd displayed to Lips Manlis. Her soft flesh was compliant under his touch, reflecting anything but the boredom she flaunted at other men in the same way she flaunted her beauty, her body.

To Lips Manlis, 88 had merely been the "funny boy" who drove Breathless around, who shopped with her, went to The Russian Tea Room with her, escorted her to the theater. It had been an easy deception, but no less dangerous for that.

He was sure part of what attracted him to her was the danger. Love was like a knife: useless if it was dull, at its best when it had a sharp edge.

88 was a natty dresser, but tonight his suitcoat was off and so was his tie. It was the middle of the night and he'd been banging at the keys since the first show at seven that evening. On the stage, just a step up off the dance floor, a troupe of chorus girls—most of whom he knew intimately, if not well—were sagging in their rehearsal clothes. Their makeup was streaking, their hairdos coming undone.

It was all because the new boss—Al "Big Boy" Caprice—had arrived around eleven, politely announced to the patrons that the Club Ritz was under new management and temporarily closed—and promptly cleared the joint out! Shortly thereafter, the new boss had begun rehearsing the girls, personally.

And whenever the club's musical director—88 himself—made a suggestion, Big Boy snarled at him to shut up.

It had begun with Big Boy's brilliant notion to do a "real peppy version of 'Brother, Can You Spare a Dime.'"

88 had tried to explain that the tune would not work effectively up-tempo, and that the patrons might consider a cheerful rendering of that particular dirge in bad taste.

"*Your* taste is in your *mouth!*" Big Boy had told him.

"Thank you very much," he'd said.

Big Boy had then turned to the girls and, flicking ashes

from his enormous cigar onto the shining dance floor, said, "You girls will come out dressed like bums, like tramps, and then you sing a little, and then strings offstage'll yank the raggedy clothes offa you . . . they'll be these, like what you-call-it, breakneck garments."

"Breakaway," 88 corrected.

"Shut-up!" Big Boy had said. "Anyway, under the rags you'll have a lot of skin and not much else. Then it'll rain balloons and confetti and everything. It'll be classy as all get-out."

Big Boy had directed 88 to play a "real peppy version" of the song, and 88 had done so . . . dozens upon dozens of times. They had alternated this exercise with rehearsing an equally peppy number called "More," an up-tempo ode to greed, which seemed fitting to 88, considering the nature of his new employer.

Big Boy, oddly enough, had a sort of childish energy; he got in the midst of the girls and demonstrated steps and kicks, his arms around the girls, getting real chummy. At first the girls, despite the late hour, were kind of charmed by their new boss and his larger-than-life presence and quaintly cornball notions. But when any chorine failed to kick at exactly the right moment, or precisely the right height, he would shout obscenities at her. He'd slapped a couple of the girls, as the night wore on.

"You're gonna do it till you do it right," he told them. "When people come here, they're gonna get something classy, something perfect. They're gonna think they're in a lousy palace. And they're gonna *know* who's king of this town."

Big Boy had just stepped out momentarily, when Breathless drifted in, in white slacks and matching halter top, trimmed in gold sequins. She strode across the dance floor, jiggling the goods, but without any of her usual studied seductiveness. She was irritated. As opposed to annoyed, which was her natural state.

88 began to play, "If There Is Someone Lovelier Than You," and it softened her as she reached the piano, and leaned against it.

She glanced with ironic disgust at the exhausted chorines who were leaning against each other, or the back stage-wall, or sitting like Indians. Some were grabbing smokes. They looked as feminine as a baseball team.

He broke back into "Brother, Can You Spare a Dime," and the girls made faces.

"You still floggin' that dead horse?" Breathless said to 88. "You been on that all night!"

"Yowsah," 88 said, and went back to noodling the ballad. "You missed the part where he had 'em lay down on the stage to make patterns, like he saw in the movies. I tried to explain it was a different medium, but His Eminence didn't see it that way."

"Next week, 'On a Waterfall,'" she leered, and shook her head, and sighed, still leaning against the piano; she looked tired, but on her, tired looked great. What a gal, he thought. He began playing "On a Waterfall."

"Cig me," she said.

He kept playing the left-hand vamp, but with his right took his deck of cigarettes from off the piano and shook a smoke toward her. She plucked it out with her lips.

"Light me," she said.

He did, using a monogrammed lighter the wife of a theater owner in Cedar Rapids gave him last year.

"It's enough to make me long for that loser Lips," she said, and took a deep drag on the cigarette.

"Lips was a beast," 88 agreed, easing into 'Cocktails for Two.' But this clown is the missing link."

She laughed; it was low and sultry. "Where *is* slopehead about now?"

"Outside." 88 smirked, his cigarette drooping as ever downward, and began playing "I Get a Kick Out of

You." He said, "He painted himself a 'Reopening Soon' sign and he took it out to the doorman. He's encouraged he can whip this sorry bunch of showgirls into shape in a day or two."

Her blue eyes were at once sleepy and alert. "I bet you'd like to blow this dump."

"Baby, we could go out on the road as a duo and make some real dough."

She shook her head no. "Without a hit platter, we'd make chickenfeed. Trust me. We can make a killing here. Big Boy may be a repellent human being, but he has an infinitely greater capacity for the acquisition of power than the late Lips. The money is going to start rolling in soon."

"For him."

She gave him a wicked smile that was mostly her upper lip. She blew out blue smoke. "We'll find a way to get our share. More than our share."

He studied her. "You sure of that, baby?"

"Sure I'm sure. Enough to go away and find that desert island, lover."

He began to play "Blue Moon." She sang along, softly, in a wispy voice. Then she made up a few lyrics: "Big Goon—why don't you leave me alone, biggest creep that I've known . . ."

That's as far as she got when 88's laughter became infectious and got her laughing, too. He stopped playing, she stopped singing, and they laughed till they cried.

Neither of them saw Big Boy coming.

The gangster hadn't heard the little song Breathless was singing, but the laughter apparently rubbed him the wrong way, anyway, because with a swift move—incredibly swift for a man of his girth—Big Boy slammed the piano lid down on the fingers of 88's right hand, which had been resting on the keys, unsuspecting.

The pain was as excruciating as it was sudden.

From above the knuckles, where the lid had come down, his fingers went white and began to throb and swell as he massaged them.

"That was stupid!" Breathless said. "He's the top piano man in town."

"I don't like people laughin' at me," Big Boy said, factually, not defensively.

"He wasn't laughing at you!"

Big Boy slapped her.

Not a vicious slap—just hard enough to express displeasure, and ownership. Her eyes went wide and wet, but she did not seem about to cry.

"Listen to me, sweetheart," Big Boy said, gesturing with a hand in which the huge cigar rested, "bein' my girl don't mean you get to lip off. Next time piano man gets wise with me, I don't rap his knuckles. I twist his little fingers off like pretzels. Understood?"

He looked at Breathless and she nodded, twice.

He looked at 88, who sat cradling his throbbing right hand in his left, and 88 nodded as well.

"And sweetheart," he told her gently, with a fatherly smile, easing an arm around her, "I'll do the same to you. Only it won't be your fingers." He touched her cheek. "Nice skin. But you know the trouble with delicate skin like that . . . it scars real easy. I recommend milk baths, baby."

The girls on the stage were taking all of this in with wide, frightened eyes.

"Keep playin', piano man," Big Boy said.

88 made himself play, throb though his fingers did.

"See?" Big Boy asked, smiling benevolently. "Sounds fine. Sounds better, even."

The gangster, looking like a big, hunched evil gnome in his gaudy dark blue shirt and suspenders and red tie, kept rehearsing the girls, maniacally. He tried singing along. Listening to Big Boy sing hurt 88 worse than his fingers.

They were taking five, when the front door sprang open and a broad-shouldered man in a yellow topcoat and matching fedora came in, hauling three of Big Boy's boys in, bodily—Itchy, Flattop and Mumbles.

88 had lived in the city long enough to know who Dick Tracy was. The detective, backed up by two more plainclothes officers, deposited the three gunmen in chairs at a table, like a bullying maitre d', and said, "Hello, Big Boy. Here's your garbage."

Big Boy Caprice's clothes, Tracy noticed as he approached the man, were as expensive as they were tasteless. The gangster was standing by the piano, talking to a beautiful, sultry-looking blonde. A platinum blonde, Tracy noted, who happened to be wearing *one* blue sapphire earring. What a coincidence.

"This is a private club, copper," Big Boy said, sneering at Tracy, then turning his glowering gaze on Patton and Catchem, as well. The blonde's face was blank, but her eyes smoldered.

"Here's my membership card," Tracy said, and slammed his warrant on the piano. The piano player winced; you would have thought Tracy slammed the lid on his fingers or something.

Big Boy unfolded the legal document, gave it a cursory read, and wadded it up and threw it at Tracy's feet.

"Murder? Lips Manlis? I didn't even know he was dead!"

"You seem all choked up about it," Tracy said. "You guys used to be pals."

"I'll bust out crying in private, if you don't mind, copper. But I'm sorry to hear old Lips is gone. Heart attack?"

"More like hardening of the arteries," Catchem said. "Head to toe."

"Somebody tailored him a cement suit," Tracy said. "Earlier tonight."

The blonde seemed to flinch, around the eyes; it was barely perceptible, but Tracy caught it.

"That's sad," Big Boy said. "What funeral parlor did they take the body to? There *is* a body, ain't there?" Big Boy smiled smugly, reaching in his pocket for a walnut, cracked it in a fist, forcefully, selected the nuts from amongst the cracked shells.

"You like walnuts," Tracy said, "don't you, Big Boy?"

Big Boy popped the nuts in his mouth and chewed arrogantly. "Lot of people like walnuts. Good for the liver."

"But bad for the brain, maybe. You're getting sloppy, Big Boy. You let one of your triggermen kill a cop. That's bad for business."

The look in Tracy's eyes made Big Boy swallow his mouthful of walnuts, hard. But he summoned a smile. "Got any evidence, Tracy? Or is this just the usual police harrassin'?"

"I'll ask the questions, Caprice. Where were you tonight?"

"Well, I been here at my new club, since maybe eleven."

"And before that?"

"I was at my dancing lesson," Big Boy said.

"Your dancing lesson?" Catchem asked with amused doubt.

"Yeah. I'm learning all about chor-e-a-graphy—so I can run my new club good. Been rehearsing the girls tonight, you know. Gotta know that stuff." He smiled magnanimously at the chorus girls, who were taking all this in with wide eyes and wider ears.

Patton's round face was crinkled with skepticism. "A dance lesson till eleven at night?" he asked.

"I got a female instructor." Big Boy shrugged

grandly. "She's Latin. She's got a thing for me. Sue me."

"No," Tracy said, turning the gangster around quickly, roughly, snapping on the bracelets, "we'll just arrest you."

Big Boy glared over his shoulder at the detective. "You've had it in for me for years, haven't you, flatfoot? You got this crazy idea I had something to do with that Trueheart dame's old man buying it. You're nuts! Off your rocker! Rousting my boys. My lawyers are gonna make mincemeat outta you."

"Just in time for Christmas," Catchem said pleasantly.

"Come on, Big Boy," Tracy said. "You're going to love the food at the county jail."

They walked him toward the door. Flattop, Itchy, and Mumbles looked menacingly at the detectives, but kept their place.

"When'd you buy this joint, Big Boy?" Catchem asked casually.

"Tonight. I got a signed contract."

"You saw Lips tonight?" Tracy snapped. "Must've been before your dance lesson."

Big Boy scowled. "I got nothin' more to say to you bums." He looked back at his three stooges and said, "Boys, call my lawyer!" Then to the chorus girls he called, "This ain't a break! Keep rehearsin'!"

Then the three detectives and the gangster were out on the street where a squad car waited, a uniformed cop driving. Catchem shoved Big Boy in the back of the car and got in with him, glancing back curiously at Tracy.

"Are you coming, Tracy?"

"No. Take Caprice to the lockup, and Pat—you get him booked. Sam, you hightail it back here. And there's something I want you to bring with you when you do. . . ."

11

Breathless Mahoney sat in her spacious, luxurious dressing room and carefully studied her face in her bulb-lined makeup mirror; she was checking for bruises or abrasions. There seemed to be none, fortunately. As she stared at herself coldly, she thought about Big Boy. Her face seemed to harden, to become a beautiful mask.

She heard the door open and knew it would be 88.

"Hi, baby," she said, not looking. "How's the hand?"

"Fine," a deep male voice said. Not 88's. "How's your face?"

She turned in the seat.

It was the cop. The younger, better-looking one with the jaw like the prow of a ship. He closed the door with one hand, his fedora in the other. She smiled. Crossed her legs.

"This is breaking and entering, you know," she said.

"Maybe you should call a cop."

Her lips pursed in amusement. "Maybe I should. You're Dick Tracy, aren't you?"

"That's right."

"You mind if I call you . . . Dick?"

"It's my name. What's yours?"

"Breathless."

"That's not a name."

"It'll just have to do, won't it?"

He drifted over to her. He didn't seem to be looking her over, like so many men did, she noted; perhaps he was just more discreet. But he was a detective: she didn't figure he'd fail to examine the evidence.

"Big Boy slapped you, didn't he?"

She nodded. "Did you see it?"

"No. One side of your cheek was blushing, and I didn't figure you embarrassed easily. Didn't take much of a detective to put that and Big Boy's rep for roughing up women together to figure you'd got a taste."

"I've been slapped before." She went to the bar; poured two martinis.

"I'd imagine," he said. "But why put up with it?"

She handed one of the drinks toward him. "What do you mean?"

He took the glass. "A few hours ago you were Lips Manlis's girl, weren't you?"

"Do you know that, or are you just guessing?"

"I'm a detective, remember."

"Are you going to arrest me?"

"If I were going to arrest you, I'd have done it by now." He smiled mirthlessly; sipped the drink. "You're in a cheery mood, for somebody whose boyfriend passed away so recently. No grief for the man?"

"I'm in mourning, sure."

"Yeah?"

"I'm wearing black lace step-ins. If you don't believe me . . ."

"I'll take your word for it."

"Listen, Tracy. Why don't you tell me what you're up to?"

"I want you to tell me who killed Lips Manlis."

"Don't you know?"

"Sure, I know. Your new boyfriend. The suave man-about-town who slapped your sweet face not so long ago, and who'll do the same again and again, unless you care to stop him."

"Or take a powder."

"Or take a powder," Tracy said, shrugging. "You know, I don't think you're such a bad kid."

"Oh?" she said archly.

"I think underneath it all, you . . ."

She stood. "I already told you, Tracy—underneath it all are black lace step-ins."

"I don't think you're as tough as you pretend to be, Breathless."

"Look who's talking," she said, and she slipped her arms around him. Pressed against him.

"I take it back," he said. "You *are* bad."

"I'm even better than that," she said, and brought her lips close to his, and he pushed her gently away.

"No," he said. "It might be nice. I won't deny it. But I understand you, Breathless. You have your weapons and I have mine. I just thought maybe you'd like to see the guy who killed Lips Manlis get his. I figured you'd be on Manlis's side, in this thing . . ."

She laughed.

That surprised him. "Whose side *are* you on?"

"The *only* side, Tracy." She smiled and gestured to her bosom. "My own."

There was a knock at the door. Tracy straightened himself and answered the knock and it was one of the other two plainclothesmen, the rumpled-face, freckled one who was always smirking. If he'd been the one come calling, Breathless thought, I'd have him leaving his wife by now.

Tracy took something from the rumpled-face detective and nodded at him and shut the door, leaving the man out in hall.

"Recognize this?" he asked.

He was holding out her blue sapphire earring

"Not really," she said.

"You're wearing its twin," he said, moving closer. "I saw you wearing it out there. So I sent for it. Figured you'd want it back."

"Thanks, but no thanks. I am missing an earring, but taking a close look at that one . . . I don't think it *is* the mate."

"A little detective work, checking local jewelers and so on, and even without your help, we'll I.D. it as yours all right."

"So what?"

"We found it at the warehouse tonight. Where Lips Manlis was killed. You know how they killed him?"

She looked at the floor.

"Actually," Tracy continued, "we don't know yet whether he was alive or dead, when the cement was poured in. Be better if he were dead first. Drowning in wet cement, ye gods. That's a rough one. Local hoods call it 'the bath.'"

"Please be quiet."

He came over and held the earring in her face. "You *were* there. You know it and I know it. Now, I can take you down to headquarters and we can sweat it out of you under the hot lights, or . . ."

She touched his lips with a fingertip. "I sweat better in the dark."

Their eyes locked together; his will was as strong as hers, and she liked that. The attraction, the pull, was magnetic; she could tell he felt it, too.

"I know how you feel, Tracy," she said, making her voice as sultry as possible—and that, she knew, was plenty sultry. "You don't know if you want to hit me, or kiss me. I get a lot of that."

He sighed, shook his head; he was clutching the earring tightly in a fist. He raised his other hand and pointed a finger at her. "I'm going to put Big Boy away. You want to help, you give me a call. You don't want to help, you might find yourself living in a room a lot smaller than this one. It won't have a makeup mirror or fancy white carpet. And your roommate won't be some man you can wrap around your pinky. More likely some hard-nosed harridan who strangled her husband."

"Stop," she said with dry sarcasm. "You're scaring me."

He grimaced, shook his head. Then more softly, he said, "Right now you're safe. Big Boy's in jail—you're the one who can keep him there. Just think about it. Okay?"

"Okay," she said.

He started out.

"Dick . . ."

He looked at her.

"See you again, Tracy."

She kissed the air.

She thought she saw him smile, ever so faintly, before he disappeared out the door.

The radio was on, softly, when Tracy entered his two room apartment—"Stay as Sweet as You Are," a crooner seemed to be advising Tess, who had fallen asleep in Tracy's favorite easy chair. A ladies' magazine lay across her lap, her head nestled sweetly against an oversized arm of the chair.

He took off his coat and hat and hung them on a hook on the wall just inside the bedroom, where the Kid lay sleeping—snoring—on Tracy's bed.

He felt a strange tug of emotions—guilt was part of it, from the encounter with the sultry saloon singer; but most of it was that feeling of warmth that Tess gave him. He went to her and knelt beside her, and gently touched her hair.

She awoke with a start.

Tracy, a little startled himself now, said, "I didn't mean to wake you."

"Oh my," Tess said, sitting up straight, yawning. "What time is it?"

"Before dawn," Tracy said. "Barely. How did you and the dead-end kid fare?"

Her smile was crinkly. "He's been sawing logs since his head hit the pillow, about two minutes after we got here.

"You gave him the bed, I see."

"Yes," she said. "I didn't figure he'd had the opportunity to sleep in one too often."

"Probably not."

"I'd better go," she said, smoothing herself, standing. Tracy got up and helped her into her coat, and moved with her toward the door. She paused to adjust the position of a vase of lilies she'd given him earlier.

"Aren't these pretty?" she said. She yawned again. "I'll have to be getting to the greenhouse before you know it. New delphiniums coming in."

"Thanks for taking care of the kid," Tracy said. He reached in his pocket for his car keys. "You take my buggy home; it's parked right in front. I'll have Pat pick me up on his way to work."

She took the keys, smiled, and said, "You needn't walk me down." She touched his face. "You look exhausted. Please get some rest."

Tracy glanced toward the bedroom. "Do you want me to make the arrangements with the orphanage . . . ?"

She squeezed his hand. "Not just yet. He's such a sweet child."

Tracy grinned. "Sweet child?"

"Listen, I only have to work half a day," she said. "You and Pat drop the boy off at the greenhouse on your way to headquarters this morning."

"What . . . ?"

"Let me have the boy. Let me show him a good time, buy him some new clothes, give him a taste of what being a *real* kid is like, not some wild boy of the road."

Tracy sighed, but he was smiling. "You know what?"

"What?"

He leaned his face to hers and kissed her. A soft, sweet kiss.

"That," he said. "I'll drop him off about eight. You just hold onto my car and I'll meet you two at Mike's for supper."

Her smile was glowing.

Tracy laughed softly. "And you wild boys and girls of the road be good, now—hear?"

"I hear," she said sweetly, gratefully.

The warmth, and the guilt, flooded him.

"Tess . . ."

"What?"

"I'd do anything in the world for you, you know. You do know that?"

"Even take me for a drive in the country?" She touched his face again. "Good night, Dick."

And she was gone.

12

The sun was shining, reflecting off the sandstone steps of the majestic County Courthouse; winter seemed held at bay, for the moment. Unfortunately, Tracy thought, the same could be said for a certain blind woman who could be seen balancing scales by way of a statue near the top of those stairs.

Tracy and District Attorney Fletcher held back for a moment, not wanting to get caught in a confrontation. A crowd of reporters had come in a tide up the steps toward the descending Al Caprice and his several expensive attorneys. Big Boy, beaming, waving his fedora to them as if he were a grand marshal and they were a parade, gesturing with the other hand in a magnanimous manner, had won a victory here today.

"What's your reaction," reporter Bush of the *News* asked, "to having your case thrown out of court?"

"Judge Debirb is a fine American," Big Boy said. "He knows police brutality when he sees it."

Charet of the *Tribune* asked, "Isn't a strong police response understandable when one of their own is slain? Specifically, Officer Lefty Moriarty?"

"What?" Big Boy blurted indignantly. "Are you sayin' the ends justifies the means? That's a shockin' way to look at this world of ours. But I will say I think Officer Moriarty's murder is an awful thing. A tragedy. I sent flowers."

"Will you be taking legal action against the city," another reporter followed up, "for false arrest?"

"Or against Dick Tracy specifically?" asked another.

Big Boy patted the air, smiled sweetly. "Fellas, these legal matters are up to my attorneys. But I'll say this." His expression darkened. "This Tracy character is outta control. He's either a fool, or flat-out crazy. The city had oughta get rid of him."

"If you don't get rid of him first, you mean?" called out a voice in back.

"Who said that?" Big Boy snarled. But then the snarl eased into a smile. The sweet one, again. "You boys have me all wrong. You believe these police lies. I'm no criminal. I'm a respectable businessman. In fact, other than a couple juvenile raps, I got a clean record."

"But dozens of arrests," Bush said.

One of the attorneys stepped forward. "And no convictions."

"I've heard that about Big Boy." Bush smiled.

"My name," Big Boy said tightly, pointing a thick finger at the reporter, "is Al Caprice. You fellas want me to keep givin' out with the colorful quotes, you better treat me with some respect, *capeesh?*"

"Mr. Caprice," Charet asked, "who do you think killed Lips Manlis?"

"Well, who's to say he's been killed? I think he left town or something. Anyway, you know what the witnesses say."

"Oh?"

"Yeah, three cops yanked him out of his club. I'd like to know if this loose-cannon of a *cop*, Tracy, has an alibi."

"Mr. Caprice," Bush said tightly, "you know as well as any of us that Tracy shot it out with those three 'cops' in the warehouse where Manlis was seen going in, but not coming out. They were torpedoes from Philadelphia."

"Sounds like Tracy covering up for himself, if you ask me," Big Boy said.

One of his lawyers, apparently distressed by his client's

public accusations about a member of the police department, whispered urgently to Big Boy, who brushed him off like a fly.

"Any other questions, gents?"

"Yes," a voice from the back of the group called out. It was Matt Masterson, the *Chronicle*'s crime-beat columnist. He was a strikingly handsome man with a full head of dark curly hair. "What about the Seventh Street Garage Massacre? The police seem to think you were involved."

"The cops want to make me their patsy for every murder since Booth popped Lincoln. Well, I was at my dancin' lesson that night. And I can prove it."

"You can?" Bush asked.

"Sure." Big Boy put a hand on his stomach and did a little mambo step, right there on the courthouse steps.

Flashbulbs popped, and the reporters smiled and laughed. Except for Bush, Charet, and Masterson, who as hardened crime reporters had seen too much suffering and murder to be amused by gangsters who got off scot-free with the press by giving them colorful quotes and snazzy pics.

Caprice moved through the reporters to his limousine, where Itchy was behind the wheel; Flattop, who'd also been riding in front, got out to open the door for his boss.

"Don't any of you boys miss the grand opening of the new Club Ritz," Big Boy called out by way of farewell. "Tomorrow night! You're all my personal guests."

He bowed, making a sweeping gesture with his hat, and climbed in back of the limo. Shutting the door for his boss, Flattop wore a tiny smug smile on his perpetually puckered lips.

Up at the top of the stairs, behind the statue of blind justice, Tracy said to Fletcher, "Those reporters aren't going away. We'd better brave it."

"You take the side exit," Fletcher said tightly, his eyes

cold behind round-lensed glasses. "Have my driver bring the car around."

Tracy nodded and went back inside.

D.A. Fletcher waited while Tracy got a head start, then moved down the stairs, the reporters swarming back up to meet him.

"Mr. District Attorney," a reporter said, as the cacophony of questions finally died down into one decipherable one, "will you be taking disciplinary action against Chief of Detectives Tracy for making this false arrest?"

Fletcher smiled gently and raised a benedictory hand. "Please. Gentlemen—please. Detective Tracy is the most honored, decorated officer this town has ever seen. He has a reputation, highly justified, for his scrupulous procedural approach. It's ludicrous for you to suggest that his actions would be anything but by-the-book."

"But isn't this a personal matter?" Bush asked. He could be just as tough with those representing the law as he was with criminals. "Doesn't Tracy blame Big Boy for the murder of his girlfriend's father, Emil Trueheart?"

"Yeah," Charet said, "isn't this starting to look a little like a vendetta on Tracy's part?"

"Detective Tracy," Fletcher said, quietly, mustache twitching, "is indeed under a good deal of strain. But I have the utmost confidence in his good judgment."

"Mr. D.A.," Masterson called out, "what's the story on Frank Redrum's escape?"

"Yeah," Bush said, "if Redrum returns to our fair city, the bullets could really start to fly!"

"I have no more facts on that matter than you do," Fletcher said. The D.A. gave them his most ingratiating smile. "All I know, gentlemen, is what I read in the papers."

And Fletcher, nodding his thanks to the press corps, moved down the steps through the throng to where a black sedan, with a police driver behind the wheel, had drawn up to the curb. Fletcher joined Tracy in back as the sedan pulled away, leaving the frustrated faces of reporters behind.

"Shall I drop you at headquarters?" Fletcher asked, as they settled into the backseat.

"I'd appreciate that," Tracy said.

The D.A. frowned. "Tell me—what's this 'Frank Redrum' business the pressboys are so worked up about?"

"I spoke to Inspector James Trailer of the F.B.I. this morning," Tracy said easily. "Apparantly Redrum escaped . . . or attempted to escape . . . from Alcatraz Prison last night. He was using a homemade raft, made of shirts from the laundry and scrapwood from the prison shop. The raft was found washed up, in pieces, on the island's shore. He would seem not to have made it."

"The wire services say he's assumed dead. What do you think?"

Tracy shrugged. "There have been no successful escapes from the Rock that I know of. On the other hand, his body hasn't been found."

"If he survived," the D.A. asked, "would he come back here?"

"I doubt it," Tracy said. "I think, whether Redrum is at the bottom of Frisco Bay or not, we've seen the last of him."

Fletcher seemed pensive. "I didn't prosecute that case."

"It was just before your term of office began, Mr. D.A. Redrum was a grotesque-looking character—a regular Phantom of the Opera, unmasked. He ran a gang in the twenties, they betrayed him, he did time, got out, kidnapped and bumped 'em off one at a time. Strictly revenge. No pieces left here for him to pick back up."

"I remember it vaguely," Fletcher said, nodding. "The newshounds had fun with it, didn't they?"

"They sure did. Like they're trying to have fun with this. Listen, I heard most of that from the car—and I appreciate you sticking up for me back there."

Fletcher looked sideways at Tracy and the look was a hard, unfriendly one. "You think that was for *you?* I only did that to minimize the embarrassment of my going into court with so little." He shook his head. "You told me you could deliver fingerprints."

"I know."

The lab had tried both the iodine transfer and the silver nitrate—twice—and could not pull Big Boy Caprice's fingerprints off the walnut shells. Like Sam said, it had been a gamble. And Tracy had lost.

"The newshounds are right, Tracy, and so is Big Boy: You're out of control. You're on a vendetta. And I won't stand for it."

"I'm in complete control."

"I don't think so. Listen, I've got a good shot at becoming Mayor, coming election. And you're in line for Chief of Police. Don't mess it up for the both of us. Back off. Cool off."

"It was a good bust, Fletcher," Tracy insisted. "I had sufficient evidence at the scene to—"

"You had nothing. You had less than nothing. When you go around beating up private citizens, kidnapping them, making false arrests, throwing them in jail . . ."

Tracy's mouth was a thin line as he said, "Private Citizen Caprice is responsible for seven deaths so far this week, including Officer Moriarty. Go back any farther, you'll start losing count, quick."

Fletcher's eyes softened; he shook his head, wearily, regretfully. "I'm sorry about Miss Trueheart's father."

"Thank you."

His face turned stern again. "But if you can't control yourself," Fletcher continued, "I'll direct Chief Brandon to remove you from the Detective Bureau. And I'll be forced to prosecute you for misconduct. And do you know something, Tracy?"

"What, Fletcher?"

"That's a case I guarantee you I won't lose." The car drew to a stop. "Here's headquarters. Go on in and see if you can get from here to your office without tearing a hole in the Constitution."

Just after dark, Tracy slid onto a stool at Mike's Diner and ordered a cup of coffee; Sam Catchem had dropped him off here. The Major Crimes squad had spent a frustrating, unfruitful afternoon examining the evidence from both the garage and warehouse shootings.

Mike set the steaming cup of black liquid before the detective.

"Back so soon, Tracy?" the counterman said. "You working a case in this neck of the woods?"

"Naw," Tracy said. He sipped the coffee; it was bitter and near scalding. He took another sip. "Meeting somebody here."

"That girl of yours?

"Yeah, and our little friend. He thinks your meat loaf is a miracle."

"Well, this is everybody's lucky night—that's the Blue Plate Special again."

Tracy smiled and sipped his coffee. He felt tired, and he felt discouraged. Big Boy was sprung, Mumbles was apparently in hiding, and Tracy felt his own job being threatened.

Nonetheless, he had managed, at several points today, to connect up with Tess and the Kid. They'd called from Marshall and Bradbury's Department Store, where Tracy had to intermediate when Tess and the boy clashed over clothes. In fact, Tracy had chased the Kid down the street, when the urchin—clad only in his underwear—made a break for it.

Tracy had rounded the boy up, telling him, "if you don't want to wear that suit, march back in that store and tell her you don't. Are you going to run away every time somebody tries to make you do something you don't want to do?"

Later, he had joined with them again, at the northside florist's shop where Tess worked, and had accompanied them to the zoo and aquarium, albeit fitfully, and for that long-promised if ultimately brief ride in the country. He'd even found time to buy the Kid a baseball and glove. But he'd been called back to headquarters and/or the courthouse five different times.

Plus, he'd dropped by the funeral home to pay his respects to Officer Moriarty's family. Chief Brandon had offered a full police funeral, but the Moriarty family had wanted to keep it small, simple, private. But the line of cops who'd come for visitation today seemed never-ending.

Now Tracy sat at the counter in the diner, sipping his coffee, enjoying a few moments of solitude. But he was glad when, a few minutes later, Tess and the Kid came bustling in. The Kid was dressed up in the little red suit Tess had selected for him—short checked pants with argyle knee socks, a blue shirt and black-and-white polka dot tie, and a little red cap, under which his reddish hair sprouted like weeds. He looked clean and vaguely miserable.

"Dick!" Tess said. "What a wonderful day we've had."

Tracy got off the stool, gave her a hug, a peck on the cheek, helped her off with her coat.

"You have a good time, too, junior?" Tracy asked him.

"Swell," he said, noncommittally.

Tess excused herself to wash up and Tracy and the Kid took their places at the booth from the night before.

"Decided to wear the clothes, huh?" Tracy said.

The Kid nodded and sighed. He gestured to himself; to his little polka dot tie, to his short pants. "Look what she done to me!"

"Yeah, I can see. Pretty tough, huh?"

"Yeah. You wear clothes like this, first thing you know, *pow*—you wind up in school."

"Wouldn't that be awful."

The Kid nodded vigorously. "I feel like a doggone sissy."

Tracy clicked in his cheek. "Yeah. Rough one."

The boy looked sharply at Tracy. "But don't say anything to Miss Tess."

"Oh?"

"Yeah, I wouldn't want to hurt her feelings."

Tess came back, and she and the Kid ordered Blue Plate specials while Tracy stuck with the chili. Tracy got filled in on what he'd missed of their adventures. Then pie for the grownups and ice cream for the Kid followed. It was a pleasant replay of their evening here last night. And was the happiest Tracy had been in some time.

Tracy drove, Tess snuggled against his shoulder. The Kid was in the backseat, curled up like a fetus, asleep. Pretty soon Tracy pulled up in front of Tess's three-story brownstone apartment building. They sat and talked in the parked car, neither of them anxious to disturb the sleeping boy.

"I could call in sick tomorrow," Tess said.

"You know, you can't call in sick everyday," Tracy said.

"I had this afternoon off, legitimately."

"But not tomorrow. You better behave yourself. You need that job."

"I know," she said. "But one little day can't hurt . . ."

"Little crimes lead to big crimes," Tracy reminded her.

She laughed and elbowed him gently. "Look who's talking. I saw the papers. I heard the radio. They're saying you're a maverick cop. Running around making false arrests, bullying people."

"What do you think?"

"Sounds just like you."

He looked sideways at her, gave her a crooked smile.

"Seriously, Dick—be careful about this. I know your heart's in the right place. I know you're thinking about . . . about Papa."

He nodded somberly.

"But, Dick—you've got a career to think of. You've got . . . the *future* to think of."

"I know, dear."

She sighed; her eyes tightened in concern. "We're going to have to turn that little boy over to the system, aren't we? He'll be in an orphanage before he knows it."

"Maybe he'll find some parents to adopt him."

"Dick . . . do you mean . . . ?"

"I'm not sure what I mean. Look, *I'll* take the Kid tonight. You got to get to work in the morning. He can hang around with me at headquarters tomorrow, till I get somebody at the Welfare Department to come over and process him through the proper channels."

"That sounds so cold."

"We can still see him. But we both have lives. We both have jobs."

"Yes, and we both live alone. I don't *mind* living alone." She glanced back tenderly at the slumbering boy. "But you know—I liked having company for a couple days."

He touched her hair. "I've got six hundred bucks saved up, Tess. Tidy little nest egg."

"What are you saying, Dick?"

"Look," he said, "maybe it's about time . . ."

"Yes?"

"We'll talk about it—as soon as this craziness with Caprice is behind me."

She sighed, shook her head, nestled against his arm. "Will it ever really be over?"

"Sure, Tess. Then maybe I can think about that . . . that other thing."

"What other thing?"

"You know—the Chief of Police slot."

She looked at him, her eyes shining. "Oh, Dick . . . that would be wonderful, but I wouldn't want you to do it just because . . ."

"Hey, the extra money would be awful nice."

She squinted in near-irritation. "I don't *care* how much money you make. That's not why I want you to consider that job."

"Why do you, then?"

"Because it would be a way for you to pursue the work you love without having to run around the streets, risking your life, every day and night."

"Tess—that *is* the work I love. The streets. The risk. The game."

"I know." She sighed. "I know, dear. Please don't think I'm a terrible nag. I'll stand behind you—*beside* you—whatever you decide. It's just . . . I'd like to have you around for a few years."

They kissed. Tracy couldn't help but think of his encounter with Breathless Mahoney yesterday; it lingered in his mind, and elsewhere in his body, a guilty pleasure.

"Is something wrong, dear?" she asked him.

"No, Tess," he said, and he kissed her again, and banished Breathless from his heart and his mind, if not his soul.

"Where are we?" the Kid said from the backseat.

Embarrassed, Tracy pulled away from Tess and said to the barely wakened boy, "Dropping Miss Tess off, is all. Go back to sleep."

He got out of the car, walked around and opened the

door for her. They walked hand in hand up the steps to the doorway of the building.

He was looking into her eyes when a voice, the Kid's voice, rang out: "Hey! Tracy! Look out!"

"Get down!" he yelled back to the boy, instinctively, and he pushed Tess back, into the recession of the doorway, and Tracy covered her body with his as tommy-gun fire ripped open the night, bullets eating chunks out of the brownstone building; he caught sight of the black sedan as it rolled by, the barrel of the weapon snorting orangely, bullets biting into the building, the tommy gun held in obscure hands. He kept her covered with his body, and the tommy-gun chatter ceased, and he moved away from her, yanking his .38 from under his arm.

Then Tracy was standing in the street, watching the red taillights disappear.

He slipped the gun back in the shoulder holster, glanced at his car—saw no bullet holes in either the body of it or the windshield, saw the bright eyes of the apparently uninjured boy as he popped up in the front seat—and rushed to Tess, sat on the stoop with her, cradling her in his arms. She was trembling. So was he.

"Are you all right, Tess? Are you all right?"

"I'm okay, I'm okay . . . is the boy . . . ?"

"I'm fine, lady," the Kid said, standing there in his new suit and tie. He shrugged. "It's just the clothes."

Tracy laughed, and so did Tess.

The boy did, too.

But then the the smell of gunpowder, and the holes the bullets ate in the brick building reminded them that nothing was funny at all.

"Jeez," the Kid said, eyes round more with wonder than fear, "I thought we was goners."

"They're just trying to scare us, Kid," Tracy said, not believing it.

"Let's go get 'em!" the Kid said eagerly. "What're we waitin' for?"

Two beat cops were approaching quickly on foot. One of them asked Tracy if he'd seen who the shooter was.

Tracy shook his head no. He spoke to them in a whisper: "Stick around here, boys, will you? A little protective custody for my girl."

The two cops nodded; one said, "Sure, Tracy."

Tracy walked Tess up the brownstone steps. "Sorry, honey," he said, embarrassed, as if this were somehow all his fault. Maybe it was, at that.

"Don't be," she said gently. She had pulled herself together, somehow. "When you play in the streets, it's all part of the game. I may not like it—but I know it."

She touched his cheek, said, "Don't worry about me, Dick," and went inside.

Tracy returned to the dark street, collected the Kid, climbed in the car, and headed back to headquarters. There'd been no license plate on that sedan, but he could identify the make and model, and that was a start.

—13—

n a pool of light from his banker's lamp, Tracy sat in his otherwise dark office, studying photos the boys from the Auto Theft squad provided him. He tapped one of them and smiled tightly; this was it: the make and model and year of sedan that the machine-gunner had fired from.

"Excuse me," a voice said.

A sultry, female voice.

Tracy looked up.

Breathless Mahoney was standing in the doorway, draped against the doorjamb like a glamour pinup come to unlikely life. She was wearing a black satin gown, tight as her skin, trimmed with black feathers, a plunging neckline revealing a wealth of bosom and a slit up the front showing off one long, lush leg. In one hand, gripped by the neck, was a bottle of champagne; in the other, clutched by their stems, were two glasses.

In the hall, asleep on a bench, was the Kid.

"You caught me rehearsing," she said, as if that explained her apparel. Her smile was a wispy, teasing thing. "So glad you called."

"Why the champagne?"

She moved slowly into the room; she was catlike, languorous in a deliberate way. "Long as I was going to drop by, I thought I might as well help you celebrate."

"Celebrate what, Miss Mahoney?"

"Being alive," she said. "I heard you almost died this evening."

"News travels fast in this town," Tracy said. "Almost as fast as bullets."

Catchem stuck his head in the door, made a slow, wide-eyed, appreciative survey of Tracy's guest, then said, "One of the boys is makin' a sandwich run at the deli over on Division. You want 'em to bring you back something, Tracy?"

"No thanks, Sam."

Catchem raised his eyebrows. "Don't do anything anything I wouldn't do, children."

And he closed the door.

She moved liquidly across the small office and perched herself on the edge of Tracy's desk; she wore black spike heels that showed most of her pretty feet. "I have a feeling your partner's admonition leaves us plenty of leeway."

Tracy said nothing.

She set the champagne bottle on the desk, the glasses as well; they looked more than a little out of place amidst the cop clutter.

"I was beginning," she said, "to wonder what a girl has to do in this town . . . to get arrested."

"Wearing that dress," Tracy said, "is a step in the right direction."

She laughed. "Who's the kid in the hall?" she asked, turning an arched eyebrow to the smoked-glass-and-wood door.

"Just a little street urchin I picked up. Trying to give him a break."

"Cute." She picked up Tess's framed picture on the desk. "Also cute. Nice hair color." She studied the picture. "She could use some help with her makeup."

"I think she looks fine."

She put Tess's picture down. She gave him a look that would've fried an egg. "Are you going to make a move, or do I have to do it all?"

"I'm on duty," Tracy said.

117

"Don't you ever get a day off?"

"Sure. This isn't it."

Then she touched one finger to the cork of the champagne bottle. "If I open this, you think it'd wake the kid?"

"Miss Mahoney . . . "

"Breathless."

"Breathless. We have regulations about alcoholic beverages in city buildings, and Central Police Headquarters certainly qualifies as a city building."

"Oh, really?" she said. She reached for the bottle; her hands caressed the neck. Then, with sudden, masculine authority, she popped the cork. It sounded like a gunshot. She poured the overflowing bottle in one of the glasses and held the brimming glass out to Tracy.

He took it.

She poured herself a glass; she raised hers in a toast.

"Here's to crime," she said. "Where would you be without it?"

She clinked the glass against his.

"So. What do you want from me, Tracy?"

He pointed to the photo on the desk. "That car look familiar to you? Know anybody who works for Big Boy who drives a car like that?

She glanced at it, shrugged. "Not really. I'm more interested in drivers than cars."

"Me, too."

"Afraid I'm no help on that subject. That can't be all you wanted . . . ?"

He reached in his desk, found what he was looking for, and dropped the item in Breathless's drained champagne glass.

It was the blue sapphire earring.

"I had a lot of bad news today," Tracy said. "But one small piece of *good* news: We identified you through the jeweler who sold you those earrings . . . though they were charged to the late Lips Manlis."

She frowned. Then she slid off the desk, the dress hiking up as she did, showing him creamy white thigh. She strolled over and stopped in the doorway, her shapely backside to him. She looked over her shoulder at him and when she spoke, the words seemed ironic, but there was no irony in her voice.

"You're right, Tracy. Why would you want to get mixed up with a cheap floozy like me? I'll be lucky if I get through the week alive. They probably followed me here." She laughed mirthlessly. She turned the champagne glass upside down and the earring tumbled to the office floor. "If you want to throw me in jail, go ahead. I'd probably be better off."

And she drifted out.

Tracy got up, knelt and plucked the earring from the floor, and returned it to a small evidence envelope in his desk. Then he got his yellow topcoat and went out in the hall, where Catchem was discussing with Patton the vision of sensuality in the tight black gown who'd just exited past them.

Tracy gestured to the boy who still slept on the bench. "Keep an eye on him," he told his two assistants.

"Where you goin', Tracy?" Catchem asked.

"I'm going to follow her," Tracy said. "That woman's in trouble."

"What?" Patton asked Tracy's back, as the detective hurried down the hall.

"That woman *is* trouble." Catchem smirked.

119

14

The conference table seemed endless, its surface as slick and reflective as glass, only red, a brilliant blood-red slash down the center of the room. The color seemed fitting, considering the amount of blood that had been spilled by the dozen gangsters seated there—amongst themselves alone.

Big Boy's spacious office—a red art-deco chamber unchanged since the departure of its previous tenant, the late Lips Manlis—was on the third floor of the Club Ritz. Tomorrow night was the club's grand reopening, but tonight was an even more special occasion.

Tonight Big Boy had gathered together the city's crime lords, the aristocracy of the local underworld. Dressed to their yellow teeth in all their colorful, wide-lapelled glory, they sat glowering at each other, their respective bodyguards lining the walls, the tension tighter than piano wire in an assassin's grip.

They were all present; a virtual Who's Who of hoodlums: Pruneface—-his long, grotesquely wrinkled mug a fright mask out of which cold dark eyes glittered—ran much of the Northside out of Ravenwood; Texie Garcia—ebony-haired, fortyish, witchily attractive in a slinky black dress—was the city-wide queen of prostitution; Northsider Lawrence "Acey-Deucey" Doucet, a razor-thin blond, had gambling in the suburbs sewn up; beaky one-time Big Boy gunman Ribs Mocca—looking sporty in his bowler hat and bow tie—now operated the city's widest-spread protection racket; Southside boy Johnny Ramm—dark, dapper, mustached—owned nightclubs perhaps less grand than the Club Ritz but many in number; Ben "Spud" Spaldoni—who might have been Ramm's brother—was the West Side slot-machine king. There were half a dozen dangerous more, seated at the blood-red table in the blood-red room, rivals in the business of crime, trading looks of suspicion and displeasure in strained silence.

Seated at the head, in a pinstripe suit as red as the table, and redder than the room, was the Big Boy himself. Smiling paternally, a thick Havana cigar in the corner of his thick lips, Caprice rose slowly and hooked his thumbs in the pockets of his vest. A gold watch chain draped itself across his belly. A carnation as red as the suit was snug in his lapel. An ashtray mingling cigar butts and walnut shells was set before him. Behind him were Itchy and several other bodyguards. Seated near him was his balding, bespectacled accountant, Numbers Norton.

"I suppose you're wonderin' why I asked you all here tonight," Big Boy said grandly.

"We're wondering," Pruneface said, in a deep, gravelly voice that suited his hideously crêped face, "why a guy who just started a war would ask for a peace conference."

"I didn't start a war," Big Boy said, smiling genially. He shrugged matter-of-factly. "Lips Manlis was importing torpedoes; he was the one getting ready to start a war. Against us all. I just took some, what do you call it . . . preventative measures."

"Yeah, and you bring the heat down on us all," Spaldoni said. He shook his head in undisguised disgust. "That's just plain stupid, Big Boy."

Big Boy frowned; but just momentarily.

Spaldoni went on. "A massacre like that, it gets Joe Q. Public all up in arms. Followed by a *cop* killing. It gets the newshounds up on their high horse. It makes the cops act crazy."

"Yeah," Mocca said. He chewed the end off his own

cigar, definitely not a Havana, and spit it on the floor. "No offense, Big Boy—you and me go way back . . . but look at the way you got Tracy all hot and bothered. That's all we need, is that guy throwin' the book out the window."

Big Boy frowned.

"I hear the bigshot flatfoot's in trouble with City Hall," Texie Garcia said, lighting up a cigarette in a long holder. "I think maybe he'll take himself out of the game."

"Don't worry about Tracy," Big Boy said. He smiled enigmatically. "I got him covered."

The door behind him opened and Big Boy glanced back and saw Flattop enter; Flattop frowned and shook his head, no, at his boss. He was conveying, silently, the news that the hit on Tracy tonight had failed.

Big Boy didn't let his disappointment show. He smiled at the group and said, "Look—leave the copper to me. *I'll* take care of him. I'll either buy him, or kill him."

"Buy Tracy?" Spaldoni asked. "Are you kidding?"

"Nobody'd like to see Tracy dead more than me," Pruneface said. "But killing another cop right now would be plenty dangerous, in a lot of ways."

"And Big Boy, you'd be the prime suspect," Mocca pointed out.

Big Boy tried to keep his impatience in check, but was not entirely successful. "Leave it to me," he said. "Just leave it to me, all right? Now. Let's deal with our other problems. Our mutual problems."

"My problem," Spaldoni said sardonically, "is everybody at this table has tried to kill me, at one time or another. That's a problem I have real trouble gettin' around."

"Hey," Big Boy said, and gestured with the huge cigar, "I could say the same thing. Pruneface, you tossed a fire bomb in my car one night, and gave me this. . . ."

Big Boy yanked his collar down and revealed a nasty red scar.

Pruneface swallowed thickly and loosened his own collar with a finger.

"But I forgive ya," Big Boy said, straightening himself. His smile was tight, pulled back over his upper teeth. "And Mocca—when we had that little fallin' out, you put three slugs into me."

"But you lived," Mocca uneasily pointed out.

Big Boy shrugged. "Yeah, and so did you. Live and let live. After all, I owe *all* you guys somethin' . . . even you, Texie, even you. That night you had your girl Daisy try to slip that shiv into me?"

"That was *her* idea, Big Boy," Texie said nervously.

"I guess we'll never know," Big Boy said philosophically. "Funny how easy a neck can snap. But, boys and girls—leave us face it. I owe you all somethin' for some past indiscretion. But I *forgive* you all—'cause the past, well . . . it's the past."

"You want a city-wide truce, then," Spaldoni said.

"No! I want a city-wide *syndicate!* And then I want to hook up with the mobs out East, and out West. I want to go national, and I want to take all of you with me."

They began to shift in their seats, interested. All but Spaldoni, who sat smirking skeptically.

"Okay, we talked about the past," Big Boy said, patting the air. "Fine. Now let's talk about the future. A boss who can't see the future is no use to nobody."

"So you're psychic, now," Spaldoni cracked. He reached into his pocket.

Everyone half rose, started for their guns; the bodyguards along the walls sprang to attention. World War Two almost broke out before Spaldoni, smiling one-sidedly, chuckling, withdrew his cigarettes and lit one up.

"What's wrong, fellas?" Spaldoni said, in a singsongy voice. "Nervous?"

"What do you mean you can see the 'future?'" Pruneface asked Big Boy.

"Let me put it this way," Big Boy said, the cigar tilting upward, his hands on the blood-red wood. "I *am* the future."

Uneasy expressions were exchanged among the gangsters.

"And so," Big Boy said, placating them, "are all of you—*if* you're smart enough to come along. Wise enough to put the past in the past, and *consolidate*."

More glances were exchanged, but now some heads were nodding, and there were a few intrigued shrugs.

"With Prohibition past, we got a choice," Big Boy said. "We can fight amongst ourselves—"

"Survival of the fittest," Spaldoni interrupted.

Big Boy nodded. "Or we throw in together and start exploring new avenues of income."

"Such as?"

"Unions. Then we get a piece of everybody's action. It's no different than your protection racket, Ribs—same principle. First thing we do is control the bartenders' union, then the other restaurant unions—waiters, chefs. Entertainment unions, too, anything involving musicians working in nightclubs. We invest in the food business, in hotel and restaurant operations, cocktail lounges, saloons, retail liquor stores, all over the country. We put our money in legal enterprises, but the kind of enterprises we understand. We give the people what they want, whether it's a steak and a highball, or a girl and a game of chance."

"Are you nuts?" Spaldoni asked.

"No," Big Boy said quietly, "I am not nuts."

"Well, I think you are. Bartenders' union? That's your bright idea of where dough can be made?"

"If the bartenders are in our pocket," Big Boy said, "then they'll push our brands of liquor. They'll push our brands of soft drink. They will get their pretzels from us. They will get their potato chips from us."

"Pretzels," Spaldoni said, laughing, "potato chips."

Acey-Deucey Doucet said thoughtfully, "Spaldoni, Big Boy's talkin' about a *lot* of pretzels. If we controlled every hotel, restaurant, cocktail lounge, and private club in these forty-eight states . . ."

"Then," Big Boy said, gesturing with his cigar, "we'll soon see the day we make a profit offa every olive in every martini served up in this fine drinkin' man's country of ours."

Ramm nodded at Doucet, and Doucet nodded back.

"I got a vision," Big Boy said. "A big boss has got to have a big vision." He painted the picture in the air with his cigar-in-hand. "In a town like this, a country like ours, you got thousands of small stores and businesses . . . people working real hard. I think they should be workin' hard for us. Every time a citizen buys a pound of hamburger, we'll get a nickel. Every time some guy gets a haircut, we'll get a dime. All by controlling unions. In the meantime, we'll join the Rotary Club. The Chamber of Commerce. We'll dress like bankers."

Pruneface looked at Texie Garcia who smiled and nodded; then Pruneface nodded back.

"We gotta stop this small-time thinking," Big Boy said, frowning. "We gotta stop thinking about truces and peace treaties. We gotta stop thinking who has what territory. We don't divvy up the town. We throw in with each other! We consolidate; we're one company, where everybody's got his position. One of us runs gambling in town. One of us runs prostitution. Another the protection racket. Another narcotics—I see a *real* future there. And so on. And we come together for planning sessions, for expansion efforts, like the board of directors of a big-time corporation."

"And you're chairman of the board, I suppose?" Spaldoni asked.

"That's right." Big Boy glanced back at Flattop and narrowed his eyes and Flattop nodded and went out. Big Boy returned his gaze to his guests. "Together, we'll own this town. And one day, the nation. What do you say, gentlemen? And lady?"

"I'm in," Pruneface said.

"Me, too," Texie Garcia said, nodding.

"And me," Doucet said.

Ramm, Mocca, and several others spoke up affirmatively as well.

"Count me out," Spaldoni said, and rose.

"It only works," Big Boy said gravely, "if we're all in."

"Tough," Spaldoni said. He pointed at himself with a thumb. "I got a good business. I ain't interested in going national, or incorporatin'. I'll take my chances all by my lonesome."

"It's a free country," Big Boy said, and shrugged. "No hard feelings."

"To hell with you, Caprice," Spaldoni said, and he went quickly out, and his pair of bodyguards followed, their eyes not leaving the faces in the room behind them.

Then the door was closed.

"Now what?" Pruneface asked.

"Aw, Spud's always flyin' off the handle," Big Boy said magnanimously. "He'll come back down to earth. Sit down, sit down, everybody. Now the reopening of the Club Ritz, gentlemen, lady, is tomorrow night, and you're all invited. *I* pick up the tab. . . ."

The city's first major underworld peace conference had an uninvited audience.

Just outside the window, on the narrow ledge, Tracy had positioned himself to eavesdrop. He'd come down the fire escape, on the alley side, stepped out onto the ledge and edged gingerly over, his fingers gripping bricks. The cold night wind was whipping his yellow topcoat and threatening to take his hat. But the trickiest part was going around the corner of the building; that was awkward, and scary, and Tracy had just enough vertigo to know not to look down.

He'd followed Breathless to the club, determining to his satisfaction that she'd not been followed—other than by him—and she was apparently in no immediate danger. While she went inside to rehearse, Tracy noticed the parade of limos bearing gangsters.

From his car he'd called Catchem on the two-way. "Every top hood in town has pulled up in front of Big Boy's club," he told Catchem. "There's more limos on the street than a millionaire's funeral."

"The club doesn't open till tomorrow," Catchem's voice said.

"That's right," Tracy said, "but so far, I've spotted Johnny Ramm, Spud Spaldoni, Texie Garcia, Joey De-Santo, Pruneface, Chuck 'the Clipper' Brown, Acey-Deucey, Ribs Mocca and . . . do I have to go on?"

"Ye gods," Catchem said. "Sounds like an underworld summit conference!"

"With Big Boy convening," Tracy said. "You and Pat better get over here."

"Right away," Catchem said.

Tracy had parked his car on a side street and found his way to a hallway in the apartment building across from the Club Ritz. He was studying the conference-room window through binoculars when Patton, en route, checked in by two-way.

"Can we bust these babies, Dick?" he asked.

"I don't know," Tracy said. "No outstanding warrants on any of 'em. . . ."

"What about a conspiracy rap?"

"What exactly are they conspiring to do?" Tracy said into the two-way.

Patton's sigh was audible over the tiny cloth-covered speaker. "Wish I was a fly on their wall."

Tracy lowered the binoculars, grinned to himself, said, "Good idea," and was on the move, even as Patton's voice was saying, "Huh?" from Tracy's wrist.

Now he'd maneuvered to the window and wasn't sure the effort, and the risk, had been worth it. All he could hear were muffled voices. He was just at the edge of the window, where he could peek in, but not really see well, nor chance taking a better look. A bodyguard had his back partially to that window, and other bodyguards lined the wall facing the window.

Tracy had come to eavesdrop, and for his trouble was getting a little night air. A little cold night air. A little cold *windy* night air . . .

He couldn't stay here long. Though there was no doorman manning the entrance below—the club was closed, after all—the beat cop might come along any minute; and while it was late, and the street seemed largely deserted, someone driving by still might spot him.

"Sam," Tracy whispered into his two-way, "afraid I've struck out. The glass on this window is thicker than a ham sandwich. Must be bulletproof."

"Tracy," Catchem's voice said from the two-way, "we're parked down below—over to your left. Have you fallen off your trolley? Get down from there!"

Catchem was right; this was pointless: he couldn't hear a thing up here.

"Pull the car up under the street light," Tracy told Catchem.

Tracy edged back around the corner of the building, out of sight; he glanced down and saw Flattop walking from the street into the alley just below him. The gunman went in a side door. Funny, Tracy thought; he hadn't seen the flatheaded hood leave in the first place.

Out front, Spaldoni and his two bodyguards were laughing and talking as they got into their car. Tracy could see them clearly, but couldn't make out anything they were saying specifically.

Then, a few moments after all three were within the car, the driver hit the starter switch.

And the car exploded in a fiery ball.

The blossom of orange made the night briefly day, the shock of it almost making Tracy lose his balance and tumble off his perch.

The car almost completely disintegrated and the three men within it were blown in the air like rag dolls; they came down the same way. The car itself was little more than thick charcoal smoke, a gnarl of steel and four very flat tires. A horrid, pungent smell wafted up to the detective.

Around the corner from him, the window he'd tried to listen at suddenly slid open.

And Big Boy leaned out.

"See?" he said, apparently to his audience within. "I told ya Spaldoni would come back down to earth."

Big Boy disappeared, and Flattop shut the window.

Still around the corner, on the ledge in the alley, Tracy whispered into the two-way. "You there, Sam?"

"I'm here." Catchem's voice seemed uncharacteristically shaken. "I take it, *that* you heard?"

"I sure did."

"I called it in. We got a pretty good view of that room with binoculars now. You better get outta there . . . the place is emptying out."

"Get ready to pull the car over."

Tracy turned and made a jump to the light pole and slid down, like a fireman answering a call. He leaped to a parked car and, just as Catchem with Patton pulled up

in an unmarked sedan, Tracy hopped aboard, clinging to
the roof of the car as it sped away down the street.

Tracy did not see the menacing figure in an oversized
coat and slouch hat watching his flashy departure. Had
he seen the man, Tracy would surely have been struck by
his face.

That is, his lack of a face.

15

A patch of sunlight fell from the bedroom window onto the Kid's face as he lay sleeping snugly beneath the covers. The light gradually nagged his eyelids open, and then he sat up with a start, not sure where he was.

Looking around, he realized he was in a bedroom, Tracy's bedroom; in a bed, Tracy's bed. On the nightstand was a small, round clock, which showed the time as a little before seven. The boy stretched, then climbed out.

He looked down at himself and made a face. He was wearing red pajamas; the idea of wearing special clothes to bed seemed pointless and even silly to him. But Miss Tess had bought these, among other clothes, for him. She'd even bought him a little suitcase, which he noticed was over in the corner, next to a dresser.

On that dresser was a picture of Miss Tess, smiling, looking real pretty in a summery dress; and a picture of a white-haired man with glasses and a strong jaw, who the Kid figured was Tracy's pa, with his arm around an older lady who had a real nice smile, who the Kid figured was Tracy's ma. In front of the framed pictures was the baseball and glove Tracy gave him yesterday. That Tracy sure was jake.

Also on the dresser was a wallet.

The Kid looked in the worn leather billfold. There was fifteen bucks in there. And some more pictures, several of Tess, and those same old people that he figured for Tracy's parents. Also, pinned to the leather was a shiny silver detective's badge. It said "Chief of Detectives" on it.

131

He caught his own reflection in the dresser mirror as he held the wallet in his hands; his face looked white, his hair was sticking out every which way, and his eyes looked real ashamed, as if he'd caught himself at something.

He swallowed and put the wallet back on the dresser.

"Are you up?" Tracy called from the other room.

The Kid went out into the little living room. For a guy with a decent job, Tracy sure didn't live fancy; just two rooms and a kitchenette and a can. Of course, the place was nicer than the Kid was used to, by a long shot—but he'd seen fancier digs. Like when he and Steve went around to sell their stuff to certain fences, for instance.

Tracy was in the bathroom brushing his teeth. He was wearing a T-shirt. He had muscular arms and wide shoulders; the Kid wouldn't mind a build like that himself someday.

"What are you doing?" the Kid asked, standing just outside the bathroom.

"What do you mean, what am I doing?" Tracy asked, turning to the Kid. Tracy's mouth was foamy white.

The Kid laughed. "Don't bite me or nothin'."

Tracy laughed back. "Look like a mad dog, do I? Well, you ought to try this stuff. Doesn't taste so bad—peppermint." He lifted his toothbrush from under the running tap water. "I don't have a spare brush, so just sprinkle some in your hand and rub it on your teeth with your fingers."

He handed the Kid a tin of tooth powder.

"Do I have to?"

"Just wash your mouth out with water after."

The Kid was looking at the tin of tooth powder with distrust. "You know, Tracy—for a tough guy, you sure do a lot of pansy things."

"Is that right? Your pal Steve—how are *his* teeth?"

"He don't have too many. They're pretty black."

Tracy shrugged. He began working his shaving brush in its mug. "That's where you're headed, if you don't use that stuff."

"Maybe tomorrow."

"Your decision. I'm not your father."

The Kid made a face and sprinkled some of the tooth powder on his fingers.

Tracy glanced at the boy. His face was kind. "You want some breakfast? I scramble a mean egg."

"Sure! Is that coffee I smell?"

Tracy was lathering his face up. "That's for *me*, junior. Milk?"

"No, that's okay. I like mine black."

Tracy shook his head and started to shave with a straight razor. "Why don't you go change your clothes. Then I'll rustle up that chow."

"Swell!"

"Oh, and junior . . ."

"Yeah?"

"Better get your things together. I'm taking you with me to headquarters today and I'm going to have to make the arrangements to . . . you know."

"You're turning me into the orphanage, huh?"

"Don't look it at that way. . . . Tess and I'll come see you this weekend. Ever go to the movies?"

He shrugged. "I snuck in a few times."

Tracy was drying his face off with a towel. "Well, we'll take you to see the new Tom Mix picture. How's that sound?"

The Kid sighed. "Swell."

Tracy went into the other room and the Kid looked at the powder on his fingers and sighed again. He was about to start rubbing the stuff onto his teeth when a sharp knock on the front door startled him.

The Kid cracked the bathroom door open and listened.

"Mr. Tracy," an old woman's voice was saying. "I'm Mrs. Skaff— from the Welfare Department."

"You'll have to excuse me," the detective said to the door. "I'm not dressed yet . . ."

"It's come to our attention that you have an orphan with you. Mr. Tracy, you're a single man . . ."

"Mrs. Skaff," Tracy said, "I have the situation in hand. It's my intention to contact the orphanage this afternoon . . ."

"I don't think you quite understand, Mr. Tracy," the woman's voice went on. "You can't just pick up a child off the streets and take him home like a stray dog."

Panic clutched the boy's chest. He slipped out of the bathroom and back into the bedroom. Miss Tess had thrown his old clothes out, so he had no choice but to put the sissy ones back on.

He went to the dresser and picked up the baseball; he forced it into his pocket. Then he grabbed the wallet and stuffed it into his other pocket and climbed out the window onto the fire escape.

"I don't appreciate you comparing that child to a dog," Tracy told the closed door tersely.

The woman's voice responded just as tersely: "He must go to the orphanage *now*. It's the law."

The irony of having that phrase tossed in his face was not lost on Tracy.

"Don't force me to get a court order, Mr. Tracy."

"All right, all right," he said.

He went to the bedroom and found the window open. On the floor, sprawled like a ten-story suicide, were the red pajamas. The Little Lord Fauntelroy getup Tess had forced on the Kid was gone.

So was the baseball. And the Kid, too.

He sighed, shook his head, and then noticed that his

wallet was also missing. He swore silently and trudged out into the living room, buttoning up his shirt, saying, "Human nature" to himself, bleakly.

"Mrs. Skaff," Tracy said, unchaining the night latch, "you frightened the boy away—but I'll find him, and take care of it . . ."

And as he opened the door, Tracy looked out at Flattop, whose cupid lips were pursed in a self-satisfied smile. The gunman reached out with one hand and pushed the door open wider; and with the other, pointed a big .45 right at Tracy.

"It's the law," Flattop said sarcastically, in the old-woman voice.

Itchy was just behind him, and laughed nasally, weasel-like, in appreciation of Flattop's mimicry; beneath the bright blue fedora, which matched his expensive topcoat, Itchy's face was bulging eyes behind pop-bottle eyeglasses, and sneering, madman's lips. Itchy dug at his neck with one hand, but in the other was a long-barreled .38 revolver with a silencer.

Both men wore gloves: not a good sign.

Flattop, looking like an undertaker in his long black topcoat, bareheaded (no fedora invented could sit on that flat skull), pushed Tracy roughly back into the little apartment. Itchy followed, shutting the door.

"Morning, fellas," Tracy said through bared teeth. "Care for a little breakfast?"

"Maybe a little hot chili?" Flattop said, raising the hand Tracy had burned.

"Or scrambled yeggs," Tracy said.

"Don't even think about it," Itchy said. He was reaching behind himself, trying to get at a spot between his shoulders. But his gunhand was steady.

"It's your play," Tracy said to both of them.

"We're not here to shoot you," Flattop said pleasantly. "This is a friendly call."

"A business call," Itchy said, digging at his neck.

"A *friendly* business call," Flattop said. He eyeballed the flat. "Jeez, copper, you call this an apartment? Secondhand furniture. Threadbare carpet. Little dinky rooms. Sad. They ought to pay you more."

"I'll take it up with the Mayor," Tracy said.

"Get your coat and hat, copper," Itchy said. "We're goin' for a ride. . . ."

"The one-way kind?"

"Depends on you, Tracy," Flattop said cheerfully, and nudged him with his .45. "Depends on you. . . ."

The Kid had scrambled down the fire escape to the alley, where he paused to empty the wallet; it was leather, but way too worn to be worth anything. He'd pocketed the money and was just about to dump the rest in a garbage can, when the wallet fell open and Tracy's badge caught the sun and glinted at him. He studied it a long time.

He felt bad. Up in that apartment was the only guy who'd ever really been halfway decent to him. And the Kid had taken his money. The boy sighed. It was a hard world.

But he slipped the whole wallet in his pocket. He couldn't quite bring himself to toss the badge, or the snapshots, either. Miss Tess was in one of them.

He was just coming around the corner of the alley when the front door to Tracy's building flew open and Tracy was prodded down the steps by the flatheaded guy and his nervous partner. The killers from the Seventh Street garage! They had guns on Tracy, but in their pockets; somebody going by casually might not make anything of this.

But the Kid sure did.

Ducking back in the alley, the Kid saw the flatheaded guy shove Tracy into the red sedan at the curb, and the nervous one jump behind the driver's seat.

He didn't know what to do. These guys were hoodlums! Murderers! What could he do, a kid? Maybe he should find a cop! But that was against the Kid's code of the street. . . .

Swallowing, summoning courage, the Kid followed the car out into the street as it began to pull away. He almost slipped twice in the rain-slicked street, before he picked up enough speed to get near the back bumper.

He dove for it.

Grabbing the bumper, he pulled himself onto the car as it began to accelerate. He held onto the bumper with all his might, pulled himself up inside the spare tire on the back of the car, curling up inside there, an unseen stowaway as the car roared off.

16

Flattop and Itchy shoved Tracy down the steps into the basement. They were in an apartment building, a good many blocks away from Tracy's own. It was not, however, just any apartment building: this was where Tess lived.

"What are we doing *here?*" Tracy demanded as he descended.

"Shut-up, flatfoot!" Flattop said, and pushed him with the gun in hand, and Tracy stumbled down a few of the steps.

At the bottom of the steps, Tracy found himself in a furnace room; it was hot in here—ungodly hot, the big old boiler furnace working overtime. It was cold out, but not cold enough to justify this. . . .

Two figures stepped out of the darkness.

Wearing a topcoat and fedora as red as the blood he'd so often shed, Al "Big Boy" Caprice moved forward, with a friendly smile on his grotesque puss. Just behind him was the bespectacled mob accountant, "Numbers" Norton, a little yellow rat in a big tan topcoat.

Nobody needed a topcoat in this inferno of a furnace room.

"Glad you could join us, Tracy," Big Boy said. He withdrew some walnuts from his pocket, cracked one, and sorted through the broken shells for the nuts.

"Those are good for the liver, I hear," Tracy said.

Big Boy popped a nut in his mouth and chewed; he gestured around the small, steamy furnace room. A tiny wooden table with a single chair was set beneath a hang-

138

ing lamp, in a cone of light—as if awaiting someone. Perhaps it was.

"We thought you'd be more comfortable in familiar surroundings," Big Boy said. "So I had you brung to your girlfriend's place."

Tracy moved forward and Flattop braced him with a tight arm around the chest. "If you've touched her . . ." Tracy began.

"Tracy!" Big Boy said, as if hurt. "What kind of guy do you take me for? She ain't here. She's down at her job. We put some candy upstairs for her, with a card from you. Thoughtful of you, wasn't it?"

"Why don't you sit down, copper?" Flattop said, and sat Tracy bodily down at the small wooden table.

Big Boy cracked another walnut. "Why don't you call me 'Al'? That's what my pals call me. You mind if I call you 'Dick'?"

"What's this about, Big Boy? Why did you send your triggers around to haul me here, if all you wanted was to small talk?"

Big Boy pretended to be offended. "My boys aren't triggers. They're messengers."

"I mistook those telegrams in their hands for a forty-five and a thirty-eight. By the way," he said, looking at Big Boy but nodding toward Itchy, "you ought to tell this nearsighted pinhead that revolvers with silencers aren't worth the trouble. Too much escaping gas."

"When I drill you," Itchy said, scratching his stomach, "you're the one gas'll escape out of."

Big Boy raised a calming hand. "Let's not be impolite to our guest, boys." He looked around the furnace room again. "Don't you think your little sweetie deserves better than a dump like this, Dick? If you were on my payroll, you could make her happy."

"She's happy enough as it is."

"I doubt that," Big Boy said with a knowing smile.

"You been going with her for years, but on your salary, how can you afford to do right by her? Sad. How I hate to see our valued civic servants suffer."

"Do tell."

"I'm a businessman, Tracy," Big Boy said, reasonably. "I think all this shooting nonsense has gotta cease. All these tommy guns and cement overcoats and bombs in cars . . . did you hear about that disgraceful murder last nght, right outside my place? Poor ol' Spaldoni."

"Somebody must've wanted to make you look bad, Big Boy, blowing up Spaldoni right outside your place like that."

"I know. I know." He shook his head sadly. "Everybody wants to make me out to be a big, bad man. I'm just in the entertainment business. My business is to serve the public."

"We have that in common, then. If there's a point to this, Big Boy, I wish you'd get to it. I'm late for work."

Big Boy exchanged smiles with his boys. "Ain't this guy a pip?" he asked them good-naturedly. Flattop and Itchy weren't smiling. "Numbers" Norton was doing his best to fade into the background.

"The point is," Big Boy continued, "I don't want trouble. I thought you might be in a position to help me out."

"Oh?"

Big Boy nodded sagely. "What I need is, Tracy, for you to go bother the real criminals. Bank robbers and embezzlers and jaywalkers. I think you should *support* a good local businessman like me. And I think a good local businessman like me should support local law enforcement."

Big Boy dropped his walnuts into one topcoat pocket and reached into the other and withdrew a large wad of bills. He threw the loose stack of bills onto the table, in front of Tracy.

Big Boy, ever the philosopher, said, "Everybody's got his price."

Tracy picked up the stack of bills and began riffling idly through them. "What's mine?"

Big Boy pointed at the money Tracy was thumbing through. "You're holding fifteen gees in your hot little hands right now. And you'll get fifteen more, at the end of every quarter. That's sixty grand a year, in case your math ain't so good."

Tracy watched the green bills flutter under his thumb. "Oh, that's a very businesslike arrangement. I'm impressed, Big Boy. When can we seal this deal?"

Big Boy shrugged grandly. "Right now."

Tracy gave him a bland smile. "All right, let's. You're under arrest for attempted bribery of an officer of the law," he said, and hurled the wad of money in Big Boy's face, and in one continuous motion, slammed an elbow into Flattop's belly, doubling the wincing-in-pain punk over even as Tracy was throwing a left hook into Itchy's chin, leaveling the pop-eyed purse-lipped gunman.

But then Big Boy had him from behind, and Flattop was on him, snarling, and swinging his massive .45, catching Tracy along the side of the head with the barrel.

Tracy, as he crumpled to the floor, felt rough hands on him, and he was hauled back to the table, where a furious Itchy was looping a thick rope around him, binding him to the chair.

Flattop held the .45 to Tracy's temple while Big Boy backhanded the detective, brutally. The gangster sneered at Tracy and Tracy looked back at him coldly.

"Hot in here, did ya notice, copper?" Big Boy walked over to the big boiler furnace behind Tracy and patted it with a gloved hand; it echoed hollowly. "This accident's just been waitin' to happen. Somebody carelessly turned it way up this morning and jimmied some of the safety valves and so on." He made a clicking sound in his cheek.

"See those trash cans in the corner? Those are your girlfriend's. You brought 'em downstairs here, after you dropped that candy off to her. You just happened to be down here, when the boiler blew . . . which it's gonna, in due time. This basement's gonna be blowed to chop suey."

Tracy shrugged. "I like Chinese food."

Then Big Boy smiled; it was a horrible, toothy thing under the skinny mustache. "You silly, stupid cop. I offer you a seat on top of the world, and you choose the gutter. I offer you the keys to the kingdom, and you tell me you're an officer of the law. I *am* the law. *Me!*"

"You're one law I look forward to breaking," Tracy said calmly.

Big Boy's sneer returned. To Itchy, who stood nearby, he said, "Let 'im have it."

Itchy picked up a nasty-looking wrench and stepped near Tracy with the wrench raised; Itchy's eyes behind the thick glasses were crazed, his lips smiling madly. His weasel-like laugh filled the small furnace room as he moved toward Tracy, who tightened his eyes, and braced himself for the blow. . . .

But Itchy had moved past Tracy, and the blow was struck beyond and behind the bound-in-the-chair detective, against the furnace itself, the glass of the safety-valve meter breaking, metal meeting metal jarringly, and the furnace began to hum and the hum began to build, quickly, to a low rumble.

The boiler was roaring as Big Boy began climbing the stairs, the mob accountant on his heels. "Hate to miss the fun," the gangster said, "but ringside seats at some events can prove dangerous. My boys'll take care of ya, proper."

"You'll fry for this, Big Boy."

"I think you're gonna do the fryin' today, Tracy." He

looked down from the stairs at the detective; steam was filling the room. He shook his head forlornly. "You shoulda made the deal. So long, sucker. . . ."

And Big Boy was gone.

"Pick up the dough," Flattop said.

"It's gonna blow, Flattop!" Itchy said.

"Shut-up," Flattop said. "Pick up the money."

Itchy, scratching his shoulder, began collecting the scattered bills; the furnace was rumbling, the room steamy, fogging the gunman's thick glasses.

Tracy looked around the furnace room, eyes darting, looking for something to use to escape as soon as these clowns had finally left; in the process, he glanced up at the window.

The Kid was framed there. Tracy looked quickly away.

"You got it all, Itchy?"

"Sure, Flattop!" Itchy was stuffing the money in his topcoat pockets. "Think I'm nuts?"

"Is that a trick question? Let's go."

"Say good-night, Tracy," Itchy said, and giggled nasally, heading for the stairs.

"Hey!" Flattop said, spotting the Kid in the window. "It's that kid!"

The Kid had watched it all through the window, wondering what he could do to help, trying to catch Tracy's attention without alerting the hoods in there, hoping a beat cop would come along . . . and then when two of the gangsters came out, one important-looking one in a red topcoat and another unimportant-looking one in a tan topcoat, he hid behind some garbage cans by the stoop, till they drove off. Then he returned to the window and, finally, Tracy saw him!

But a few seconds later, so did that flatheaded killer.

From within the basement room Tracy shouted, and through the glass window his voice was muffled but the words were unmistakable: "*Get out of here! Run!*"

If he could only break the window—but the glass was thick, and a fist or even a kick wouldn't do the trick, and if he stayed close to that window, that flatheaded guy would *shoot* him. What could he do? What should he do?

The baseball!

He dug it out of his pocket and backed up and he brought his arm back and he pitched the pitch of his life, the pitch of all-time, and the glass shattered; it was the most beautiful sound the Kid had ever heard.

But down in the cellar, the flatheaded guy was shouting, "Let's get him!"

And he knew they were coming up out of there to grab him, maybe kill him, and he knew he should run, like Tracy said; but he just couldn't leave Tracy down there, where that boiler looked like it was going to go *ka-blooie* any second!

So he hopped inside one of the garbage cans and huddled there.

And when the two killers made it onto the street, the Kid was nowhere to be seen.

"That thing's going to blow any second," Flattop said. "Let's get the hell outta here."

The Kid heard their car roar away.

He scrambled out of the garbage can and went back to the shattered window and reached in through the jagged glass-teeth to open it and dropped himself down into the steam-filled basement.

"Get outta here, son!" Tracy said. He was trying to drag his chair toward some of the glass shards, to try to cut his ropes; but the Kid could see there was no time for that. And it looked like Tracy was getting groggy from the steam . . .

"I'm not goin' anywheres without you," the boy said, and worked at the big knots on the ropes. It was no problem for the Kid—Steve had taught him how to untie all sorts of things. It came in handy when you were a thief.

The ropes fell loose around the man, and the Kid slipped an arm around Tracy and used every ounce of his strength to help the heavy adult up.

When he got to his feet, Tracy seemed to come to life. He grabbed the boy's hand, and said, "Come on, junior!" and they clambered out of there, up the stairs, and out onto the street. They ran and ran and behind them the explosion rocked the building, sending glass and wood and other rubble flying; the man and the boy hit the deck, the debris raining down on them.

Still on the pavement, Tracy looked back at the building; smoke and fire billowed from basement windows.

"You okay, kid?" he asked.

"Sure. How 'bout you?"

"All in one piece." He sat up and so did the Kid. "How did you wind up here?"

"I was comin' back." the Kid said shyly, "and saw those goons kidnap ya. I hopped the spare tire and went along for the ride."

"You came back to my place?" Tracy asked.

"Yeah, well," the Kid said. "I forgot my jammies. And what's the idea, turnin' down fifteen thousand bucks?"

Tracy hugged the boy, hugged him tight; and the boy hugged back. Their tears were partly from the drifting smoke.

Partly not.

17

Tracy sat at his desk, loading cartridges into his .38 Police Special. Out his office windows, the night awaited—a night that Tracy was confident would spell the beginning of the end for one Al "Big Boy" Caprice. Tonight was the grand reopening of the Club Ritz; but, if Tracy's plan succeeded, the gangster's moment of glory would be followed by days and nights of frustration and defeat.

And Tracy knew all about frustration and defeat. Today had been a prime example of that.

"You're saying," Tracy had said to District Attorney Fletcher earlier that day, following the latter down a bustling hallway at the County Courthouse, "that if I pull Caprice in, you won't prosecute? The man tried to have me killed!"

"It's your word against his," Fletcher had said irritably, walking fast, making Tracy work to keep up. "*And* the word of his two cronies.

"Flattop and Itchy! You can't be saying you're taking their word seriously. . . ."

Fletcher paused and looked at Tracy with frank disgust. "After you so recently arrested Caprice under specious circumstances, you can hardly do it again on anything less than the solidest of grounds."

"The bribe was real. The threat was real. The attempt on my life was real."

They were moving down the hall again. Fletcher's face tightened; he seemed annoyed to have Tracy wasting his time. "Were there any fingerprints in your apartment? Any witnesses in your building, or on the street, or at Miss Trueheart's building, who saw any of these people?"

"I don't know if he got a good look at 'em," Tracy said, "but that street kid that I took in, the one who saved my bacon, saw 'em all."

Fletcher stopped. He seemed both amazed and weary. "Well, then it would be your word and that of a delinquent child against thirty-five respectable witnesses who place the three men at a fund-raising prayer breakfast."

"A what?"

The D.A. sighed heavily. "A favorite charity of Big Boy's. Saint Catherine's Church is building a home for unwed mothers."

"Oh, brother. Mr. D.A., don't you want to get rid of this scum that's fouling our town? Do you really expect to run successfully for Mayor if Big Boy has the city in his grip?"

Fletcher scowled. "If you want me to prosecute Big Boy, then ye gods, man— give me something solid to go on! Have your detectives scour the rubble of that basement for fingerprints; comb the streets and find some witnesses. But I won't waste my time, and the city's money, for you to chase windmills, just because your girlfriend's father got killed a hundred years ago!"

Fletcher's courtroom baritone was echoing in the high ceiling hallway; it had attracted the embarrassed attention of more than a few passersby.

Tracy grabbed the D.A.'s arm; through clenched teeth, he said, "That was unnecessary, Fletcher. I'll give you something solid, all right—since attempts on my life aren't enough for you. And when you *get* this solid evidence, I'm going to be watching you. And if you don't prosecute, if you find some excuse not to, the next case I investigate is going to be *you*."

Fletcher had shaken the arm off; he was angry, and so was Tracy. This was developing into a public scene, but neither man at this point cared.

"Do it, then," Fletcher had almost shouted. "But you better behave like a *cop* and not some mindless thug, no better than the riffraff you're chasing."

The D.A. had stormed off, his footsteps echoing down the marble hall.

Now it was evening, in the office at HQ, and Tracy—putting his cleaned and loaded .38 in his shoulder harness—told Sam Catchem about the encounter with the D.A.

Catchem had spent much of the day on a fruitless search for fingerprint evidence in the rubble of the explosion in the basement of Tess's building, while Patton had canvassed both Tracy's neighborhood and Tess's, looking for witnesses, but there had been none, at least none willing to go up against Big Boy Caprice.

Catchem said, "You don't really suspect the D.A. of bein' connected, do you?"

"He's a politician." Tracy shrugged. "Of course I suspect him."

Catchem was standing, leaning a hand on Tracy's desk; he gestured open-handedly with the other. "He's got a real good conviction record."

"Sure. But you'll note that none of that flesh-and-blood rogues' gallery that met with Big Boy last night has done any time at all in recent years. And God knows we've tried: we've made the arrests, but the D.A.'s office has consistently found the evidence insufficient to prosecute."

Catchem's eyes narrowed. "Is that why you didn't tell Fletcher we're going to hit Caprice tonight? And what we're going to do with Bug Bailey, once we get there?"

"That"—Tracy nodded—"and that maybe he'd find some legal reason to stop us."

Pat Patton wandered into the office. "Say, Dick," Patton said, noting the Kid curled up on the bench in the hall, snoozing, "weren't you going to call the Welfare Department about your little pal here?"

Tracy admitted he simply hadn't had the heart to make the call. Not after the Kid had saved his life. . . .

Through this day and now early evening, the Kid had been Tracy's constant office companion, except for a couple hours when Tracy fixed the boy up with the public-affairs officer for a tour of the police station. The Kid had been anything but a pest, amusing himself reading newspapers, the funnies mostly, and filling up a tablet of paper (usually used for crime-scene diagrams) with all sorts of grease-pencil drawings.

The highlight of the day had been an impromptu late-afternoon ceremony here in the office, when Tracy and Tess watched Chief Brandon present the boy with a scroll.

"For action in the face of grave danger," Brandon had imperiously intoned, "the recipient is awarded this Honorary Detective's Certificate."

The Kid had tried to conceal that he was touched by the honor, but couldn't quite pull it off.

"Best-looking officer on the force," Tess had said, mussing the boy's hair.

"This is just a temporary certificate," the Chief told the boy, "till you pick a name out for yourself. Got one in mind, son?"

"Not really," the Kid had said.

Tracy had pinned a small badge on the boy, telling him, "Now, don't take this as encouragement to go jumping on the back of any more cars."

"Okay, Mr. Tracy. Listen . . . uh, maybe I'll have a badge for you sometime."

"What do you mean?"

"Nothin'."

Now they were waiting at the office for Tess to get back from some grocery shopping; she was going to prepare dinner at Tracy's apartment, where Tracy hoped to catch a nap before returning to HQ for the evening's festivities.

In the meantime, the lights off in the hall, the boy had succumbed to his own nap. His sketches were scattered around him and by a chair in Tracy's office where the boy had sat earlier, doodling.

"Hey," Catchem said, picking up off the floor a scratchy, lively picture of a dog, a terrierlike mutt, "this is pretty good!"

"Yeah," Tracy said, "the boy's got real talent."

Catchem examined drawings of himself, Tracy, Patton, and other cops from the squad room; they were good likenesses. "I wonder if he's ever put it to use."

"He sure has," Tracy said. "He said sometimes Steve had him sit on a street corner and do sketches of people for a nickel."

Catchem, admiring his own portrait, smiled warmly. "Jeez, that's kinda nice. You wouldn't think a crumbum like Steve would think of something as nice as that."

Tracy grunted a laugh. "He thought of it all right. He'd be in the crowd picking pockets."

Patton picked up another drawing. "Hey—look at this!"

He brought it over to the desk where Tracy was going through Catchem's field notes. It was a self-portrait, but in the portrait the Kid was wearing a fedora just like Tracy. And written below the picture it said, "Ace Detective."

"For a kid who's never been to school," Catchem said, "he seems to spell pretty good. You think he can read?"

"I know he can," Tracy said. "He claims he taught himself. He's got quite a native intelligence."

Patton was grinning. "He may not have a name picked out, but's got his eye on your job, Tracy."

"Pretty corny," Tracy said, and stood and took the self-portrait back to lay it beside the sleeping boy with his other scattered drawings.

"Corny?" Catchem said. "You think that kid is tops."

"Yeah, I would if . . . well . . ."

"What?"

"Sam, the little bum stole my wallet."

"Yeah? What's that lump in your back pocket? Big Boy's bribe money?"

Tracy felt behind him and, sure enough, there was a lump there all right. He withdrew the wallet; flipped it open, saw his badge, photos, and even his fifteen dollars, all intact. He smiled slowly.

"Shifty little pickpocket," Tracy said. "He *said* he had a badge for me. Slipped it back to me. I wonder what other secrets he's keeping?"

Tracy sat at his rolltop desk in the bedroom of his apartment, studying mug shots.

He and Tess and the Kid had come back here, and Tess had prepared supper—featuring her own meat loaf, which the boy professed to like as much as Mike's.

Tracy had convinced Tess to stay at his apartment, with the Kid, until her own apartment building was inhabitable again. There had been no damage to her apartment, or the building structurally, but there was the stench of smoke and, of course, no heat.

"I'll sleep on the couch and fix a cot up for the Kid," he told her.

"What if people talk?" she asked.

"Let 'em."

Her smile was a beauty. "We'll be like a little family, won't we?"

"Sort of," Tracy admitted.

Now, Tess and the boy had gone down to the corner ice cream parlor to get themselves a couple of cones; and Tracy, rather than catching that much-needed nap, found himself obsessively filing through the ugly faces of the city's underworld elite.

A knock at the front door interrupted them; it was a little early for Tess and the Kid to be back. The last knock at his door had been Flattop and Itchy.

He took his gun with him.

"Is that you, dear?" he said to the door.

"Yes, darling."

He opened the door, but after experiencing Flattop's female mimicry, did not put the gun away. "How was the ice cream?" he asked.

"Melts in your mouth," Breathless Mahoney said.

She was standing there wearing a black painted-on gown with a neckline that stopped short of her navel. Just.

He glanced out in the hall; no bad guys. No Tess and the Kid, either.

She stepped in and he pushed the door closed behind her. She moved through the room lightly touching things—a lamp shade, the overstuffed arm of his chair, his beat-up radio.

"Aren't you going to frisk me, Tracy?"

"What do you want, Breathless?"

She shrugged. "What does any woman want? A real man."

"I'd think you would've had enough of men."

"Oh, not at all. I've seldom encountered any. What I've had enough of is worms, weasels, and welshers. This town isn't treating you very well, is it?"

"I don't have any complaints."

She approached him slowly, touched his cheek. "What would you say to a desert island?"

"Nothing. I never speak to land masses."

She laughed. "You're as cute as that kid you took in. As cute as your milk-fed honeybunch. What if I had money, Tracy? What if I had more money than we could spend in a lifetime?"

"Money has a certain appeal, I guess."

Suddenly there was sadness in her eyes. "Would you come with me, and be my love, and . . ."

"I'm not much for poetry."

She paused, a melancholy smile tickling her lips. "Yet you want me to sing, don't you? And I don't mean at the club."

"On the witness stand. Yes. You can bring him down."

She shook her head; her platinum curls shimmered. "Is that all you can think about? Big Boy? Nailing Big Boy? Is that what you want most in life?"

"Yes."

"*Then* what?"

"What do you mean?"

Her face was amused and disgusted, at once. "Do you start over? Do you take on Big Boy's successor? Or maybe you move on to another city and take on *their* Big Boy?"

"What's your point?"

"That there *is* no point!" Irritation bordering on anger did something to the beautiful face that made it suddenly not so beautiful. "You *can't* clean up a city like this. Why bother trying? It's a cesspool by nature. The people like it that way. They want their booze, their broads, their gambling, their dope."

"I don't believe that."

She sighed. "Tracy—Tracy. Then believe what you're

feeling now. You do feel it. You feel the chemistry—the electricity, between us. How often does that happen in this lousy world?"

"Probably about every second and a half."

"Does it?"

She plastered herself to him and kissed him, hard and deep. Her mouth was hot, her mouth was wet, her mouth was sweet. The flesh of her bare back on his hands was cool and yet it burned. He tried to remain impassive, but she caught him; her kiss caught him like some crook backed up against a dead-end alley wall.

Still in his arms, but not looking at him, she said, "If I testify against Big Boy, he'll have me bumped off, you know."

"No, he wouldn't."

"You sound confident."

"I'd guard you myself, twenty-four hours a day, if necessary."

She liked the sound of that. "And if I helped take Big Boy down . . . what's in it for me? You?"

"Breathless, I . . ."

There were footsteps in the hall. Voices—Tess and the Kid.

Tracy pushed Breathless gently away, quickly wiped the lipstick off his face with a handkerchief, stuffed it in his pocket, and went to the door, which was ajar, he discovered. Had Tess seen anything?

He opened it.

Tess and the boy entered, nibbling at ice cream cones; her red-and-black coat and the boy's red outfit made them seem connected, somehow. Tess held an extra cone in the same hand as hers.

"I brought you one," she said softly. Her voice had a bruised sound.

The Kid's eyes were bugging out as he took in Breathless's provocatively underclad form. He whistled.

"Some babe!" the Kid said.

"Junior!" Tracy snapped.

"What a cute little boy," Breathless said, smiling, enjoying herself.

"Uh, Tess," Tracy said, "this is . . ."

"I know who she is," Tess said crisply. "Hello, Miss Mahoney."

Breathless greeted Tess with a knowing smile. "You must be Tess Trueheart. Dick has told me so much about you."

"Really," Tess said. She was smiling, too, but it was glazed.

"You're a very lucky woman, Miss Trueheart," Breathless breathed. She looked at the embarrassed detective. "I'll be in touch, Tracy." She patted the Kid on the head. "Cute little boy."

Then Breathless was out the door, which Tracy shut quickly behind her.

Tess stuck the dripping ice cream cone in his hand. "Undercover agent of yours?"

He gestured with his free hand. "I'm trying to get her to testify against Caprice."

"I'm sure the men on the jury will find her most convincing, whatever she says."

"Tess, don't get any ideas . . ."

"That's good advice, Dick."

The Kid was at the window watching Breathless below, as she blended into the night.

"Some babe," he said wistfully.

Tess went to the window; she put a hand on the child's shoulder. She stood by him, looking out into the darkness.

Tracy, feeling uncomfortable, sat in his overstuffed chair and ate the ice cream cone. Pistachio. The sweetness caught in his throat.

"I sure had a swell day, Miss Tess," the boy told her, as they moved to the couch and sat. "Lineups and fingerprints and mug books. You know, before this, I always thought cops were bums."

"Yeah, well a bum told you that," Tracy said. "Consider the source."

"How about we take in a movie tonight?" Tess asked the boy. "There's a Jack Holt detective picture at the Rialto."

"Sure!" the Kid said. "That'd be great! Can you come with us, Mr. Tracy?"

Tracy, still working on the dripping cone, smiled and shook his head. "Afraid not. This is going to be a busy night."

Tess glanced at him searchingly.

"Take my car," he told her.

She nodded.

"We better get going," Tess said, sitting up straight, "or we'll miss the cartoon."

"I hate cartoons," the Kid said.

"Well, I bet you like popcorn."

"Yeah!"

Tess gave the boy her hand and they rose from the couch and headed for the door. She glanced over her shoulder and said, "Good-bye, Dick."

He went to her and kissed her on the cheek. She smiled, but the smile seemed sad to him.

"Wash your face," she told him.

"Pistachio." He grinned.

Tess and the boy went out into the hall, but then the Kid said, "I forgot something!"

He ran back in to Tracy. He curled his finger, so that Tracy would bend down to him; then he whispered: "Mr. Tracy, I think you oughta know you didn't get away with it."

"What do you mean, junior?"

"You still got lipstick on ya."

Tracy touched his face.

"And it ain't Miss Tess's, neither."

"What . . ."

The Kid smirked. He kept his voice a whisper. "Look, I don't blame ya. That blonde is a real tomato. But you got somethin' good going with Miss Tess. Don't be a dumb dick."

And the boy went out and took Tess's hand and they were gone.

18

Big Boy shrugged out of the black-and-red dressing gown and allowed Flattop to help him slip his dinner jacket on. The accountant, Numbers Norton, placed a white carnation in Big Boy's lapel with the grace and skill of a baker putting one last frosting flower on a wedding cake.

Breathless sat by the fireplace, dressed in the low-cut black gown she would wear onstage tonight; she seemed lost in thought, staring into the flames.

Big Boy was a little worried. "None of our contacts at headquarters got a line on nothin'?"

"That's right, boss," Flattop said, brushing Big Boy's tux off with a little whisk broom. "I think after the D.A. chewed out his tail, Tracy's gonna be smart enough to lay off us for once."

Big Boy wagged his big head. "The big grand opening, and I gotta worry about that copper. I'd hate to embarrass the judges and congressmen and other high-hat bums. I don't even know if I dare open up the casino room! Can't afford to have my joint busted up into kindling, first night open . . ."

A knock at the door broke Big Boy's paranoid reverie.

"Get that," he said to Norton.

The little accountant scurried to the door.

It was 88 Keys. He was wearing a sporty yellow cap and a sky-blue overcoat over street clothes.

"Why ain't you in your tux?" Big Boy demanded. "You gotta go on 'fore ya know it!"

Keys took the off the cap, held it in his hand. "It's important, Mr. Caprice."

Big Boy, annoyed by the intrusion of the pansy piano player, particularly at a time like this, almost shouted at him. "What do *you* want? You don't come to me, I come to *you*, piano man!"

"This is different," 88 said. The pianist's Oriental eyes were languid, yet they glittered. "This isn't show business. It's just plain business . . . *your* business."

There was something about Keys's tone that made Big Boy take him seriously. "You got one second to make your point," Big Boy said, and gestured for him to come in and sit down.

The gangster and the piano player took seats at one end of the gleaming red conference table and spoke privately.

"I can help you get rid of Tracy," Keys said. He lit up a cigarette; it drooped insolently from the middle of his upper lip as the piano player smiled mysteriously, blowing smoke through his nostrils. "And nothing will come back on you. At all."

Big Boy studied the man. "Spill."

"I got a torn-in-half C-note in an envelope last night," Keys said. He left the cigarette in his mouth when he talked. "Slipped it under my door. I don't know where it came from."

"This better get interesting, fast."

"It does." Keys lifted an eyebrow, smiled on one side of his face, cigarette drooping. "There was a note with the torn hundred that said if I wanted the other half, I'd find a cab waitin' out front of the club this evening. It was."

Big Boy crushed a walnut in his fist; he popped the nuts in his mouth and chewed them fiercely. "You still got the note?"

"Yeah." He reached in his pocket and got it, handed to Big Boy, who looked it over. "The cabbie drove me to that industrial area off Seventh . . . around Fairfax? I don't know that neighborhood too good, and honest, I could never find my way back to the specific building. But I got dropped off at this car barn; it was all dark. The cabbie said go in—he'd been paid to wait. So I did."

Big Boy was unwrapping a Havana from its cellophane. "You did all this for a C-note?"

Keys shrugged. "Times are hard, Mr. Caprice. I work all week for a C-note from you, don't I? Anyway, the car barn was empty, except for a little table."

Big Boy was puffing his Havana, getting it going. "Then what? They served you corn-beef hash?"

"Not hardly. There was a briefcase on the table, and an envelope beside it. So I stood there and waited—there was no chair—and then this guy came in. That is, he walked out onto this catwalk above me, and looked down at me. I never seen anything like it. I would've laughed, frankly, if it hadn't given me the creeps."

Big Boy's features contorted. "What are you talkin' about?"

Keys gestured with one hand. "He was all in black, like some kid's idea of a bad guy. Black floppy hat, a black coat he wore like a cape. The thing that got to me, though, the thing that made all that man-in-black stuff disturbing not laughable, was his face."

"What about his face?"

"He didn't have one." Keys raised an eyebrow; he sucked on his cigarette, blew smoke out through his nose again. "It must've been a mask, but it didn't look like one. His face just looked like a lump of featureless flesh under that hat."

Big Boy sat and tried to make sense of it. Keys waited patiently till Big Boy asked, "What did he call himself?"

"He said his name was the Blank."

"I wonder . . ."

"What, boss?"

"Ever hear of a guy named Redrum?"

"No. Should I have?"

"How long you been in this town?"

"Just a year. This faceless guy is somebody you know?"

"Maybe," Big Boy said, exhaled smoke. "Didn't you see it in the papers, few days ago? Frank Redrum escaped from Alcatraz. Tough cookie. He had a bootleg outfit back in the twenties. His boys betrayed him, he did some time, then he got out and knocked 'em off one at a time."

"And he had no face?"

"He had a face, all right. A face that'd stop a clock. Two clocks."

Keys almost shivered. "Well, this face is worse than that—it was no face at all! And his voice—it was just as weird. Weirder. All hoarse, distorted. Some of it was the speaker."

"Speaker?"

"Yeah. He talked into a microphone; whispered, actually, but it came out of a speaker, amplified and distorted, though I don't know where it was positioned in the room. The voice seemed to come from everywhere. . . ."

"Disguising his voice, same way he was disguising his face," Big Boy said, mulling it over. Then looked sharply at Keys. "So. Give with the rest of it."

Keys shrugged. "He said I'd be the go-between. He said open up that briefcase, and I did, and it was full of money. The other half of the C-note was on top—but that was a drop in the bucket."

"How much cash was there?"

"I haven't counted it yet."

"How much, Keys? I ain't gonna take it away from you or nothin'."

Keys swallowed. "Five grand. At least that's what

the Blank claimed. Like I said, I haven't counted it yet."

"This is *your* fee?"

"First payment of it, anyway," Keys said.

Big Boy's eyes were moving back and forth, fast. "Why didn't he come to me direct?"

"I don't know. All I know is, he wants to help you get rid of Dick Tracy."

Big Boy thought about that. "Well, Tracy *was* the guy that put Frank Redrum away. Tracy's put a *lot* of guys away. Whether it's Redrum or not, it sounds like somebody wants to get even. . . ."

"Yeah—for a price."

"What?"

"If it's revenge, it's revenge for a price. Here's the message I'm supposed to pass along." He got out another piece of paper and read the typewritten words: " 'If you kill Dick Tracy, you will be the prime suspect and the city police will mobilize against you. But for one hundred thousand dollars, I will guarantee Dick Tracy will not be a problem for you, anymore. And you will not be suspected of a thing. Fifty now. Fifty later.' " Keys shrugged. "What do you think?"

Big Boy crushed the cigar in his hand. His brow was creased in thought. "You got a way to get in touch with this Blank?"

Keys shrugged. "No. But he chose me as a go-between, didn't he? He'll get in touch."

Big Boy sat and smoked and considered. Then he got up and pointed a thick finger at Keys and said, "Piano man, if this is some scam of yours, keep in mind I can snap my fingers and you're a hamburger. Rare."

Fear flickered in Keys' eyes. "It's no scam, Mr. Caprice. . . ."

He laughed harshly. "I'm gonna make a deal with some bum I never saw, and *you* never really saw, and don't know how to get to?" He shook his head. Then he waved an arm and Keys drew back.

"Get outta here!" Big Boy raved. "Go put on your tux and play your piano."

The pianist got up and quickly left.

Big Boy shook his head disgustedly as Flattop approached. "Want me to follow him, boss?"

"Where to? The piano?" He snorted a laugh. "He's a bug. Forget about him."

Breathless rose from her seat near the fire and drifted over to Big Boy. "What was that about?"

"None of your business."

Her lip nearly sneered; not quite. "So what *is* my business, then?"

He slapped her, gently. "Me. I'm your business. And don't ever forget it."

He took her throat in one of his big hands and kissed her greedily.

"Opening night, baby," he said. "Break a leg."

Gallantly, Big Boy offered her his arm to walk her from the conference room to the showroom.

"You, too," she said, wiping off her mouth with the back of a hand.

And took his arm.

See P. 27

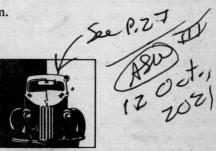

19

A gray-haired, gray-mustached man with a round face considerably younger than his hair moved cautiously along the periphery of the private garage adjacent to the Club Ritz. Behind a parked limousine, he removed his long topcoat and revealed a formal waiter's uniform—red jacket trimmed with black and gold, and high collar with tuxedo tie. He left the topcoat behind and moved to a doorway beyond which was a bustling, crowded kitchen, the staff frantically doing its best to keep up with a capacity opening-night crowd. The gray-haired, gray-mustached man with the round, young face slipped into the hubbub, blending immediately in.

Just another waiter.

In the showroom of the club, the quiet elegance of Lips Manlis had been replaced by the wild revelry of Big Boy Caprice—a carnival-type atmosphere that made opening night—and one might suppose, *any* night at the Club Ritz—a rowdy, no-holds-barred New-Year's-Eve-like celebration. Scantily clad showgirls kicked and shimmied as the band on stage, elegant in their white tuxes, beat out a blaring brand of swing.

At the center of it all was Big Boy, a ruling monarch surrounded by rivals who had become his subjects—Pruneface, Texie Garcia, Johnny Ramm, Ribs Mocca, and the rest, resplendent in their formal attire, looking like a ghoulish wedding party. The queen of the madams, Texie Garcia, the lone female among these wolves, dripping with jewels, cigarette holder in hand, had poured

164

herself into a tight red dress that announced her as a literal scarlet woman. Her matching red pillbox hat with veil was an absurdly tasteful touch. Flattop wore his black gloves, as usual, as if everything he did in life were criminal, making him afraid to leave his fingerprints on even a champagne glass.

"So what do you think?" Big Boy asked Pruneface proudly. "Is this a joint or is this a joint?"

The hideously wrinkled gangster was gazing droolingly at the showgirls. "Gotta hand it to you, Big Boy," Pruneface said admiringly, "they're the classiest broads in town."

"That's a matter of opinion," Texie put in, and Itchy, who was sitting next to the madam, cozying up to her, laughed his weasel laugh. Texie seemed to like it.

Across the room, the gray-haired, gray-mustached waiter with the young, round face was keeping busy, without really serving anyone anything. He was also keeping his eye on the entryway to the stairs that led up to the conference room. Right now a pair of tuxedoed goons stood guard there.

Bathed in a blue spotlight, Breathless Mahoney took the stage; her skintight backless black gown shimmered. So did her hair. So, seemingly, did her hauntingly pale skin, the bright red lipstick startling against the ghostly complexion. Though the casino room at the rear remained boisterous, the showroom quieted as the chanteuse began to sing her torchy ballad.

Outside, in a moonless overcast night lit only by neon, a police car slid silently to the curb across the street from the Club Ritz.

Within the car, Tracy, in the driver's seat, spoke softly into his two-way.

"Move in, men," he said. "Take your positions."

Even as police cars were moving in, to cordon off the area, Catchem and a small, bespectacled individual named Bug Bailey had maneuvered up the Club Ritz building's fire escape and up onto the rooftop. Their dark topcoats blending into the night, they stood near one of several skylights; Bailey carried a heavy black satchel—it was as if he were on a trip.

Catchem knelt and began to jimmy the lock on the skylight. Soon he had knotted a rope on a pipe and began lowering Bailey down.

Then Catchem followed.

With flashlights, they made their way through the dark attic, which was directly above Caprice's conference room; with a knowledge of the layout of the building, garnered from blueprints on record at the county recorder's office, Catchem directed Bailey to the precise position.

The little electronics expert began unloading and setting up a series of microphones encased in a compact wooden box; these included a wire recorder as well as the most sophisticated sound devices available.

Bailey was, after all, the police sound technician who had consulted with Diet Smith's staff in the creation of the most technologically advanced device currently in use: the two-way wrist radio.

And that device was, in fact, *literally* currently in use.

Because Sam Catchem was checking in with Dick Tracy, letting him know that he and Bailey were safely inside.

"Make it snappy, Sam," Tracy said into his two-way.

The detective sat in the unmarked car studying the watch portion of the two-way, and the next time the second hand climbed to "twelve," he spoke into it again: "Okay, boys—let's go!"

The police cars pulled in closer and uniformed cops began to stream out of them, heading for the building on all sides.

One of those sides was the front door, where the

grandly uniformed doorman frowned and quickly hit a concealed button.

Within the club, a loud shrill bell rang, and the clientele—among them, many of the city's and the state's elite—began rising in panic; silverware and plates collided, chairs scooted noisily against the floor, gasps and curses mingled in the mounting din.

Big Boy rose quickly from his table and moved to the casino room in back; like a musical director, he waved his arms as he spoke, a thick cigar between the just-as-thick fingers of his left hand.

"Take it easy, folks!" he assured them in his grating voice. "Everything's under control!"

By way of demonstration, the gangster suavely moved two customers away from a 21 table; it revolved into the wall, and was replaced by a dining table for two. Gracious host that he was, Big Boy gestured regally to the table and the stunned, rather pleased customers sat back down.

A central roulette table disappeared under a hardwood panel that was clicked into place; atop it a pair of tuxedoed waiters quickly threw a white tablecloth and a centerpiece of artificial flowers. A wall of slot machines soon became concealed behind another wall that dropped down into place. Within a minute, the entire casino was converted to an innocent dining room.

Uniformed police began pouring into the room through the front entrance; then cops began moving in through every other doorway as well. The bluecoats were everywhere. In the confusion, the tuxedoed guards stepped away from the entrance to the second-floor stairway, as they tried to catch Big Boy's attention, to find out what they should do.

In that confusion, the gray-haired, gray-mustached waiter with the young, round face slipped up the stairs. At the same time, in the attic two and a half stories above,

Bug Bailey was about to drill a hole in the floor. He would not begin, however, until the gray-haired waiter below had signaled him with knocks on the ceiling, to confirm the precise position of a certain light fixture.

In the showroom, Big Boy had returned to his table and resumed his regal pose with his cronies. He sat watching as if disinterested, as Tracy finally shouldered his way into the club, like a general checking up on his troops, to see how they'd fared with the foe.

Every eye was on the detective as he slowly crossed the room. He would tip his hat, in mock-politeness, to various dignitaries as he made his way to Big Boy's table: "Judge Debirb—how you are, sir? Judge Harper—it's nice to see you out of your robes. How are you, Congressman Retfarg? My, your daughter looks lovely tonight. . . ."

Of course, the blonde in the low-cut gown sitting with the congressman was probably not his daughter.

"Looks like a class reunion," Tracy said, with a small nasty smile, positioning himself before Big Boy and his table of gruesome cronies. "Maybe we should sing 'Hail Hail, the Gang's All Here'?"

"This is a private club," Big Boy said, not rising, doing his best to sound bored. "This is a private party."

"I decided to crash it." Tracy shrugged. "This lets me."

He tossed a folded document on the table.

"So you got yourself a search warrant," Big Boy said, not looking at it. "So search. But consider. . . ." He lifted an advisory finger. "You're gonna make some enemies out of some very important people. Better think twice about how *careful* you look, Dick."

Tracy laughed shortly. "You're sweating, Big Boy."

Big Boy twitched a shrug. "It's a little warm in here."

"Maybe you ought to check the safety gauge on your furnace."

Big Boy said nothing.

Tracy glanced around; the uniformed cops were checking the place out. In front of the bandstand, Breathless stood singing. She wore a black gown, but not the one she'd worn to his apartment earlier. Their eyes locked. For a moment he couldn't pull away.

But he did.

"Tracy," a uniformed cop said, "no sign of any gambling devices."

"You've checked thoroughly, Cochran?"

"Yes. There's nothing."

Tracy sighed. He glanced toward the stairway entrance and saw the gray-haired, gray-mustached waiter slipping back into the room.

Pruneface, Texie Garcia, Flattop, and the rest were laughing, toasting each other, making cracks about Tracy under their breath. Having a great time at the detective's expense.

"That's it then," Tracy told the officer. "You and Sergeant Matetsky round up the boys and head out."

"Aren't you gonna join us, Tracy?" Big Boy asked with an ugly grin, gesturing to the table.

Tracy looked sharply at the gangster. "Not just now. But I'll be back."

"Let us know in advance next time," Big Boy said with a magnanimous wave of his Havana. "We'll toss you a great big party."

"The next party's going to be for you, Big Boy," Tracy said. "We'll reserve you a seat of honor at the big house—a hot seat."

Tracy and the uniformed cops left as quickly as they had come.

"Some raid," Flattop said.

Itchy giggled nasally. "Big Boy scared 'im off—when he saw all the high-hats here, the copper knew he'd get in hot water."

"He sure didn't look around too close," Big Boy said, suddenly troubled. "I don't get it. . . ."

Pruneface's mask of merriment had dropped away; he was watching the door where Tracy went out. "I thought you were going to take care of that bum."

"He didn't really look around," Big Boy said, puzzled.

"Relax, Big Boy," Texie said. She put an arm around him, her generous bosom rubbing up against him. "He was just tryin' to louse up your grand opening."

Breathless continued singing, and Big Boy—and the room—responded to her soothing, sensual sound. The front of the room quieted, even as the casino in back came to loud life, and the party was again underway.

In his car, Tracy spoke into his two-way. "We're out, Sam."

And in the attic, Catchem prepared to ascend the rope, as Bug Bailey was settled on the floor, sitting Indian-style, attending his listening devices.

"You're on your own, Bug," Catchem said. "Call home if you're in a jam."

"That's what I invented this for," Bug said cheerily, holding up his wrist with its two-way.

As Tracy pulled away, he slowed as he neared the club's garage. He reached over and swung open the door on the rider's side.

The gray-haired, gray-mustached waiter hopped into the car, peeling off the gray hair and mustache as he did.

"How'd it go?" Tracy asked.

"The light fixture hides the microphone perfectly," Pat Patton said. "Bug should hear—and record—plenty from there."

"It's a dangerous assignment."

"We'll have a man posted in the building across the way," Patton said. "Anything goes wrong, Bug's got his two-way."

"Brave little guy," Tracy said admiringly. He turned the corner. "Let's hope we get away with it. You think Big Boy thinks I'm too stupid to look under a false tabletop?"

"Maybe he thinks you were afraid of getting in trouble with those judges and the other high-hats in attendance."

"Yeah," Tracy said. "He did mention that himself."

"Kind of embarrassing, isn't it?" Patton admitted. "Letting Big Boy think we're that stupid, or that scared."

"Yeah," Tracy said. "It's embarrassing." He grinned at his assistant, who looked more than a little silly in the red waiter's jacket. "But no more embarrassing than you in that outfit."

Patton looked at himself and laughed, and said, "I'll get over it."

"So will I," Tracy said, pointing. "There's Sam . . . let's give the man a lift. . . ."

See p.27

171

20

Big Boy slammed his fist down on the front page that stared up at him, taunting him, from the blood-red conference-room table; the table shook, the very room seemed to shake, and the newspaper below the fist tore and crinkled. Big Boy's fist had landed directly on a smiling photograph of Detective Dick Tracy, seen hauling away a sullen, handcuffed Ribs Mocca.

"Everywhere I turn," Big Boy raved, "it's Tracy, Tracy, Tracy!"

The newspaper headline, in print of a size and boldness usually reserved for the outbreak of war (and in fact that was, in a way, what the *Tribune* was reporting), said: TRACY ATTACKS GANGLAND, with a secondary head stating: BIG BOY FEELS THE SQUEEZE. Several other papers were scattered about the table; the headline on the *Chronicle* said: TRACY'S WRECKING CREW BRINGS GAMBLERS BAD LUCK, accompanied by photographs of axe-wielding plainclothesmen smashing slot machines, overturning gambling tables, and escorting hoodlums into paddy wagons.

The *News* had focused on the arrest of Texie Garcia and the shuttering of various of her brothels. That headline read: TRACY CRACKS DOWN ON WHITE SLAVERY RING. Smaller headlines referred to the various judges, aldermen, city council members, and socially prominent citizens among the patrons of the various illicit establishments raided, gambling and prostitution alike. Tracy had graciously chosen not to arrest any of these luminaries, but did leak their names to the press.

"He invited the newshounds along!" Big Boy said. "Publicity-seeking son of a . . ."

And the room rang with invectives as obscene as they were heartfelt.

Seated at the shining red table, making a very disgruntled audience for this symphony of rage, were Pruneface and his chief bodyguard, Influence, whose mashed-looking skeletal face rivaled his boss's in sheer hideousness. Seated across from them, watching them with hooded-eyed care, were Flattop and Itchy, their coats unbuttoned, their shoulder holsters showing.

"Consolidate, you say," Pruneface growled. "You're the future, you tell us. And the day after we start all this mutual planning, this 'coordinating' like a 'big-time corporation'—with *you* our 'chairman of the board'—we suffer our worst setbacks, the most damaging raids, in history!"

"It's like that lousy dick's readin' my mind!" Big Boy said, and he wadded up the newspaper with Tracy's face on it and hurled the ball into the fireplace across the room, where the paper crackled and burned.

Pruneface seemed unimpressed by Big Boy's display of temper. "Tracy threw Ramm in the slam; he nailed Texie, too. Mocca's in the jug, so's DeSanto and Clipper Brown. They'll all be out on bond by noon, but still, it's real inconvenient. Worse, nearly every gambling joint in the city is in pieces."

"Don't you think I know that?" Big Boy snarled. He slammed his fist on the table. Again and again.

"All this show of emotion," Pruneface said coldly, "doesn't hide one fact."

"Oh, yeah? Which is *what*?"

"*You* didn't get raided last night."

"I got raided the night before! You was there!"

"Yeah. Compared to the rest of us, your club got a free pass. You'll be the only game in town tonight. The only casino up and running. The question being asked in certain nasty circles is, Did Big Boy sell out his competition to the cops?"

Big Boy waved his arms. "That's crazy! Tracy'll probably hit me tonight, which means maybe I don't even dare open the casino—I probably oughta put the wheels and slots and such in storage."

"Is that what're you gonna do?"

"I don't know. I don't know what I'm gonna do." Big Boy shook his head. "Tracy. This one lousy cop, Tracy . . ."

Pruneface's dark eyes were crazed and glittery in the rough-creased mask of his features. "I'll hand you your head, if you're playing me for a patsy. And if you got a canary singin' in your organization, tipping Tracy off, then you better *find* that bird, and find yourself a big *cat* to feed him to. Or your grand and glorious scheme about all of us 'businessmen' throwing in together and goin' national is going to blow up in your face. And it'll make Spaldoni's demise look like a firecracker goin' off."

Big Boy's lip curled. "Don't threaten *me*, old man . . ."

"You said you had a way of taking care of Tracy," Pruneface said in his hoarse, hollow voice. "You told me you'd either buy him, or take him out and make it look like an accident. But instead you screwed up royal."

Big Boy glared at Flattop and Itchy; Flattop remained impassive, but Itchy began scratching over his ear, like he was digging out a tick.

Pruneface sneered with disgust. "I wanted to just bump him off, plain and simple—but no. You had to outsmart yourself."

"I *am* gonna take care of Tracy," Big Boy said, almost pleading. "But you gotta leave it to me." ·

"No," Pruneface said, standing suddenly. "I'm takin' this bum out of the headlines myself."

Flattop and Itchy rose a fraction of a second thereafter, as did Pruneface's bodyguard Influence. The men glowered at each other like the Earps and Clantons trying to decide who was going to draw first.

"Not so fast," Big Boy said, holding up a fat palm in a stop motion. "You rub Tracy out, the finger's gonna point at me."

"My finger's pointing at you now," Pruneface said, and it was. It was as gnarled as the branch of a tree; an old, ugly tree. "I'm rubbin' him out! And you can't stop me."

"Pruneface," Big Boy said, "we got to keep our heads . . ."

And as he extended his hand in a gesture of reasonableness, Big Boy felt something damp.

A drop of something.

Something brown and warm.

He looked up, saw nothing. Pruneface was looking at him like he was crazy; Flattop, Itchy, and Influence were similarly transfixed by Big Boy's sudden distraction.

Then Big Boy glanced down, where one of the newspapers on the table was getting damp. A picture of Tracy, in fact, was pearled with brown moisture.

Bug Bailey was, as Tracy had described, a brave little man. Little in life fazed him, and he had pulled hazardous surveillance duty more times than the rest of the department put together. But he had one, ironic phobia.

He was afraid of bugs.

Not the electronic kind, obviously. Ever since he was a little kid, whose bug-eyed physiognomy had earned him his nickname, he'd been good with all things mechanical and electrical. He had an affinity for science that had led to his involvement in helping Chief Brandon initiate a city-wide system of radio patrol cars, well ahead of much of the country; and with the encouragement of Tracy, Bug had connected with billionaire Diet Smith and, together with Smith's inventor son Brilliant, they had come up with the two-way wrist radio.

But if science was his friend, biology was not. At least not entomology.

Perhaps it was inevitable that a four-eyed, goofy kid nicknamed Bug would have some bully put insects down his shirt. One nightmare after-school encounter with a sadistic lout and his rat pack of equally brutish chums had moved Bug's aversion to things creepy and crawly into a full-blown phobia. A spider had been put down his shirt, and a cockroach dropped into his mouth.

A cockroach not unlike the one that was, at this moment, moving inexorably toward his ham-and-cheese sandwich.

Bug spotted it, and, though gripped with horror, looked for something to swat it with. His fingers found his notebook and he tried to flick the cockroach away from his sandwich, but to his dismay and terror, Bug determined the bug was only millimeters from slithering between the white slices, apparently planning to nestle between the ham and the cheese.

This was not the first meal the Bug had taken here. On both days at this listening post, he'd brought sandwiches and a full thermos of coffee to help him through the night. His surveillance stint was a long haul, albeit not a twenty-four hour one. Big Boy's business was, after all, primarily conducted in the evenings—it had been Tracy's primary intent to track and interrupt Big Boy's various bagmen as they made their payoffs and collections. So Catchem would return before dawn each day, collect the Bug, and bring him back again, to be lowered into the attic via the skylight, well after dark.

Bug had enjoyed himself; he didn't mind the dark, and there was plenty of entertainment. He sat crosslegged, looking very buglike, heavy headphones over his ears, in his black-and-yellow striped sportcoat with black-and-yellow tie. Listening to Big Boy blusteringly ordering people around was like listening to a radio melodrama. Though he was only one floor above, Bug felt detached, removed, entirely safe.

He sat like a mischievous elf, eavesdropping, then tattling, via two-way. He'd been especially amused, a few moments ago, when Big Boy began raving about "Tracy, Tracy, Tracy," and that it was as if Tracy could "read his mind." That made Bug smile. It had been fun duty, and the danger hadn't bothered him a bit. Hadn't even occurred to him.

He didn't like the sound of Pruneface wanting to "rub Tracy out," but Big Boy, oddly, seemed to have talked the older gangster out of it.

But now, as he frantically swatted the dreaded cockroach, he lost composure. He didn't notice that his thermos-cap cup of coffee had spilled.

The bug banished, Bug returned to his listening post, scribbling notes as he monitored Big Boy's fulminations.

He was shivering, the thought of that insect crawling into his sandwich a frightening image that he couldn't dispel. Intent on his work, shaken by his phobia, Bug did not notice the coffee silently dripping into the microphone hole, and down.

The white light fixture, with its deco concentric circles, had hidden the microphone and its hole well. So Big Boy observed, having climbed up on the red table to get a peek. He could see from whence the brown rain had fallen. He began to reach for his gun, but something, somebody, tugged his pantleg. Flattop.

"Boss," Flattop said, and made a shushing gesture with the forefinger of a black-gloved hand. Then the gunman curled the finger and nodded to the door.

Big Boy's eyes narrowed, then he nodded back, and climbed down off the table.

"What . . . ?" Pruneface began.

But Big Boy raised a hand. He pointed upward, and Pruneface nodded, too.

"Be with you in a second," Big Boy told him. "Gotta sign for some meat."

In the hall, Big Boy said, "Tracy's got somebody up there listening!"

Flattop, ever composed, nodded sagely. "That's right, boss."

"The attic, right over us! The nerve of the bum! Let's get up there and smash the son of a . . ."

"No, boss!" Flattop touched Big Boy's arm, gently. "The cops don't know we're onto 'em. We should use it *against* 'em, before we put a stop to it. Feed 'em some wrong info or something."

Big Boy's eyes narrowed shrewdly. Then he said, "Go get that wrinkled lunatic for me."

"Sure, boss."

In a moment, Pruneface had joined the hallway confab.

"You want to rub Tracy out?" Big Boy asked the older gangster. "With my blessing?"

"I'd like nothing better." He shook his head. "But finding him's going to be the trick. He's moving so fast, we're getting hit everyplace in town. . . ."

"So why don't we send him an invitation?"

Big Boy walked Pruneface back into the office. Flattop, pulling his black gloves tight, smiled smugly, following them in, as Big Boy went to the phone. Pruneface stood and smiled up at the light fixture. Influence gazed upward, as well, though his was a face that never smiled.

"Okay, Freddie," Big Boy said into the receiver, his thumb holding the cradle button down, keeping the line dead. "Get down to the Southside warehouse. Time for the *big* pay off. . . ."

21

We have to talk," Tess said.

"I know," Tracy said, and dipped his spoon into a bowl of Mike's chili.

Outside the night was a dark hand gripping the city; not a good night to wish upon a star, because there wasn't a star in the sky. Within the electric radiance of the diner—its chrome trim glistening, enamel countertop and tables gleaming, booths and stools covered in ersatz leather as red as a circus clown's nose—the world seemed brighter. But it was an illusion.

The Kid was curled up in one of the booths while Tracy and Tess sat at the counter, having moved there not to disturb the boy after he dropped off to sleep.

"The Welfare Department called about you-know-who," Tracy said glumly.

"He is a swell kid." Tess sighed. She wasn't eating her food.

"Not hungry?" he asked.

She shook her head.

"It's probably better for him," Tracy said not too convincingly. He ate the chili; he was hungry, wolfing it down—it was the first time he'd eaten since breakfast.

"Probably," Tess allowed. She didn't sound very convinced, either.

Mike was pouring Tracy some coffee. Tracy swallowed a spoonful of chili and asked, "What's the ratio of beans and meat to melted rubber in this concoction, Mike?"

"Trade secret," Mike said good-naturedly, and moved away.

"You may be right," Tess said.

"What?" Tracy asked.

"About the child. We can't keep passing him around between us like a puppy. Spends half his time at the greenhouse with me, the rest at police headquarters with you. . . ."

He nodded, embarrassed. "I've stuck you with him a lot, the last two days. . . ."

"I don't consider myself *stuck* with him."

"I know, I know. But I haven't been able to do my share. The case is really heating up. We've been knocking off mob operations left and right . . . we've intercepted half a dozen of Big Boy's payoffs. One more major sting and we can cripple his cash flow."

She smiled faintly. "You've really got him on the run, don't you? That's good. I'm very proud of you, Dick."

He looked at her shyly. "You know, I might be able to spend time with you two this evening. Since it looks like the orphanage is in the cards for the little guy tomorrow."

"Dick, we *have* to *talk*."

"Well, sure." He put the spoon down; he touched her hand. "What is it, dear?"

She seemed to be having difficulty finding the words; then she was about to begin when his two-way spoke up.

"Tracy!" Bug Bailey's voice said. "Come in, Tracy. . . ."

She sighed; not angry, just frustrated, and a little sad.

"Honey," he said, patting her hand, ignoring the two-way, "don't worry about it. I'm sure Sam or Pat will intercept that call. I'm off-duty."

"Are you sure?"

He made a sweeping gesture of finality with one hand. "Positive. Now, what is it?"

"Dick . . . I can't stay at your place any longer."

"Well, I can understand that. For appearance' sake . . ."

"No. It's not that." She sighed again; averted his gaze. "My apartment isn't really habitable right now, so I'm . . . leaving."

"Leaving?"

"Going to my mother's, in Homewood."

After the murder of her husband, Mrs. Trueheart had sold the delicatessen and moved from the city to a bungalow in one of the outlying suburbs.

"Well, Tess, that's an awful long commute into the city to get to your job."

"I know. But it'll only be temporary."

"Good. Until you can find a new apartment."

"No. I mean, until I find a new job, closer to Mama's."

"Tess. I don't understand. . . ."

Her eyes were tragic. "Dick, I used to dream that someday maybe things would settle down. That you'd be able to take the time to really live a normal life. Now . . . now I know that's never going to happen."

"Tess . . ."

"I wouldn't want you to give up what you love doing. I'd never ask that."

The wrist radio interrupted again, in its obnoxious, staticky way: "Come in, Tracy . . . come in!"

Bug's voice.

"Sam'll cover it," Tracy said.

"No. It's all right. I understand."

"Tracy," Bug's voice said, "please come in. . . ."

"I'll just tell him to call Sam," Tracy said, and raised his wrist near his face, as if lifting a great weight. "What is it, Bug?"

"Tracy," Bug's voice said, "you better get down to the Southside Warehouse right away—sounds like a *big* payoff is comin' down."

"Bug," Tracy began, "check in with Pat or Sam. I'm indisposed."

"No," Tess said quietly, touching his arm. "It's all right. Go."

"You're sure?" he asked her.

She nodded.

"I'm on my way, Bug," Tracy said. He took Tess's hand and squeezed it. "I'll be back. We'll talk this out."

"Go," she said, and her smile was faint, but supportive.

The industrial area near the river was blacker than the inside of a fist. Tracy parked and walked to the massive redbrick warehouse, thinking he'd probably go in that same window in the alleyway, where he'd found Patton unconscious a few nights ago.

But when he tried a door on the Front Street side, and it quietly opened, he slipped on in—why stand on ceremony? As long as he had his gun in hand, that is.

Stacked crates loomed, throwing inky shadows; the stockpiled boxes along the periphery provided good cover, and he ducked behind them, moving down an aisle, edging quietly along, listening for voices, for any sound.

He didn't hear voices, but he did hear a mechanical rumbling; and the guttural purr of an engine.

Moving cautiously, he headed toward the source of the sound, and then, between stacked boxes, he got a view of something.

He saw Bug Bailey.

Bailey was visible only from the chest up; he was gagged, a bright red handkerchief like a gash across his lower face, his eyes buggy and filled with no hope.

Though he could see no ropes, Tracy knew the little man was bound.

Bug Bailey was standing in an iron-chain-draped crate,

the upper portion of which was open, and above him was the spout of a cement mixer.

Tracy drew a sudden breath, afraid for his friend.

At the same time, the detective saw Bailey's captors, standing on the platform just to the left of the churning truck: two men in dark fedoras and topcoats—the wrinkled human nightmare that was Pruneface, backed up by his chief enforcer, the skeletal-faced Influence, whose hauntingly hideous gaze bespoke his days as a carnival hypnotist.

Both of them had tommy guns.

Influence's staring eyes caught Tracy, and Tracy ducked out of sight, as Influence signaled his withered boss that they had company.

"Come save your little friend, Tracy!" Pruneface called out tauntingly. "Be a hero! That's what you're so good at, isn't it?"

And Pruneface nodded to Influence, who reached up and threw a lever on the truck. Its huge mixer tumbled and churned and began to cascade wet cement down upon Bug Bailey, covering his head like thick gray molasses, splattering his yellow-and-black coat with the same blobby gray.

Ye gods, Tracy thought, *he's going to drown in that stuff!*

The detective had changed positions and was fashioning an impromptu scarecrow, hanging his yellow topcoat on a mop and using a bucket for a head, on which he snugged his fedora. He propped the Tracy-like figure between two crates not far from where Influence had spotted him.

Hunkered down, he quickly, carefully moved along an aisle between walls of stacked crates, leaving the scarecrow behind, circling around to get at Bailey from the other side.

While he was doing this, Pruneface and Influence were

stalking him—or so they thought. They moved slowly down an aisle of boxes, where the yellow of Tracy's coat and fedora attracted the attention of their combined tommy guns.

Tracy smiled tightly at the sound of machine-gun fire elsewhere in the warehouse, as the bullets chewed up the wood of the crates, and killed a topcoat, hat, bucket, and mop. With that cacophony as a backdrop, Tracy was getting bathed in cement while he worked at untying the Bug.

But it wasn't easy. The bonds were tight, the cement was sloppy and flooding down on them both, and the groggy little man was wedged down inside that upended crate.

"I hate heroes," somebody said.

Tracy, his face, his hair, his black suit, splotchy with wet cement, glanced back to see Pruneface, his shriveled face cracked apart in a smile. The ancient gangster was pointing a .45 automatic right at him. Influence, his tommy gun empty, smoke curling out its barrel, stood watching with glazed, contented eyes.

"Somebody should have done this years ago," Pruneface said, and a shot echoed through the warehouse, but it wasn't his.

Nor was it Tracy's.

A figure in a black topcoat with a black slouch hat had emerged, just barely, from a gap between stacked crates, a smoking .38 in his black-gloved hand.

A man with no face.

"Ye gods," Tracy said softly.

Influence, armed only with an empty tommy gun, scrambled for the Front Street door, and Tracy watched as the faceless figure seemed to consider putting a hole in the fleeing man's back. But it didn't happen. The door opened and closed, and Influence was gone.

Tracy looked back at his savior, but the man with no face had receded into the darkness.

Tracy didn't pursue the faceless man; he couldn't—he had to proceed with rescuing his little friend, who thank God was alive. He wrestled Bailey out of the crate, and the gray men looked like statues come to life, doing a bizarre dance in the dimly lit warehouse, their only audience a wrinkled gangster who lay on the floor, his staring eyes as blank as the face of the man who had killed him.

22

Big Boy sat at the conference-room table with a full-course meal laid out in front of him, a feast fit for a king—only the king was fit to be tied. Utensils clutched in his fists like weapons, a lobster bib tucked in his collar as if he were a tot, Big Boy was fuming, his eyes flashing dangerously as he spoke to Flattop.

"The *Blank* bailed Tracy out?" Big Boy asked incredulously.

"So Influence says." Flattop shrugged. He laughed shortly. "Old skeleton-face has scurried into his rat hole, shakin' like a little girl."

Breathless was buffing her nails by the fire. Her black gown glittered in the glow.

"What the hell's goin' on?" Big Boy said, eyes flickering with confusion. "Is he working for Tracy, this no-face bum?"

"Who says he's working for Tracy?" Flattop said.

"What sort of man has no face?" Breathless asked.

"Keep out of this," Big Boy snapped. "If I want your opinion, I'll slap it out of you."

Her smile was wicked as she studied her red nails. "That Dick Tracy really gets under your skin, doesn't he?"

Big Boy grabbed a glass of wine and, half standing, flung it wildly at the mirror over the fireplace; the wineglass and the mirror shattered into shards and rained near Breathless, who backed away, shaken. Red wine dripped like blood down the broken remains of the mirror.

"Get out!" the gangster ordered her. "Go find your pansy piano player and rehearse or something! What do I pay you for?"

"That's an embarrassing question," Breathless said coldly, and, her blue eyes mingling fear and rancor, she moved to the door, exiting as fluidly as the wine Big Boy had spilled.

"All right, all right," Big Boy told Flattop and Itchy. Numbers Norton stood on the sidelines, as well. "That's enough of this garbage. I want 'em dead, *both* of 'em! I want the Blank blanked, and I want Tracy deader than this here steak!" He stuck his fork in his rare steak and it quivered there.

Itchy and Norton exchanged nervous glances; Flattop remained impervious.

"What's the deal anyway?" Big Boy ranted. "Did you bums forget how to *kill* people? Don't you have any pride in your work anymore? Have you no sense of duty? I want Dick Tracy dead! Dead, dead, dead!"

"It was Pruneface and Influence that screwed up, boss," Flattop said, gesturing casually, trying to get Big Boy to be reasonable. "You want us to do the job, we'll do it."

"But you wanted it to look like an accident, boss," Itchy said, in a pleadingly nasal tone, gesturing with his palms up.

"That's right, boss," Norton said. "We got to be careful. We're running a business here. Killing cops brings down the heat. Look at how worked up they got over that harness bull getting it at the warehouse!"

"Yeah," Big Boy said, calming himself, his seething turning into scheming. "Yeah. You're right. When you're right, you're right, and you're right. Listen . . . Flattop. Tell that funny-boy piano player I want to talk to him. . . ."

* * *

By the time Tracy got back to the diner, Tess was gone.

He'd stopped by headquarters to shower away the cement and generally clean up, as well as grab his spare topcoat and hat (placing another bullet-riddled fedora on the shelf for Pat's wall-display collection). But he'd done all that as quickly as humanly possible and he was sure Tess would understand.

Chief Brandon sat at the counter with the Kid. They were polishing off pieces of pie.

"Where's Tess?" Tracy asked.

"She's gone to stay with her mother," Brandon said, surprised that Tracy would ask. "She called and asked me to stop by and mind the boy, here, till you got back."

"She's gone?" Tracy said, sitting on stool, stunned.

"Sorry, Tracy," Brandon said. His rugged face had gone soft with sympathy. "She said you knew. . . ."

"Yeah. Well, uh, thanks, Chief. Thanks for pinch-hitting for me."

Brandon's face tightened; his eyes were hard and strictly business now. "What's this about some mystery man shooting Pruneface and saving your tail?"

Tracy clued him in. The Chief reacted with the same skeptical surprise as had Catchem and Patton when Tracy had filled them in at the scene. In the darkness on the dock, with a foghorn making its ghostly wail from somewhere out where the river met the lake, the tale of the faceless man saving him had seemed less than credible to Tracy himself. But both his assistants had bought his story.

"If you say there was a man with no face," Patton had said, "I'll bet the mortgage there was. But who is he workin' for?"

And now the Chief was asking the same thing.

Tracy told Brandon what he'd told Pat at the scene: "I don't know. But somehow I don't think he's working for me."

The Chief raised his eyebrows, then hauled himself off the stool; he smiled and patted the Kid on the back. "You take care of this big lug, son."

"Will do, sir," the boy said. He was still eating his pie, though with less enthusiasm, now. He was studying Tracy's face.

The Chief walked out into the night.

"You look sad, Mr. Tracy," the boy said.

"It's that kind of night, junior," he said. "Are you done with that pie?"

"Yeah."

"Come on. Let's walk."

He'd left his car at headquarters, which was only half a dozen blocks away. It was midevening. It had rained, a brief but world-shaking thunderstorm; in the aftermath, the streets were shiny and slick under an ink-black sky. The city was a mass of rectangles with occasional dots of light; geometric, unreal, as cold as a blueprint, and every bit as inviting. The sidewalks were largely empty, but for the occasional street person stumbling in the dampness, searching for the recession of a doorway to duck into, or a soup kitchen open for business.

"You can make her like you again," the Kid said with a touching urgency in his voice, so close to the man that their clothing brushed as they walked. "Just tell her that dame didn't mean nothin' to you."

"Thanks, kid," Tracy said gently. "That's good advice."

"I'll talk to her for ya. I'll tell her it wasn't your fault that babe plastered her lips on ya."

Tracy had to laugh a little. "With you as my defense counsel," he said, "I just may get the chair."

The Kid frowned, but then he laughed. "Yeah, I guess that did sound kinda bad. I mean, the babe kissed *you*, you don't kiss *her*—right?"

"Right. How did you know?"

"Tracy, you got nerve when it comes to crooks. But with dames, you're putty in their hands."

"Thanks a bunch. But you're right. *She* kissed *me*."

"Yeah, but you aided and abetted." He patted Tracy's arm. "Don't let it get ya down. Miss Tess is nuts about ya. You can get back on her good side. I got faith in ya."

Tracy smiled at the Kid; he felt a warmth for this little roughneck that went beyond simple compassion. He slipped his arm around the boy. "You come up to the office with me. We need to talk about this orphanage business."

"I know." The boy shook his head, glumly. "It's a lousy world, ain't it?"

"Sometimes."

Tracy could understand why Tess would be hurt, would be angry; he was angry with himself. How could he let Breathless vamp him like that? She'd played him like a two-cent kazoo. At the same time, the memory of kissing her remained something he could not throw off; the sensation of it lingered, like a dream you couldn't shake upon awakening. The heat of her, the coolness, her body so soft, so firm; was that it? Was that the fascination? The contradictory nature of the woman? The sweetness and the wickedness?

With Breathless on his mind, but Tess in his heart, Tracy neared the front steps of the police station, with the well-dressed ragamuffin at his side. Puddles on the sidewalk reflected light from the nearby street lamp; but even with that, the world was dark.

"Look," the boy said, "Miss Tess is still comin' into town to work at the greenhouse, right? So stop by and see her in a day or so, and con her into coming to see me at that orphanage, why don't you?"

"Yeah?"

"Sure! She'll go along for my sake—then you can take me for a picnic or something, and I'll pretend to fall asleep . . . and, you know—you let nature take 'er course."

Tracy laughed. He took off the boy's red cap and ruffled his wild mop of reddish hair. "Junior, you're a pal."

They were going up the steps when Sergeant Crane came out.

"Tracy!" the uniformed man said. He worked the receiving desk, and his shift had just ended. "A message just came in for you . . . some woman wants to meet you somewhere."

Tracy glanced at the boy, who grinned and said, "Miss Tess!"

"No," the sergeant said. "I think it's a Miss Mahoney."

Tracy swallowed. He turned to the boy. "I'll take you upstairs."

"Maybe I oughta come along for this one," the boy said.

"I can handle myself," Tracy said.

The Kid laughed humorlessly. "Sure. Putty, I tell ya."

The detective said nothing more as he walked the boy in and up the stairs to the office.

Even with the Bug and his bugging devices pulled from the conference room, Big Boy was taking no chances; he sat parked in his limousine, on a dark, quiet side-street, conferring with 88 Keys.

The gangster sat thoughtfully smoking a big Havana. "You tell this 'Blank' character I accept his offer—only there's no down payment. He has to deliver."

Keys, in street clothes, his cap snugged down on his high forehead, was lighting up a cigarette; he nodded.

"He puts Tracy out of commission," Big Boy continued, "without any suspicion comin' back to me, I'll give 'im his hundred thousand bucks, and kiss him on the lips, if he has any."

"You've been using force," Keys said calmly. "The Blank's gonna use finesse."

"I don't care what he uses. If he wants to play bridge, that's okay with me. Just so Tracy's out, and I ain't incriminated."

Keys blew smoke. "The price has gone up, Big Boy."

"What?"

"It's ten percent, now. Ten percent of your business."

Big Boy's eyes popped. "Is he kidding? Who does this no-faced—"

Keys gestured in the air. "What have *you* been getting lately? Besides one hundred percent of nothin'. Your money's been going straight into Tracy's evidence lockers for days now. You think he's gonna let up?"

Big Boy scowled.

Keys continued. "The Blank gets rid of the cop, and you're left smellin' like a rose . . . *plus* the boys on the inside know you got the Blank workin' out on the fringes as a secret enforcer. So nobody ever gets outta line again."

Big Boy's eyes bulged with thought; he puffed the Havana like a train engine burning coal uphill. "Ten percent is a lot of dough."

"You only pay if Tracy's out of the picture and you're not implicated. What can you lose?"

"Okay," Big Boy said impulsively. "Okay, piano player. Tell no-face we got a deal."

On an otherwise empty dock, Tracy stood and studied the city's skyline. The dark clouds had skipped town as suddenly as a thief on the lam. Now the moon glowed yellowly, and the stars had made a late, dramatic appearance, a surprise witness in the courtroom of the night. The buildings of the city against the sky looked flat, like cutout cardboard; the occasional lights of buildings made irregular black-and-white checkerboards of their rectangular shapes. The harbor lights and the belated moonbeams shimmered on the dark water, streaks of white relieving the blackness.

He heard her car pull in and turned to watch as she moved from the sleek lavender sports car, hugging her black mink to her, and somehow he knew she was shielding herself from more than just the cold.

She stood and looked at him and her expression was one he'd never seen on her before. She was just as beautiful, but her eyes were troubled. The strong woman was revealing an unexpected vulnerability.

"I'm scared," she said.

All the masks seemed to have been dropped; her voice had a quiet, lonely quality in the stillness of the night, as water lapped gently against the pier, no other sounds intruding. They were two people isolated, alone in the world, for this one moment.

"Why?" Tracy asked. "Does Big Boy know we've talked?

"It's not Big Boy." She shuddered. "It's this man with no face. . . ."

Tracy smiled faintly. "I can handle him."

"I don't think so. Dick, I hear things I'm not supposed to hear. I listen. I observe. And he's out to get you."

"Big Boy?"

"Both of them. Big Boy *and* the faceless one."

"Breathless . . ."

She touched his shoulder. "Tracy . . . Dick. Get out of town before they kill you. And take me with you."

"To that desert island?"

"Anywhere."

"Breathless. There's only one thing I want from you. . . ."

She looked at him expectantly; she moved closer, lips wet and parted. "Yes?"

"I want to know," he said, "if you're ready to testify against Caprice."

That seemed to hurt her; it was as if he'd slapped her. "Tracy . . . please . . ."

"If you're not going to testify against him, this is the last time we're going to meet."

She looked at him with desperation in her lovely eyes. "Tracy, trust me. You have to leave town. Trust me . . . I'm the only one you can trust in this town."

"Why is that?"

"You *know* why.

He shook his head. "I'm in love with someone else."

She looked into his eyes, hard and deep.

And then her eyes welled with tears.

He touched her arm, but there was no passion in it— just compassion.

"You do, don't you?" she said, as if confirming a dark fear. "You do love her. . . ."

She turned and left.

He didn't watch her go. He couldn't quite bear to.

He stood for a while and watched the reflection of the city, and the moon, on the water.

Then he drove back to headquarters. There was much left to do tonight.

23

The decision to leave had taken time.

Tess had spent hours mulling the matter over, torturing herself over it. Despite what she'd told Dick, she knew it wasn't just the long hours he put in, or even the danger of the streets that had sent her away. Machine-gun bullets in front of her own apartment house had not been the last straw.

The woman had.

And neither of them had been open enough, or brave enough, to mention it—much less admit it.

She blamed herself for that. Dick was the shy one, after all, where affairs of the heart were concerned. She should have been straightforward enough, honest enough, to tell him how much a certain Miss Breathless Mahoney had to do with her decision to leave the city and stay at her mother's.

Then maybe they would have gotten it all out in the open and talked it out. Maybe he would have told her *his* side of it, assuming he had a side.

On the drive to her mother's in Homewood, she'd had a sudden thought, a thought that planted some doubt about her decision to leave. A calming solitude had settled on her as she drove in darkness, the whirl of her thoughts slowing, her emotions ceasing to churn. And in that solitude, that darkness, it occurred to her that as reticent about romance as Tracy was, it was highly unlikely he'd initiated anything romantic between himself and that woman.

Tess had been around the city's most celebrated detective long enough to pick up on a few of the finer points of deduction. And looking at the facts like a detective gave Tess a fresh perspective.

Anything that had happened between Tracy and that Breathless Mahoney would've had to have been the woman's doing. That lipstick on Dick's face was evidence only that *he* had been kissed; not that he'd done any kissing. After all, Tracy hardly would have invited Breathless to his apartment for an amorous liaison, with Tess and the boy due back momentarily.

The only verdict that could reasonably be reached was that Tracy was not the kind of man who would run around on a girl.

So doubts about her decision to leave were already nagging Tess when she arrived at her mother's house. And an evening with her mother had served to further undermine her resolve.

Her mother, helping her unpack, told her how glad she was to have her "little girl back home" (even though Tess had only lived in this house briefly, before moving back to the city).

"You can stay right here in your old room," her mother had said, as if Tess had lived there since childhood and not just a few months. "I think you've done the right thing. That city is getting more and more dangerous to live in."

Such an attitude was understandable coming from the widow of a small businessman shot down in his own store.

But Tess was less understanding of her mother turning against Dick.

"That man could be President of the United States," Mrs. Trueheart huffed, removing a tin of muffins from the oven, "and he'd consider it a desk job. He's like a child who's never going to grow up."

Tess bit her tongue as she sat at the kitchen table, stirring cream into her coffee.

"He'll never take that position as Chief of Police," Mrs. Trueheart said, emptying the muffins from their pan. "He's the kind of man who always has to be on the line of fire."

"Mother," Tess said stiffly, "how can you say those things? How can you be critical of Dick? You're talking about the man who's devoted his life to bringing Papa's killers to justice."

"I know," she said, somewhat guiltily. She sat at the table and shook her head. "I know, and no one thinks more highly of that boy than I do."

"Well, you don't sound like it."

Mrs. Trueheart touched her daughter's hand. "Dear . . . it's just that I don't want you to go through what I did."

"What do you mean, Mama?"

"To lose the man you love. To lose him to . . . violence. Like I did." Mrs. Trueheart swallowed; behind her wire-rimmed glasses her eyes were moist. "Your Dick Tracy is a hero, dear. A real hero."

"I know he is."

The older woman sighed. "Yes. And real heroes always run out of luck."

"What . . . what did you say, Mama?"

"Real heroes always run out of luck, dear."

Tess looked at her mother long and hard. "Mama— those muffins smell wonderful. You know, Dick always loved your cooking."

Mrs. Trueheart smiled sadly and nodded.

"Can I take some of your prize-winning baked goods with me?" Tess asked.

"When you drive into work tomorrow morning? Certainly."

"No. I mean right now."

"Right now?"

"I'm going back *tonight*, Mama. This minute. Those muffins of yours will be a kind of peace offering."

Mrs. Trueheart's face registered shock, then dismay; but as she studied her daughter's face, the older woman's expression softened into a knowing smile.

"I'll get a brown paper bag," her mother said.

Now that brown paper bag was in Tess's hand as she entered the greenhouse. She had stopped impulsively, passing the florist's on her way into the city. It was well after business hours, but her boss, Mr. Rewolf, wouldn't mind if she used her key to slip inside and pick up a few fresh calla lilies to brighten up Dick's apartment.

She entered and began to gather the lilies, humming pleasantly to herself, anxious to see Dick, to make up with him; anxious to see the Kid, too, whom she felt she'd virtually abandoned. She would make it up to them both.

She was so absorbed in her floral selection that she didn't hear the figure at first. And when she finally did, and turned, it was too late.

The knife was at her throat.

And the face under the slouch hat was not a face at all.

Nor was the voice like any human voice—rather, it was a rasping moan.

"I knew you'd come back," the nonvoice said.

The faceless one touched her face with a gloved hand; the touch was a caressing one, but sinisterly so. It was as if the man with no face envied her for having features.

"I'm working for Big Boy," the Blank said. "He wants you. . . ."

Tracy was afraid.

Being afraid was nothing new in his job; any cop, like any soldier in any war, knew fear. But he would have much rather been shooting it out with some hood than doing what he was about to do now: drive across town to the greenhouse and face Tess Trueheart.

Ironic that after so much triumph—arrests by night, arraignments by day, accompanied by interviews to a glowingly supportive press contingent—he should hit such a personal low. Congratulatory phone calls from the Mayor and the Governor meant nothing at all when the woman Tracy loved had left him.

Even defeating Big Boy would be an empty victory if he lost Tess. If he lost her, he lost everything.

Not that defeating Big Boy was a *fait accompli*. Not now that Bug Bailey had been found out and removed from his roost above Big Boy's chamber—although, thank God, at least the Bug had not been squashed. But the inside line on what Big Boy was up to was closed.

And the reporters had got wind of the faceless gunman intervening for him at the Southside Warehouse, which had already changed the tone of the press coverage. On the street in front of headquarters, when he'd finally gotten back to the station from his harborside meeting with Breathless, Tracy had passed a newsie hawking the late edition of the *Chronicle*, the headline on which was TRACY SAVED BY FACELESS AIDE. The newsie was calling out, "Tracy in league with mystery man! Read all about it. . . ."

All of this had gotten to him. At HQ, he'd been uncharacteristically ill-tempered to his staff, barking commands to Patton and Catchem, demanding sketches of the mystery gunman be worked up.

"What exactly is there to draw, Tracy?" Catchem had asked, his hands spread.

"The shape of the head," Tracy said, "the shape of the ears!"

"We're circulating photos of Frank Redrum," Patton said proudly. "Sam and I think he's your best suspect. . . ."

"That's not good enough!" Tracy said. He took a sip of his coffee and made a face. "And could we get some fresh coffee around here? How can we expect to nail Big Boy if we can't track down a lousy cup of coffee?"

It had gone on like that for some time. Reflecting on it now, as he drove across the city, Tracy was embarrassed. He'd even handled the Kid dismissively, when the subject of the orphanage came up. He shook his head.

What had snapped him out of his blue funk was the arrival of a long yellow cardboard box tied with an attractive red ribbon.

Inside had been flowers—lilies—and a note in a flowing feminine hand: "Dear Dick—We really should talk this out. Please come over to the greenhouse right away." There was no signature, but he knew who it was from.

"Not every day a cop gets flowers," Catchem had said with a friendly smirk, cigarette drooping.

Tracy was relieved Tess had changed her mind, but he was apprehensive. What could he tell her? That he'd quit his job for her? She'd already said she didn't want that of him. What if she asked him about Breathless? Would she believe him if he told her that the woman's kiss had been meaningless? Did he believe that himself?

The florist's shop was dark, but the front door was open, and a few lights were on in the greenhouse. He went in, wandering among the flowers, breathing in their pleasant, heady fragrance.

"Tess?" he called.

She must be here because a radio was on; appropriately enough, "Love in Bloom" was playing, an instrumental version heavy on the violins. Nice.

But the scent of the flowers seemed almost overpowering. His legs felt weak. Had it been that long and hard a day? He found a chair and sat, to wait for Tess.

Then he saw them: the muffins spilled from the brown paper sack onto the cement floor.

And he knew at once Tess had been here, and there had been trouble. A wave of guilt flooded him, nauseating him even more than the overpowering floral scent. It wasn't bad enough that he'd hurt Tess emotionally; now she was suffering physical peril because she'd had the bad sense to be his girl.

He tried to stand, but his legs were too wobbly, and he tumbled to his knees.

When he looked up, a bright light hit him in the face; a spotlight!

He tried to cover his eyes, but he was too weak to do so, and the light was so all-pervasive he couldn't block it out. What was this, the third-degree treatment?

He was trying to make his hand reach inside his coat for his gun, but his fingers weren't responsive; he felt dizzy as a kid on an out-of-control carousel.

And then, abruptly, the dance music on the radio ended in a burst of static, and was replaced by a weirdly filtered voice: "Relax, Tracy."

"Who . . . what . . . ?"

"Relax," the voice from the radio speaker said.

"If you've hurt Tess, you son of a . . ."

"Relax, I said." Breathy—distorted. "Do what your girl always wanted you to."

"What are you . . . ."

"Take a little time out to smell the roses. . . ."

Only it wasn't roses.

It was gas.

A sickeningly sweet gas that was already filling the room and Tracy's lungs. And somebody had turned it up. Jets of the stuff shot out and around the surrounding flowers, the force of it ruffling Tracy's clothes as he tried to get on his feet. As weak as he was from the effect of the stuff, he might as well have been trying to stand up in a wind tunnel.

The distorted voice was almost soothing as it said, "It

won't hurt. It won't even kill you. Just relax. Go to sleep."

"Go to blazes!" Tracy shouted defiantly, and he'd won, he'd made it to his feet! Next stop, the door. "If you're working for Big Boy, you're *both* making a big mistake!"

And with that, Dick Tracy fell on his face, unconscious.

A figure in a yellow trench coat and matching fedora burst through the front doors into the dingy, shabby lobby of the Midway Hotel. The hotel was a fleabag on the corner of Conway Avenue and Byrd Boulevard, in a seedy section that was just a step up from skid row—and not much of a step. Half a century ago it had been the lavish Marschall Arms—now, it was the Midway, a graveyard for dying potted plants and threadbare armchairs and sofas that were losing their stuffing.

The clerk behind the check-in desk looked up crankily from the crime pulp magazine he was reading; he had several strands of white hair combed haphazardly across a sickly pink skull, his thin white shirt spotted with tobacco juice about the same color brown as his suspenders.

"Shut the door!" the clerk yelled at the figure in the yellow topcoat.

An old guy in a derby and a red plaid coat, who lived at the Midway, was sitting in the lobby reading a racing form; he felt the cold night come in the open door and looked up irritably as the figure in the yellow topcoat moved quickly by, ignoring the clerk's request, going up the garishly blue-painted stairs against the side wall, two steps at a time.

Muttering, the clerk got out from behind his counter to close the door; the old man in the derby returned to his racing form.

The figure in the yellow trench coat went to the fourth

floor, where numbers on the door were tarnished brass nailed on: 429. The figure unlocked the door and went in.

Inside the room, the city's District Attorney was waiting, none too patiently.

"Tracy," Fletcher said tightly, standing as the figure in the yellow coat entered, "what's the meaning of this? If you think I can be blackmailed . . ."

The figure in the yellow topcoat, having shut the door, turned so that the District Attorney could see the face under the fedora.

Only there was no face.

"Who are you?" the D.A. demanded indignantly, but the fear came through. His cigarette in its holder, held tight in his teeth, wobbled as he spoke. "What's the meaning of—"

The cross-examination, however, had already ended. Two silenced shots sent the D.A. over backward, dead when he hit the wooden floor.

Tracy heard a voice. The voice was shouting. It was faint, as if in another room, or another world; yet faint as it was, groggy as he was, he somehow knew the voice was shouting.

"Are you insane, trying to blackmail me?" the voice shouted. "If I go to jail, you'll go to jail! I'll have you run off the police force! You won't get a dime out of me, Tracy . . ."

Tracy?

The detective tried to force himself awake.

The voice was still shouting: "Put that gun away, Tracy! Put that gun away. . . ."

As groggy as a drunk coming home New Year's Eve, Tracy opened his eyes as best he could; the room was black. Did he remember someone carrying him, did he remember being hauled over someone's shoulder like a sack of grain and deposited here? Carried up a hill, or was it up endless flights of stairs? Or had he dreamt it?

The shouting had stopped. His night vision began to take hold and he could see a bed, a figure on the floor alongside it, on its back; a male figure, in a coat and tie and dark pants. A man on his back with a cigarette in a holder still in his lips.

And two other figures moved in the room. Indistinct figures. Was the room this dark, or was it him?

Someone whispered in his ear; the voice was a hoarse, muffled, somehow theatrical voice, not the speaker's natural one.

"You were right about the D.A.," the voice said. "He *was* dirty. . . ."

The figure passed a bottle of ammonia under Tracy's nose and the detective sat up sharply.

He didn't see the Blank slipping out the window behind him, past the ghostlike flutter of the sheer curtain, joining accomplice 88 Keys on the fire escape.

He saw only himself, sitting in a chair in a shabby hotel room, with his topcoat and hat on. All dressed up, no place to go.

Except down.

Because he could now see that the prone male figure was District Attorney Fletcher. And soon he was not alone in seeing this: the night clerk and two uniformed cops rushed into the room to see the same tableau.

And all of them, Tracy included, saw the gun in Tracy's hand.

All of them saw it, that is, except the District Attorney, who—like Blind Justice—was seeing nothing at all.

24

The County Orphanage was in the city.

In this dreary institution in the shadow of the El tracks, an overcast sky adding to the gloom, the Kid had to himself a cold, vast dormitory, with paint-peeling pale green walls and wooden floors and facing rows of metal beds with wafer-thin mattresses and one horsehair blanket each. He stood looking out the window at the courtyard of the orphanage, and its pitiful scattering of ill-maintained playground equipment, wishing he were anywhere else.

This was his third day here—actually, his second full day. The people had been nice enough—the lady in charge, Mrs. Plett, was kind and spent a lot of time talking to him. Or anyway, trying to talk to him. He didn't mean to be mean, or even disobedient, but he had no intention of fitting in here.

The other kids seemed all right, though they were mostly keeping their distance from him, and he was doing the same with them. The tow-headed kid who had the next bed was ten years old and a tough little character who'd ridden the rails himself for a couple years. He cornered the Kid and made a big speech about how he was the boss of the dorm, and anybody who didn't like it could lump it. The Kid let him get away with that noise, only 'cause the Kid didn't figure to be around here long enough to make a scrap worthwhile.

Today was Saturday, and day after tomorrow they would expect him to start school classes. But he'd be out of here and have found himself a freight to hop by that time. Mrs. Plett had figured out he could read after he asked if he could see a newspaper (to check up on how Tracy was doing), and the class he was supposed to go into would be for second- and third-graders.

"You're a bright young man," she'd said as he sat in her office yesterday morning. "Despite the fact that you've never attended school proper, I think you'll fit in best with children your own age."

"Yes, ma'am," he'd said. He was polite to Mrs. Plett, even though he didn't say much or answer her questions very good. She was nice, and he didn't want to hurt her feelings; besides, he wanted her guard down, so he could bust out of the joint. It ought to be a cinch.

"Now, we'll need a name for you," she said, a big record book spread open in front of her on her desk. "We have no records on you, whatsoever. And the caseworker informs me that you claim not to have a name."

"I don't have, 'xactly," he admitted. "People just call me 'Kid.'" He shrugged. "It's a name, far as I'm concerned."

"Well, it's not enough for our purposes. Why don't you select a more proper name?"

"Okay," he said. "Put my name down as 'Dick Tracy, Junior'"

The headmistress winced. "'Dick Tracy' is a well-known name, in these parts. Do you really think it prudent to select the name of a policeman? We have some boys here that don't like policemen much."

"I can take care of myself."

"And Detective Tracy is in a good deal of trouble right now."

"I know that, ma'am. I saw it in those newspapers you give me."

"Gave me," she corrected gently. Her kind face was creased with doubt, with worry. "You put yourself at risk of being teased, being an object of ridicule. . . ."

"I didn't pick the name 'cause he's a cop, or 'cause he's famous."

"Why did you then?"

"Because, 'cept for Steve the tramp, he's the closest thing to a pop I ever had. And I don't fancy bein' called Steve the Tramp, Junior."

Now, a day later, as the Kid stared out the window—through the crosshatch of wire that reminded him he was, for all of Mrs. Plett's kindness, nothing more than a prisoner here—he thought about Tracy. He knew he should help Tracy, but he wasn't sure he could.

The night Tracy got in all that trouble, the Kid had sat with Sam Catchem in Tracy's office. While the caseworker waited impatiently to haul the Kid off to the orphanage, the freckled, rumpled-face detective leveled with the boy.

"Tracy's in a real jam, son," Catchem said. "Me and Pat Patton are gonna do everything we can to get him out of it, but it ain't gonna be easy."

"What happened, anyway?"

"It's a frame-up," Catchem said, lips tight over his teeth. "Some people who want Tracy out of the way bumped off the District Attorney and made it look like Tracy pulled the trigger."

"That's crazy!"

"You know it, and I know it. But the evidence, so far, is stacked against him. I gotta give my all to this, kid. I'd like to take you under my wing, like Dick did—but I just can't do it. I gotta turn you over to that welfare worker out there."

"Yeah," he'd said fatalistically. "I figured as much. What can I do to help Tracy?"

"Just stick it out," he said. "Don't bolt from the orphan home. Tracy'll get out of this fix and come after you. He and Tess think the world of you, kid."

"Really?"

"Really."

"Well, will you ask Miss Tess to come see me at the orphanage?"

"Uh . . . well, sure, kid."

But the Kid could read it in Catchem's face: something was wrong.

"Is something the matter with Miss Tess?"

"Look, son. We're not sure. We can't locate her, and Tracy thinks she's been kidnapped by the 'mystery man,' as the papers put it."

"What? You mean, that faceless guy has her?"

"Like I said, we don't know anything for sure. We're lookin' for her . . . and we got every available man on the case. We'll find her, all right. You can take that to the bank."

"I don't know, Mr. Catchem," the Kid had said glumly. "Banks fail, sometimes."

Catchem hadn't denied it.

Now the Kid was staring out the wire-mesh window, wondering if he'd be letting Tracy down if he ran off. But what could he do for Tracy? How could he help him?

It was true that he had held out on Tracy on one thing. He never told the detective about seeing that flat-headed guy, the nervous hood, and that mushy-mouthed creep at the garage; he never told Tracy he'd been an eyewitness to that massacre.

It wasn't that he was afraid that the gangsters would try to get even with him if he ratted them out. It was the concept of ratting them out, period. Tracy was a great guy, but the Kid had lived on the streets his whole life. One of the things you learned on the street, one of the first things Steve taught him, was that you didn't squeal.

There was an unwritten code on the streets, and this was a major entry in the invisible rulebook: You did not rat anybody out to the cops, under no circumstances whatsoever.

Anyway, the Kid didn't see how telling Tracy about that flat-headed guy and his pals would help the detective out of the jam he was in now. Besides, the Kid thought, who would believe a little juvenile delinquent like him?

Footsteps on the hardwood floor caught his attention. He turned and saw Mrs. Plett, portly, attractive, in a floral-print dress, her salt-and-pepper hair back in a tidy bun, approaching with a small tray on which were a glass of milk and two cookies.

"Are you sure you won't join us downstairs?" she said. "The entertainment is really quite good this afternoon."

"No thanks, Mrs. Plett. Is that for me?"

"Of course it's for you." She put the tray on his bed. "I realize it isn't fancy here, but we are a kind of a family. I want you to know you're welcome here."

"Thanks, ma'am."

"Sure you won't come downstairs now?"

"No. Thank you."

"We do want you to feel at home. School days are devoted to work, but Saturdays and Sundays you can have a little fun. What do you like to do?"

"Well . . . I like to draw."

"Really?" She smiled. "Do we have a budding artist amongst us? That's wonderful. Would you like me to get you some paper, and perhaps some pencils, or crayons?"

"Well, uh . . . that would be real nice, Mrs. Plett."

She nodded and went out. He lay on the bed and gobbled the two chocolate chip cookies and gulped the milk. He'd skipped breakfast because he was feeling so low; but now he was starving.

Before long, Mrs. Plett returned with a tablet and some crayons.

"These are yours," she said. "Please understand that you can always come to me for help. There are a lot of children here, and nobody gets pampered—and we do not spare the rod, when necessary. But my door is always open to you." She smiled but it was a sad smile. She put her fingers in his hair and ruffled it. "This is your home now, Dick Tracy, Junior," she said.

Not hardly, he thought.

"Thank you, ma'am," he said.

Idly, sprawled on the saggy bed, he began to sketch. He drew the flat-headed guy; he drew several pictures of him, including one of him shooting a machine gun. The guy was really creepy and, in a weird way, fun to draw. Then he drew that guy that was always scratching himself—an odd-looking bird; took a while to get the glasses right. He was using a black crayon, so he couldn't erase, and had to start over when he didn't get something the way he wanted.

Next he drew the squinty-eyed blond guy who mumbled; he was easy to catch, even though he'd only got a glimpse of him sitting in that car.

He was just putting some finishing touches on, when he heard footsteps again. Thinking it was Mrs. Plett, he glanced up and was about to thank her once more when he saw a tall creature with the body of a bear and the head of a man.

Startled, even frightened, he sat up, and then he realized it was a guy in a bear costume; the man was holding the bear's head, or anyway the headpiece of the costume, under his arm, like a basketball. It was an old guy, with a mustache; his hair was white, and real messed up, probably from being inside that bear-head.

"Young man!" he called. "Are you the young protégé of Richard Tracy?"

"Huh?" the Kid said.

The mustached guy in the bear costume padded over to him.

"My name, lad," the bear-man said, gesturing grandly with a clawed paw, "is Vitamin Flintheart. Perhaps you've heard of me."

The old guy said this proudly, but his face fell when the Kid said, "No. Sorry, mister."

"It's of no great import," he said, though it obviously was to him, and he sat down on the bed next to the Kid. Now the bed *really* sagged. "I've been sent here on a mission."

"In a bear suit?"

He touched a paw to his shaggy brown chest. "I arranged for my theatrical group to give a presentation here, this afternoon, of 'The Three Bears.' I, of course, am Papa Bear. I had expected you to be in the audience, but when I inquired, I found you were not."

"What are you talkin' about?"

"My great and good friend Richard Tracy, America's answer to Sherlock Holmes, has recruited me to give you a message."

"Are you talking about Dick Tracy the cop?"

Flintheart's eyes under shaggy white eyebrows flared. "Have you no ears, lad? That's precisely what I just uttered."

"Uttered?"

"Said, lad! Said!"

"What does Mr. Tracy want?"

Flintheart pointed a bear paw at the boy. "He wants you stay put. He beseeches you not to hie to the highway—he implores you to resist the siren song of the railways."

"Huh?"

"Don't run away, lad. Tracy says he'll come for you."

"Mr. Tracy is in big trouble, mister."

"The name is Flintheart, lad. And yes he is."

"The papers say he's up for the murder of the D.A.

They got two witnesses at that hotel who saw him go in, and he was seen arguing at City Hall with the guy they say he killed."

"Alas, you speak the truth. There's also the matter of a blackmail note written in Richard's handwriting, found in the pocket of the deceased prosecutor."

"Well, it's not the truth that Tracy's goin' around *murdering* people. That's not the way he does things. And he's no blackmailer, neither! He's tough, but he's fair."

"As well I know. But Richard has prevailed over many a scrape indeed in the past, and he will overcome these dire circumstances, as well. Do as he says: wait for him. He will come for you."

"Baloney! They got 'im cold! And where's Miss Tess? The papers say nobody can find her!"

Flintheart shrugged his shaggy shoulders. "Miss Trueheart's mother indicates that her daughter returned to the city the night of Richard's unfortunate arrest. Apparently Miss Trueheart and Richard had encountered difficulties in their relationship . . ."

"She caught him with another dame."

"Do tell. At any rate, there are those who think she has gone off somewhere, to be with herself."

"That's the bunk! Miss Tess didn't take no powder. It's a snatch. Big Boy grabbed her!"

"In fact," Flintheart said, "that is indeed largely the opinion Richard has shared with his fellow gendarmes, though as yet the fourth estate is not aware of it."

"Fourth estate?"

"The newspapers, lad." Flintheart noticed the drawings. "What's this, boy? These are quite remarkable."

"I draw."

"Ah!" Flintheart raised a paw grandly. "You will never regret pursuing a life in the arts, my lad. It's a difficult life, but so rewarding." He looked at the drawings carefully. "My boy, these really are outstanding. Your gift is truly singular. But tell me . . . why this gallery of grotesqueries?"

"Well . . . Mr. Flintheart, can you tell me something? I mean, you got lots of experience; you're an old guy."

Flintheart blinked. "It's the costume, lad. I consider it maturity, not age."

"Yeah. Right. Anyway, you been around. Do you think it's wrong to squeal?"

"My boy, I'm performing in 'The Three Bears,' not 'The Three Little Pigs.' "

"No, no—I mean, is it wrong to rat guys out? What if you saw somebody do something real bad, would you tell? 'Specially if you thought ratting 'em out might help somebody else, somebody you liked."

Flintheart nodded sagely. "I believe I would, lad. It's the socially responsible thing to do."

"I don't know if this would help or not. But let me tell you what I saw. . . ."

So the Kid told Vitamin the whole story, pointing to each individual drawing as if reading an illustrated tale to a young child.

And Flintheart, sitting in his bear costume, the bear's head under his arm, listened with the rapt attention of a very young child, indeed.

25

Flat on his back on the uncomfortable cot, Tracy
stared at the cement ceiling of the cell, hands
behind his head; but he didn't notice the dis-
comfort, nor did he see the ceiling: he saw
Tess's face.

The small holding cell, one of a dozen such cubicles on
the third floor of Central Headquarters, and the only one
presently occupied, consisted of the cot he lay on, a small
table with a Bible, and a toilet sans seat (and no sink). It
was cold, rather dank, and for the first time in his life,
Tracy felt a certain sympathy for the many felons he'd
sent here.

It was quiet right now. It was usually quiet here,
though postmidnight the previous two nights, he'd been
serenaded by the discordant music of the current residents of the drunk tank around the corner from him.

His accommodations would soon improve: he was due
to be shifted to the county jail, where (he'd already been
assured) he'd be kept away from the general population.
Putting him in among those he'd sent up could be dangerous for all concerned.

Bail had been denied him, but he felt confident he'd be
out on the street soon. His wealthy friend Diet Smith was
providing the best lawyer in the city, Kenneth Levin, who
ironically had been Tracy's adversary in many a past
case. But at the arraignment, Judge Debirb—who had
long been a legal thorn in Tracy's side—found the evidence "simply too overwhelming" to set bail.

Levin should eventually prevail over Debirb's ruling,

but for the time being, this holding cell and another, slightly roomier one at the county jail, would be his home.

He understood, for the first time, the meaning of despair. Part of him wanted to kick these concrete walls down so that he could find those who'd put him here—and he knew who that was: Al "Big Boy" Caprice joined in an unholy alliance with that faceless gunman, who in all likelihood was this year's model of one Frank Redrum.

But another part of him wanted to curl up in a fetal ball, and die. Because as much as he wanted to believe that Tess was still alive, he couldn't conceive of how she could be.

Today, Saturday, had been the second full day to slip by since Tess's disappearance. There had been, of course, no ransom demand. The motive of the kidnapping was an unusual one: Tess had served as bait.

She'd been kidnapped to lure Tracy to that greenhouse. So that Tracy could be fitted for his frame. That had been accomplished, and then some.

Her kidnapper or kidnappers, their objective reached, had only two options where Tess was concerned: spring her loose, assuming she'd not seen any of their faces (and with the blank-faced guy, how much face was there to see anyway?); or they could do what so many kidnappers ruthlessly did—dispose of their victim.

The only small solace was (he hated even to form these words in his mind) her body had not been found.

But so many never were.

Was Tess, even now, in a wooden-crate coffin, encased in cement? Was she at the bottom of the river, or the lake, where so many of Big Boy's vanquished rivals kept the fish company?

Was she with Lips Manlis right now?

In the silence, in the darkness, in the coldness of the

cell, Dick Tracy did something that might have surprised or perhaps amused his foes: he wept.

He was not out of control, however; he did this almost willfully, purging his system of the emotions. Similarly, he'd made himself sleep—despite the dreams, in which the grotesque countenances of the likes of Flattop, Itchy, and Pruneface, as well as the void that was the mystery man's blurred face, haunted and taunted him.

He had to be ready. Three times a day, he'd done pushups and sit-ups on the cold concrete floor. He would, eventually, in hours or anyway days, be out on bail. Of that he was confident. And he would look for Tess, however hopeless that seemed, and he—despite the fact that at the first misstep bail would be revoked—would bring Big Boy down.

In fact, his plan to find out what happened to Tess consisted mainly of putting a gun in Big Boy's face and inviting him to speak.

The door down the hall clanged and footsteps moved toward his cell. He sat up. Through the bars appeared the massive blue-uniformed shape and sad, friendly face of Chief Brandon.

"How are you, son? Bearing up okay?"

He nodded. "I'll make it, Chief. Any news?"

Brandon winced, but then shook his head.

Tracy got up, met the Chief at the bars. "Look—I don't want you to pull any punches. If you find Tess's body, I want you to tell me. Understand?"

Brandon nodded. "She may not be . . . that is, she may still be alive."

"There's little hope of that. This frame Big Boy hung on me, probably with the help of Frank Redrum, can only fit this tight if Tess never turns up. Alive *or* dead."

"Dick . . . ." Brandon looked at the floor.

"What aren't you telling me?"

Brandon sighed. "Dick. The authorities in San Francisco . . . they found Frank Redrum. He washed up on the rocks of Alcatraz. Deader than McKinley."

"What?" He gripped a bar with one hand. He grimaced, shook his head. "I *told* Pat and Sam the shape of the head and the ears were different! Check the police sketches I had made, Chief."

"Dick—the papers were half buying your story about the faceless man because of speculation that Frank Redrum was back in circulation. But now . . ."

Tracy smiled humorlessly. "Now they'll say I just made up this business about the mystery man. That I conveniently implied an old enemy of mine had framed me . . . a trigger-happy nutcase with a track record for revenge."

Brandon nodded. "Yes, a man who was unlikely to really turn up and contradict your story. Chances were good Redrum was at the bottom of Frisco Bay, leaving you free to pretend he'd returned for revenge."

Tracy shook his head, laughed mirthlessly, but said nothing.

"After all," Brandon concluded, "nobody saw your faceless friend shoot Pruneface at the Southside Warehouse, except Influence, who's not likely to back your story up; even Bug Bailey didn't see anything—he was drenched in wet cement."

Tracy's mouth was a thin firm line. "I'm going to beat this, Chief. Nobody's going to buy blackmail as a motive. I didn't write that note in Fletcher's pocket, no matter what the handwriting experts say."

"There are those who are speculating that you didn't intend to blackmail Fletcher," Brandon said, playing devil's advocate. "That you were just pretending to, to get evidence on him, to prove he was crooked."

"Okay, in which case, why in heaven's name would I kill the man?"

Brandon shrugged. "You were seen arguing at City

Hall. There was no love lost between you—let's face it. So you lured him to that hotel room, to flush him and his crookedness out—but somehow things got out of hand. After all, Tracy—shortly after two witnesses saw someone they think is you going into the hotel, voices were heard heatedly arguing in that same room where Fletcher turned up dead."

Tracy sighed in frustration. "Yeah, dead from bullets from my gun."

"You also had the powder burns; the paraffin test indicates you did fire a gun recently."

"Chief, they must've fired a gun off in my hand, when I was unconscious!"

"You don't have to convince *me*," Brandon said. "It's a judge and a jury you have to worry about. And I think they *can* be convinced. I think you can beat this. I believe you, and I believe in you."

"I . . . thanks, Chief."

"But it's not going to happen today. It's going to happen in court, weeks, maybe months from now. It's going to be a long, hard-fought battle. You've got to stop thinking about nailing Big Boy—and you've even got to stop planning to try to find Tess."

Tracy said nothing.

"Your job right now," Brandon said, "is to work with your attorney to clear yourself. If, when you finally *do* get bail, you insist on going out and playing tough detective, you're going to foul up the whole damn case—and your whole damn life, as well."

"Chief . . ."

"Dick. This is *our* case, now. We're looking for Tess. The F.B.I. is lending a hand, too—your friend Inspector Trailer is rallying his forces."

"I'm grateful, and it's a kidnapping case all right—but no state line was crossed."

"We don't know that. Trailer is taking the position that

it's a federal matter. And as for Big Boy, we'll get that louse. Sam Catchem and Pat Patton are first-rate men and they want nothing more than to clear you and nail Big Boy and all the mobster lowlifes. Trust us to do our job."

"Sure, Chief."

Brandon's smile was a thin wrinkle. "You didn't hear a word I said, did you?"

Tracy smiled back, faintly; his first smile in days. "Oh, I heard you."

"You just didn't listen."

Tracy lifted an eyebrow in a shrug.

"Well," the Chief said wearily, "I tried."

"You know, Chief—Big Boy's having the big horse-laugh on all of us. Can you deny there's been an upsurge of mob activity in the last forty-eight hours? I've seen the papers."

Brandon's embarrassment was apparent. The Chief knew as well as Tracy that the gambling joints were back in full swing, houses of prostitution had reopened, small store owners were again being muscled for extortion money. All the key figures Tracy had jailed were out on bail and back in action; even Mumbles—lying low since his third-degree encounter with Tracy the night of the garage massacre—had surfaced, openly rejoining Big Boy's retinue.

"We were on the verge of putting Caprice out of business," Tracy said with bitter irony. "Instead, we got the rug pulled out from under us, and he's flourishing. Champagne flowing like water; money flowing into his pockets, the same way."

"We'll get him.

"A bullet would do it quicker."

Brandon's face tensed. "That isn't how we do things. That isn't how *you* do things." He touched Tracy's hand where it gripped the bar. "Hold onto yourself, son. Don't let them turn you into what they are."

Tracy swallowed.

Brandon smiled, reached a hand through the bars and tousled Tracy's hair, like a kid. Then the big old copper moved back down the corridor, his footsteps echoing.

Tracy sat on the cot. Was the Chief right? Was Big Boy's viciousness contagious? If Tess really were gone, Tracy would have nothing left, *nothing*, if he threw away what he was. And what was he, but a public servant who respected and upheld the law?

But what *was* the role of a police detective in a world where district attorneys and judges and even cops were frequently corrupt? What was his role in a world where holders of high political office and half the city's social register were among Big Boy's favored patrons at his illegal casino? A world that gave its tacit approval to lawlessness and vice? Was there a place for Dick Tracy in that world?

He had almost drifted off to sleep when he heard the clang of the door down the hall again, and footsteps moving quickly—too light, too swift a step, for the Chief to be returning.

Tracy got to his feet instinctively and was to the bars of the cell by the time Sam Catchem's rumpled face appeared there.

And Catchem was smiling.

"You got a visitor," Catchem said.

"A visitor?"

"He's just outside."

"Who . . ."

Catchem remained evasive, playing it cute. "The Chief's bringin' 'em in. And I've put a call in for the Acting D.A. I think he's going to be as interested in this new development as you are."

"New development . . . ?"

But Catchem was gone.

Moments later, the Chief had returned, and with him

was the Kid, standing just beyond the bars; the man and child had mutually bright, eager eyes.

"Your actor pal called me to pick the kid up at the orphanage," the Chief explained, "and bring him around to see you."

Brandon had the keys and opened the cell door and stepped inside with the boy. Tracy sat on the cot with him, while the Chief stood in the doorway of the cell.

"Tracy," the Chief said, "your young friend is quite an artist. As Vitamin Flintheart says, 'The stripling has a remarkable ability to capture the human physiognomy with his pen.'"

"Crayon," the Kid corrected.

"Although, in this case," the Chief continued, "we're using the term 'human' loosely." The Chief unfolded a piece of paper he'd been concealing in one hand. "Who is this, lad?"

"That's the flat-headed creep who shot everybody at the garage on Seventh Street." The boy looked sheepishly at Tracy, who couldn't have been more stunned if he'd been hit in the head with a two-by-four. "I seen it all. I was a, what-do-you-call-it . . . eyewitness."

"Why didn't you ever say anything, junior?"

"Where I come from, you learn to keep your mouth shut about things like that. I'm sorry, Mr. Tracy. I didn't know it had anything to do with you. But . . . well, I guess I figured it did, later—when him and that guy that's always scratchin' snatched you and stuck ya in that boiler room."

"He's drawn equally good likenesses of Itchy and Mumbles," the Chief said. "They were at the garage massacre, too."

Tracy slipped his arm around the boy. "Son, this is very important. God bless you, we've got 'em, now."

"But I'm just a juvie . . . a street kid. Who's going to listen to me?"

"Everybody," Tracy said. "Look—when all of this is over, I've got a job for you."

"A job?

"Yeah. We're going to make you the country's youngest police artist."

"Really?"

"Really. You're on my team, junior. From now on. Shake on it?"

He extended his hand, and the Kid took it and shook it, eagerly.

"Well," Brandon said, pleased by what he'd seen, "I'll leave the two of you alone for a minute. We need to try to get through to the Acting D.A. again. I'd like to connect with him before the county jail boys arrive to make your transfer."

"Can't you spring me, Chief?" Tracy said, standing, gesturing with both hands. "We've got Big Boy, now . . ."

The Chief's big head shook no. "Not really, Dick. You have enough to go after Flattop and company, and Flattop works for Big Boy . . . but that's not enough to go after Big Boy himself, is it?"

"Damn it, Chief, if I could get back out on the street, I could find Tess and crack this case in the bargain."

Brandon thought about that. Then, softly, mysteriously, he said, "I'll see what I can do."

A strange sensation rushed through Tracy in a wave; at first he couldn't identify it. Hope. It was hope.

Brandon nodded to the guard outside the cell as he left.

Tracy sat back down next to the Kid and said, "I'm surprised the orphanage lets you stay up this late."

"It's not so bad there." The Kid shrugged. "Good food. And they let you out if a grown-up picks you up."

"Like Chief Brandon, you mean, or Mr. Flintheart."

"Yeah. Or like you and Miss Tess—when you find her. And I know you're gonna find her."

Tracy said nothing; just tried to smile bravely at the Kid.

"You know," the boy said, "Chief Brandon gave me my permanent certificate, upstairs, when I gave him them sketches I made."

"Yeah? You finally picked out a name, huh?"

"Yeah . . . ." He got the scrolled certificate out of his pocket and unrolled it. He let Tracy read it.

"Dick Tracy, Junior," the detective read aloud, in a hushed voice.

"I hope," the Kid said tentatively, "it's okay with you. . . ."

Tracy put his hand on the boy's shoulder. The boy threw his arms around Tracy's neck and the detective hugged the boy; and the boy smiled and hugged back.

Then suddenly Chief Brandon was just beyond the bars again. His face was intense.

"I couldn't get through to the Acting D.A.," Brandon said. "We'll make the transfer to county jail ourselves. A couple of boys are waiting out back."

Tracy patted the Kid on the shoulder, and the boy stayed behind with the Chief while the detective was escorted by two guards. They cuffed him first, hands in front of him.

"You should always cuff a prisoner's hands behind him, fellas," Tracy said. "A guy can do a lot of damage with his hands in front of him, cuffed or not."

One of the guards, embarrassed, said, "We trust you, Tracy."

They ushered him into the backseat of a squad car waiting at the rear of the building. Then they shut the door and he was alone in back.

The two plainclothesmen in the front seat turned and the faces of Sam Catchem and Pat Patton beamed at him, a couple of cats who ate a couple of canaries.

"What are you two doing here?" Tracy asked, dazed.

"It's a long ride to county jail," Patton said with a shrug. "Could take all night."

"It's only five miles," Tracy said. "What . . . ?"

Catchem was leaning back over the seat, unlocking Tracy's handcuffs.

"You said you could crack this case if you could get back out on the street," Catchem said. "Well, welcome to the street, courtesy of the Chief. Your gun, two-way, and your badge are on the seat next to you."

Tracy glanced to his left, and there they were, in a neat stack. He slipped the .38 in his topcoat pocket and began strapping the two-way on.

"Call for a car to meet us at Thirty-fourth and Central," he told Patton crisply.

"Isn't that Mumbles's apartment building?" Catchem asked.

"Yes, it is. And tell 'em, step on it. Oh, and Pat, tell 'em to bring something along. . . ."

"What?" Patton asked.

Tracy told him, and Patton's round face broke into a grin.

"Let's go, boys," Tracy said to his two chauffeurs, and they went.

"I only wish Brandon were here," Tracy said absently.

"Yeah?" Catchem said. "Why?"

"I'd like to kiss his big red Irish face," Tracy said.

26

Grabbing him by his expensive purple suitcoat, Tracy shoved Mumbles up against the wall. Hard.

"Talk to me, Mumbles," Tracy said.

"Whadyawanfrmetrz?" Sweat pearled Mumbles's forehead; his blond hair was already damp from it. "Whadyawan?"

"I want you," Tracy said through clenched teeth, "to tell me who set me up."

Catchem, smoking nonchalantly, and a stocky uniformed cop, thumbs hooked in his gun belt, were watching from the sidelines in Mumbles's well-furnished flat.

"Whatdyatalkintomeabouditfur?" Mumbles asked pitifully, the detective right in his face.

"*What* did he say?" the uniformed cop asked Catchem, who shrugged.

"I'm talking to you about it," Tracy replied calmly to Mumbles, "because you sit at Big Boy's right hand. He likes you. You're the king's favorite jester."

"IdintsetyuptrazIdinsetyup!"

Tracy smiled; he could smell bourbon on the hood's breath. "I know you didn't set me up, Mumbles. But you know who did."

"Cntyufiggritoowwtfryrsf?" Mumbles said, half sneering, half pouting.

"*What* did he say?" Catchem asked the uniformed cop, who shrugged.

"Sure I can figure it out for myself," Tracy said. "But I need confirmation. I need a witness."

"Idnwitnsnuthin!"

"Sure you did. You witnessed plenty." Tracy drew back a step, glanced over his shoulder. "Ah. Here's Pat."

Patton had entered; in his hands, perched on its hind legs, was the shiny decorative gray-blue polar bear, the water dispenser that had been on the table in the interrogation booth many days before, when Tracy had given Mumbles the third degree.

"Thirsty, Mumbles?" Tracy said, taking the rather large figurine from Patton. He thrust the object in the hood's face and the hood recoiled, as if it were a bomb with a lit fuse. "Pretty, isn't it?"

Mumbles said nothing; he swallowed nervously.

"What do you make of this thing?" Tracy pondered, as if he didn't know the answer. "Looks more like a cookie jar than a water jug, doesn't it? You're the original kid who got caught getting in the cookie jar, aren't you, Mumbles?"

And Tracy lifted the top off the polar bear; inside were several controls and switches near two slightly raised metal cylinders, around which was wound a wire.

"Whdthelzat?" Mumbles wondered. It sounded like his mouth had gone dry.

"*What* did he say?" Patton asked Catchem and the uniformed cop, who both shrugged.

"That," Tracy explained, tipping the polar bear's beheaded form to give Mumbles a good look, "is a wire recorder. Something Bug Bailey devised for us—the principle is that when you speak into a transmitter, sound is recorded on a steel wire as it's rotated between the poles of an electromagnet."

"Sndsfaznatin," Mumbles said with a sneer.

"It does sound fascinating, Mumbles," Tracy said pleasantly. "Literally."

The detective flipped one of the switches within the polar bear.

Mumbles's eyes went wide in his head as he heard his own voice: "Bgbykldlpsmnls."

"You know, Mumbles," Tracy said thoughtfully, "I'm not sure this would hold up in court—there are those who might say I coerced this statement."

Casually, Tracy rewound the wire and played it back again, this time cutting some of the slack with his finger.

"BbByklldLips Manlis," the wire recorder said.

"Just the same," Tracy said gently, "I wonder what Big Boy would say if he heard that?"

Mumbles stared at the recorder, paralyzed.

"What do you think, Mumbles?" Tracy asked, and he played it back once more, his fingers tight around the wire, further slowing it down.

"Big Boy killed Lips Manlis," the wire recorder said.

Mumbles swallowed.

Tracy repeated the process: "Big Boy killed Lips Manlis," said the headless bear.

Mumbles was shaking, but he remained silent.

"Okay, boys," Tracy said, smiling at Catchem, Patton, and the uniformed man. He nodded toward the door. "Let's go play this for Big Boy."

"Wait!" Mumbles said. Suddenly he was the epitome of elocution. "88 Keys set you up."

"The piano man?" Catchem asked.

"Yeah," Mumbles said. He carefully formed the words: "Big Boy paid him to get you out of the way."

"Officer Horvitz," Tracy said to the uniformed man, "take him in."

The stocky cop cuffed Mumbles, who stood with his head hanging low, muttering to himself. This time nobody bothered asking the hood what he was saying.

Down on the street, Tracy said with no small satisfaction, "*Now* we have enough."

Patton and Catchem exchanged glances, nodding.

"We can pick up 88 Keys, Flattop, Itchy . . . and Big Boy, too." Tracy looked at Catchem. "Sam, I want you to contact the chief by two-way, and organize a raiding party. A dozen cars, but the front line should be plainclothes officers only."

"Plainclothes?"

"You can tell Brandon to stuff some uniformed boys in street clothes if he likes. But we have to go to the Club Ritz and make those arrests. And when we do, I want the whole place surrounded."

"I got you," Catchem said. "These babies are tough— this time, they ain' goin' with us without a fight."

"Right," Tracy said. "And right now, the Club Ritz is open for business—Saturday's a big night for 'em. If Big Boy and his stooges see the place surrounded by cops, they'll have a club full of hostages to shield themselves with."

Catchem nodded and took several steps away and called in on his two-way.

In the meantime, Tracy rocked on his feet, hands in his pockets, lost in thought. Deep within himself.

"You okay, Tracy?" Patton asked.

"Is the enemy of my friend my enemy?" Tracy asked.

"Huh?"

"Or is the enemy of my enemy my friend?"

"*What* did he say?" Patton asked Catchem as the latter returned.

Catchem ignored the question, saying to Tracy, "Brandon's already on his way to the Club Ritz."

"What did you say?" Tracy said, eyes confused.

"The Chief had an anonymous phone tip," Catchem said, "that Big Boy is holding Tess at the club."

Tracy's eyes hardened. "The enemy of my enemy *is* my enemy," he said with finality.

"*What* did he say?" Catchem asked Patton, who shrugged and rolled his eyes.

But Tracy was already climbing in back of the car.

Catchem quickly took the driver's seat, and Patton got in back with Tracy, and the squad car roared into the night, taking the next corner on two wheels.

27

The night was clear and cold, handfuls of stars flung across the sky like diamonds glittering on black velvet. An icy wind blew in off the lake, but it was no hindrance to Tracy and Patton as the latter lifted the former up to the roof of the building whose first floor was the Club Ritz. To Tracy, the wind, with its wintry bite, was bracing—a reminder that he was alive and well and not in a cell. He was outside, in the cold, clean air. And a cop again.

They'd gone up the fire escape in the alley, the same one Tracy had used to get to the ledge where he'd eavesdropped on that underworld summit not so long ago. And when they ran out of 'scape, Patton made a step out of his interlaced hands, palms up, and lifted Tracy onto the rooftop. Then Tracy leaned over the edge of the roof and lent his assistant his hand, hauling him up.

The flat expanse of the roof was broken three times: once, off to one side, by the dormerlike projection of a door to (and from) the rooftop; and twice, by a pair of many-paned skylights angled for maximum effect—and with the spilled jewel box of stars in the sky tonight, it would be a quite a view.

But it was quite a view tonight looking down through the nearest skylight, as well.

In the dark attic below sat Tess Trueheart, gagged, hands bound at the wrist, ankles tied, the ropes starkly white looping around her simple black-and-red-print dress, binding her to a wooden chair. She was slumped in the chair; she could have been dead.

231

Tracy pushed his hands against the glass, like a street urchin pressed up against a Christmas window at Macy's. The attic was otherwise largely empty—a trash barrel, a long, low table, a few discarded sticks of furniture. The only illumination in the room came from the pair of skylights.

Patton gripped Tracy's arm, hard; the simple gesture conveyed both hope and apprehension.

Tracy glanced around the rooftop. Sam Catchem had told Tracy that he'd left a rope up here, tied to a pipe— the rope Sam had used to lower himself and Bug into the attic for surveillance duty. Tracy had expected it still to be up here.

It was gone.

And the skylight, which Sam had jimmied open, was shut tight and had been recaulked.

Tracy silently cursed his own misjudgment. "We could use a grappling hook and some rope right about now," he said.

"Want to send for—"

"No." Tracy, breathing hard, pulled away from the window, but his eyes were round and frozen downward at the (he hoped merely) unconscious Tess.

"I could break the glass," Tracy said, "but she's right below us—the shards would rain right down on her."

"I have a pocketknife we can use to remove panes," Patton said. "We can cut away at the caulking . . ."

Tracy shook his head. "We're better off going in that door over there," he said reluctantly, "and finding our way down to her."

But before he and Patton could move to the dormer doorway, light spilled into the dark attic as two figures moved quickly into the room—Flattop and Big Boy himself.

"Where did this dame come from?" Big Boy shouted. He sounded like a stuck pig. The voice was muffled through the glass, but the words were clear. He was standing beside the chair, looming over Tess, his arms spread and his palms open in a gesture of dismay. "We've been had! Get her outta here!"

Tess lifted her head, opened her eyes.

She was *alive*, Tracy thought; thank God! For that much.

And then she looked away from the repulsive countenance of Big Boy, looking up, where she saw Tracy in the window above her; her eyes widened, at first startled, then they communicated a wave of emotions to her man: relief, fright, love, concern, sorrow. . . .

The look lasted only a moment, less than a moment— but Flattop caught it.

Tracy saw the flat-headed gunman pointing his automatic up at the skylight and pulled Patton out of the line of fire as the shot exploded in the room below and spider-webbed a pane of the skylight glass.

Flattop untied Tess and held the gagged woman in his arms like a groom carrying his bride over the threshold.

Or a monster carrying its victim.

"If they get us on kidnapping, we're finished!" Big Boy raved, his arms flailing. "Get her out of here, get rid of her, before any more cops show!"

Tracy waited till Flattop, Tess in his arms, had moved away from the wooden chair; then, like a kid about to cannonball into a swimming pool, Tracy hurled himself feet first through that skylight, the wooden frame splintering and panes of glass tumbling out, some fragmenting, others shattering.

In the seconds this took, Flattop shifted Tess over to Big Boy, and fired another round up at the skylight, just as Tracy was crashing through. The bullet whizzed up past Patton, striking nothing but the night.

Tracy landed on his feet, then tumbled onto his side, on his right shoulder, losing his hat on the ride, but despite the glass, he landed well, the thick yellow topcoat protecting him. He came up off the floor with the gun in his hand, bareheaded, face nicked from fragmented glass, topcoat slashed from shards he'd landed on.

But all he got for his trouble was a door slammed in his face, as Flattop and Big Boy, with a wide-eyed Tess still in his arms, moved out of the attic. As he reached the door, Tracy heard locks being thrown and he found himself facing a heavy steel barrier that would have done any prison proud.

"Damn," he said through his teeth.

"Dick!" Patton called down from the gaping glass-toothed hole where the skylight had been. "Are you all right?"

Tracy stuck his .38 back in the shoulder holster, retrieved his hat. "Yeah," he said. "Nothing wrong with me a battering ram wouldn't cure."

"You want me to go get a rope or something . . . ?"

"No. Too much time. Caprice has Tess!" He was moving around the dark, mostly empty attic restlessly. "I'll find something."

He did. A discarded, scarred-up sideboard table, which he hauled under the skylight and overturned, its legs up.

Patton looked down in confusion. "Tracy . . . are you sure you didn't land funny? Like on your head, maybe?"

"Sit tight, Pat. I'll get to you.

Patton watched, befuddled, as Tracy rolled a trash barrel into view, lifting the long table and sliding the barrel underneath, as a fulcrum. With one end of the table raised, and the other lowered by the weight of Tracy standing on it, an impromptu teeter-totter of sorts had been created.

"Tracy, have you cracked up?"

"No. But you're going to jump down."

"Jump down?"

Tracy pointed above him; he was directly under the second skylight. "That's the exit."

"Oh, no, Tracy . . . you can't be serious."

"Pat, how often do I pull rank on you?"

"All the time!"

"Well, then, jump, Detective!"

Tracy grabbed onto either side of his hat, pulling it down protectively over his skull.

Patton swallowed, licked his lips, took the deepest breath of his life, and leaped through the jagged-glass opening Tracy had made on his trip down. . . .

When Patton's feet hit the table, the teeter-totter swung up and catapulted Tracy through the glass of the second skylight, exploding him onto the roof. He landed on his side, and lay there stunned for a moment; but then he rose, shaking the wood fragments and slivers of glass off himself like a wet dog drying itself off.

He looked down through the hole he'd made and saw Patton sitting on the floor near the makeshift teeter-totter with his legs stretched out, like a kid playing jacks—glass fragments and wood pieces scattered about him.

"Are you okay, Pat?" he called down.

"I will be," Patton said, "after my rest cure."

"Sit tight," Tracy advised.

"I'll do that," Patton said.

But in fact Tracy's assistant was getting to his feet, and filling his hand with his gun, ready for whatever might come through that steel door.

Tracy, meanwhile, had moved to the edge of the roof, to lower himself to the fire escape, when he heard Brandon's familiar voice, amplified by a bullhorn: "All right, Big Boy! This is it!"

Big Boy knew he'd been had.

He'd been sitting at the crimson conference table with Johnny Ramm, several other bailed-out mob chieftains, and assorted bodyguards, when the phone call came in.

"It's for you, boss," Itchy had said.

"Who is it?"

"Says his name is the Blank."

Big Boy went to the phone and said, "You been paid, Blankie boy. You did good. Now, be a nice no-face and fade away."

The voice on the other end was hoarse and hollow as it laughed.

"What's so funny, Blank?"

"Look in your attic," the voice said.

"Boss," Flattop said. He was at the window. "There's some cars parked out front, in the yellow."

"Yeah, so?" Shrugging, he hung up.

"Five or six guys per vehicle. Sitting in parked cars. It's either a heist or a raid."

Big Boy went quickly to the window. "Let me see." He looked out and noted the trio of black sedans parked across the way, well-spaced out.

"Something wrong?" Ramm wanted to know.

Big Boy patted the air. "No, no. Fellas, enjoy yourselves. We'll all go down and hear Breathless sing real pretty in a few minutes. Meantime, I got to check something out."

He had taken Flattop up to the attic, where they'd discovered Tracy's girlfriend—who the papers said was missing, who Tracy was claiming had been kidnapped—trussed up like a virgin waiting to be sacrificed to some heathen god.

He knew at once the Blank had crossed him; set him up—stowed the kidnapped girl in Big Boy's own building and undoubtedly tipped off the police. And kidnapping was a capital crime in this state!

Then Tracy had come crashing down through the skylight, but they'd managed to lock the flatfoot in. Big Boy had turned to the Trueheart dame who he held in his arms; her eyes, above the slash of white over her mouth, were as wide as Big Boy's horizons weren't.

"You're comin' with me, baby," Big Boy said to her, removing the gag. "Anybody shoots me, they shoot you."

He hauled her down into the conference room; sat her down in a chair. The vast blood-red table was empty—Ramm and his two bodyguards and several more of Big Boy's own retinue, the accountant Numbers Norton included, had moved to the windows.

Ramm turned to Big Boy. "Plainclothes cops." He snorted, turned back to the window. "Who do they think they're fooling? Why do they bother with these pointless raids?"

"Johnny," Big Boy said carefully, "this isn't just another raid. I been framed on a kidnapping rap. See that frail over there? That's Tracy's missing girlfriend, who I just found tied up in my attic, thank you very much."

Every pair of eyes in every hoodlum face in the room fixed widely and whitely on Big Boy. Every hoodlum's mouth was dropped open, as if awaiting a dentist's drill.

"Tracy's out of stir," Big Boy said calmly, but it was the calm before the storm, "all stirred up, and he could be in this building right now, coming after us. The only thing keeping those cops outside from charging in is all my civilian guests downstairs in the club."

From outside came a booming voice: "All right, Big Boy! This is it!"

Big Boy peeked out the window and saw the Chief of Police and that plainclothes cop Catchem standing out in the street; Catchem had a tommy gun.

And just in back of them was a wall of squad cars behind which an army of heavily armed boys in blue were poised for action.

The other hoods took all this in as well.

Ramm's mouth was an ugly, sneering thing; he grabbed the front of Big Boy's tuxedo and wadded it with both hands. "You stupid greaseball! What have you done—"

But Big Boy's automatic was now in Ramm's stomach; the dapper gangster backed off slowly.

"Now," Big Boy said, giving everybody a good look at the gun in his hands, "we can lose our heads and fight amongst ourselves, or we can use what little advantage we got left in this situation."

Ramm's frown turned thoughtful. "You mean, go downstairs and take hostages?"

"No," Big Boy said. He pointed at the floor. "We go to our cars—right now. And make a fast getaway, before the cops make their move. They're not going to hit us till they figure out what to do about all those customers downstairs, *capeesh?* So we move. Now."

Ramm breathed in deeply. Nodded curtly.

The hoods went to the ammunition closet and began arming themselves with machine guns and shotguns.

"They've got *my* number," Big Boy told them. "But the rest of you guys got a chance."

Doucet was getting his gun out. "Let's make a break for it then," he said philosophically.

"You boys know where the garage is," Big Boy said, opening the door for them. "I'll be right there. Try not to let the patrons see your rods, or tip 'em to anything bein' wrong. Okay? Keep it calm, cool, and collected, girls."

Ramm was still seething. But he went along with the others as they quickly exited the conference room. Norton, the accountant, lingered.

"What about me, boss?"

Big Boy placed a hand on the smaller man's shoulder. "This is it, Numbers. Lock all the doors. Burn the records. Have the boys downstairs break out the guns."

Norton shook his head sadly and sighed. "Jeez, boss—Tracy's dame?" And Norton looked at Tess and shook his head again, as if witnessing the act of a stubbornly wayward child.

Then he went out.

While Tess watched with silent contempt, Big Boy crouched at his safe, unlocking it and removing packets of money. He stuffed as many of these into his pockets as he could manage. He had upwards of a cool half million on him. Enough to take an early retirement.

Then he took Tess roughly by the hand and pulled her to her feet. "Come on, baby," he said. "We gotta get outta this joint."

"You animal," she snarled, "let go of me!"

"Don't make me slap you, baby," he advised, raising a palm. "I hate hittin' dames."

Then he paused in the empty office, surveyed this throne room he was now reluctantly vacating.

"Look what your boyfriend done to me," he said to her, as if his feelings were hurt.

And he dragged her out of there.

Back down on the street, in front of the club, Tracy joined Chief Brandon and Sam Catchem behind a barricade of police cars. The club's neon merged with the cherry tops of the squad cars, tinting the night red.

"You've got the area cordoned off?" Tracy asked.

Brandon, bullhorn in hand, nodded. "No fish are getting out of this net. We were positioned two blocks away with those plainclothes men you requested staking out the place in unmarked cars. But once we heard those shots from the roof, I moved in with the uniformed troops."

"Wise," Tracy said, and filled Brandon in.

"Thank God, Tess is alive," the Chief said. Then the relief on his face was replaced with concern, even fear. "What if Caprice tries to bust out of there and brings Tess with him?"

"Big Boy's too smart for suicide," Tracy said. "My instinct is we've got to go in after him."

"Tracy's right, Chief," Catchem said, a tommy gun cradled in his arms. "The only way we'll get inside this joint is bust our way in."

"I don't know," Brandon said, troubled. "So many civilians in there . . . Tess included."

"The longer we wait," Tracy said, "the more danger the potential hostages are in."

Brandon's face flinched in thought. Then, suddenly, he spoke into the bullhorn: "Big Boy Caprice! You and your men, come out with your hands up! Everybody else— stay put! You're all under arrest. Remain calm!"

Catchem, wide-eyed, said to Tracy, "The Chief just arrested the whole nightclub."

"Not a bad idea," Tracy allowed. The detective nodded toward the club building. "Sam, you come with the Chief and me."

They were crossing the street to the front door when a car horn sounded within the garage over at their left; Tracy stopped momentarily and held up a cautionary hand, and then all hell broke loose.

The garage doors flew off their hinges as a car smashed through and tommy-gun fire ripped through the night, stitching bullet holes in the side of the nearest police car.

Tracy dove behind the front fender of the Chief's car, while the Chief and Catchem scurried behind the line of cars, joining the uniformed men there, whose hands were filled with revolvers and riot guns, but who were holding fire till Tracy, the Chief, and Sam got out of their way.

"Here they come, boys!" Tracy yelled over the bursts of gunfire.

No sooner had he taken cover than Tracy stepped back out into the line of fire, with his .38 thrust forward; he moved out into the street, like a western sheriff, aiming and firing, cool and methodical. One of his first shots punctured the speeding car's front tire. The vehicle swerved out of control and rolled over onto its left side and onto its hood and skidded across the pavement into the front of a warehouse across the street, which it hit like a metal fist, and exploded into flames.

The red night was truly an inferno now.

A second car rocketed out of the garage and Tracy rolled for cover again. From behind the left bumper of the Chief's squad car, Tracy unloaded on the speeding sedan as it swung around, a gunman with a tommy gun catching a bullet before he'd fired a single shot and dropping the gun reflexively; it fired a few rounds on its own, spinning, then fell silent. The car, meanwhile, found several of its tires blown by Tracy's well-placed rounds and fishtailed its way into a telephone pole, which it cracked like a toothpick, and then into a water hydrant, which geysered but was not close enough to the other burning car to put the fire out.

Tracy stood between flames that licked the sky and a fountain of water and fired his gun at the third fleeing car, which Itchy was driving, Flattop leaning out the window with a tommy gun, his cupid lips peeled back over babylike teeth, his normally hooded eyes round as silver dollars.

"I've got you now, Tracy!" Flattop screamed. "I've got you now!"

Then Tracy's gun was empty, and the pavement around him was getting chewed up; he dove out of the way, rolled, bumped against something.

The tommy gun that the one gunman had dropped.

Tracy filled his arms with it and, on his back in the street, arching up to aim, he let the tommy gun fly; the recoil was incredible.

So were the results.

Itchy caught several rounds, the car went out of control, veered into the Chief's car, sideswiping it; a badly wounded Itchy tried to back up and only crashed again, abutting and locking with the rear of one of the barricaded police cars. The car ground to a halt; stalled. Hunched behind the wheel, Itchy reached a hand back over his shoulder where he'd caught a bullet; it was as if he were trying to scratch a place he couldn't quite get at. Then he fell forward, on the horn, adding to the pandemonium even as he was subtracted from it.

"Give it up, Flattop!" Tracy yelled.

But Flattop climbed out, the tommy gun in his arms; his face was bruised, bloodied, dirty, his hair askew, making an odd contrast with his tux and white carnation.

"Where's Big Boy?" Tracy demanded, moving forward with the tommy gun in hand. "Where's Tess?"

Flattop responded by firing a wild volley.

Tracy ducked behind a front fender for cover, then stepped back out and let the tommy gun rip.

Flattop did a jerky dance as he took the slugs and began to shoot at the pavement; the weapon was like a jackhammer in the hands of a madman, the recoil of the tommy gun propelling him about. But when the ammo ran out, so did Flattop: he hit the pavement hard, spread out on his back like a kid making an angel in the snow. Only there was no snow, and Flattop was no angel, even in death.

"Tracy," Catchem said, rushing up beside him, tommy gun still in hand, a question mark of smoke curling out the barrel. "You all right?"

Lowering his own tommy gun, Tracy nodded curtly and surveyed the after-battle landscape. No sign of Tess or Big Boy among the cars that crashed out of the garage. The night was suddenly quiet. The crackle of flames and the gush of the hydrant were the only sounds.

Then he heard another sound; faint, but he heard it: a rumbling—metal on metal. Faint, but distinct. He knelt at the pavement, put his ear to it, like a frontier tracker.

"Tracy?" Catchem asked, looking curiously at his kneeling partner. "What are you . . . ?"

Tracy stood and stared at the pavement; he rubbed his chin.

Sirens split the silence; then came the voices of cops rounding up the surviving crooks. Soon paddy wagons, ambulances, and a fire truck or two would roll in. It was over.

But it wasn't.

– 28 –

Big Boy dragged Tess Trueheart through the showroom where the socially elite patrons of the Club Ritz cowered panic-stricken under tables and against walls. Outside, the squeal of tires and the tattoo of tommy-gun fire provided a muffled but distinct backdrop. Inside, an insectlike murmuring filled the air; but not a soul confronted Big Boy about the situation, perhaps because he was wild-eyed and had a revolver in one hand even as he dragged a bound-and-gagged woman across the shiny floor, as if in a parody of an Apache dance.

88 Keys, a cigarette insolently dangling, sat on his piano bench; he looked spiffy in his black dinner jacket with red carnation, and bored. As Big Boy passed, hauling Tess Trueheart, Keys played a brisk rendition of "Brother, Can You Spare a Dime," smirking to himself. Big Boy knew he was getting razzed, but he resisted the urge to blow the bum's smug face off.

He did take time, as he dragged the dame, to look sharply back at Keys.

"If you was in on this frame-up," Big Boy snarled at the pianist, whose fingers now had frozen over the keys, the sarcastic serenade halted, "you'd be better off practicin' a funeral march."

Keys swallowed and said nothing.

The muffled sound of gunfire continued outside; there were occasional sounds vaguely recognizable as screams. The customers clung to each other under their tables;

some of the women were sobbing. Most of the men were wanting to.

Watching with seeming dispassion as Big Boy and his pretty package moved in her direction, Breathless remained seated at the bar, ravishing in a silver gown, her lush legs crossed, her generous bosom dripping with diamonds.

"Cig me," she said to the bartender, who was crouching behind the counter.

Without moving, he said, "Cig yourself, honey."

Her beautiful mouth twitched with disgust.

An arm around the waist of the captive Tess, Big Boy was moving behind the bar, toward the wine-cellar door. He opened it, then paused to look back at Breathless. "You want to come along, baby?"

"Looks like you already have a girl."

"You change your mind, you know the way."

She laughed at him. "Bon voyage, tough guy," she told him, with quiet contempt.

Big Boy would have shot her, but he was too busy. He clomped down the cellar stairs, dragging Tess behind him. Yanking her by her bound hands, he led her through the rows of racked wine bottles. He moved to the far end of the low-ceilinged cellar and sat her down on a wine barrel, while he went to a wall covered by a wine rack, the bottles on which were secured and filled with nothing.

The wall was movable—a heavy cement door that yawned groaningly open onto darkness, but the cellar was well enough lit to reveal what lay beyond: a small flatbed railroad car on tracks in a low-ceilinged tunnel. Just inside the tunnel was the switch that turned on electric bulbs strung sporadically along its ceiling.

He hauled Tess into the tunnel, which was barely tall enough to stand in, and picked her up bodily and laid her on her stomach on the flatbed of the dolly. After putting the wine rack back in place as best he could, wedging several loose boards in front of the wall to keep the opening obstructed, he situated himself next to her, half on top of her. She smelled good.

Up to this point he'd said almost nothing to the woman; now, he turned to her and whispered almost tenderly, "You got nothin' to worry about. You just behave yourself. I never hurt a dame in my life."

That was a lie, of course, but what she didn't know wouldn't hurt her. Yet.

Big Boy released the brake and the dolly moved quickly down the incline of the tracks, but not too quickly; he'd only used the thing once before, on a practice run. Keeping this little getaway cart handy was one of the few smart moves Lips Manlis had ever made. The tunnel—which connected the nightclub with Manlis's warehouse and a riverfront loading point—had been useless since prohibition ended; it had even been blocked off from the rest of the city's underground railroad system.

But as a means of back-door escape, it was useful indeed. He would end up near the dock, near a waiting motor launch. From the river he could head to the lake, where he could go any number of places. A foghorn echoed down the tunnel, beckoning them. The sound made him smile; it was comforting, somehow.

As Caprice and his unwilling passenger coasted down the tracks—which were a pretty straight shot to the riverfront, only a matter of half a dozen or so city blocks—he felt calm again, confident again. His pockets stuffed with money, he was starting to feel like Big Boy once more.

But in the recesses of his mind he was beginning to wonder: Why did the Blank do this to him? Was the Blank in fact Frank Redrum, and had Redrum been planning all along to depose him and take over?

The overhead lights were spread out, so eerie shadows

were cast on the rounded, smoothed concrete walls of the tunnel. Now and then the foghorn called out to them from their destination. The rumble of the steel wheels on the tracks echoed down the gently snaking passageway. The woman wasn't making any noise at all; no sobbing, no moaning, no nothing. She had pride, this dame; moxie, too. It was a crying shame he had to ice her.

But once he was well away, she'd be excess baggage; and living evidence. It almost made him sad. *He* didn't kidnap her, after all! Well—he didn't kidnap her *first*. . . .

Now the tunnel moved through the basement of the Manlis warehouse; up ahead there was, finally, light at the end of the tunnel for Big Boy.

If not for Tess.

Tracy knelt at the pavement; the sound of metal on metal had faded, but he thought he might know what it was.

"Don't you think," Catchem said, confused by Tracy's behavior, "we ought get inside that joint?"

He stood. "Yes."

And the detective stormed into the Club Ritz, past patrons cowering under tables, and stopped before Breathless Mahoney, who sat regally at the bar, drinking a cocktail as casually as if at a country-club soirée.

"Where are they?" he said

"Who?" Breathless asked innocently. She didn't meet his eyes.

He heard something; not the metallic sound this time: something else. Something faint, something mellow, like a musical instrument.

"Where's the basement?" he demanded.

She nodded behind the bar. "Door leads down to the wine cellar." She pointed halfheartedly. "He took her through there."

Tracy just looked at her.

"What's wrong?" she asked with no apparent irony. "Don't you trust me?"

His eyes tightened as he heard the sound again: mellow but commanding.

He moved behind the bar, to the door, and hurtled down the steps, where he found himself in a shadowy dank cellar. Almost immediately he noticed a certain wall engulfed by a well-stocked wine rack. A wall that was slightly ajar . . .

He put both shoulders into it, but something on the other side was wedging it so that the wall simply would not budge.

And then, as he stood helplessly facing that wall, he heard the sound again, coming from behind it: a *foghorn*.

He ran up the stairs, past Breathless, without looking at her or giving her a single word; he burst out the entrance, where Catchem was cuffing a sullen 88 Keys.

"I'm going after Big Boy!" Tracy yelled as he ran. "He's got Tess, and I think I know where he's taken her. . . ."

And he sprinted down the street, toward the riverfront.

Catchem exchanged glances and shrugs with Chief Brandon; neither of them knew what to make of it.

Nor did the boy who had earlier hopped the Chief's spare tire and, unseen by anyone, witnessed the entire shoot-out. A boy who, still unseen, staying in the shadows, ran along after the man whose name he'd taken.

The tunnel ended at the riverbank, and Big Boy helped the doll off the dolly, and ushered her out of the viaductlike opening into the chill of the night. The foghorn welcomed them; the harbor lights winked on the surface of the river, but the fog was such that you couldn't see across to the other side.

While his own tux seemed none the worse for wear, the dame's red-and-black dress was dirty now, and ripped here and there; her reddish blond hair was mussed. But she was a good-looker. Nice shape on her. It was a pity, but once they were out on the lake, she'd have to be fish food.

He held her by the arm and she walked along with him, her head held high; he didn't have to drag her anymore.

"Gonna be fine, missy," he said, dragging her by the elbow toward the limestone stairs of the massive municipal drawbridge. On the other side of the bridge was the private dock where Big Boy, unknown to even his closest cronies, kept a getaway boat waiting. "Don't you worry. You'll be back with that square-jawed boyfriend of yours 'fore you know it."

"You may be right," Tess said with a tight, defiant smile, as he pulled her up the steps.

"*Let go of her, Big Boy!*"

Tracy's voice!

Big Boy, at the top of the stairs now, up on the pedestrian walkway of the bridge where he was leading Tess across, looked back and to his dismay saw the detective, in that stupid yellow topcoat, running down the embankment near the tunnel opening. His eyes bulged.

A brightly lit cruise ship was heading toward the bridge. The sound of gears meshing announced that the bridge was separating to allow the ship to pass.

The cement-and-steel leaves of the drawbridge were raising on Big Boy's one side, with Dick Tracy sprinting toward him below, and a cityful of cops waiting, back in the other direction. Cornered and then some, Big Boy glanced around desperately, looking for any alternative. Someplace to shoot from behind, if nothing else. A doorway in the nearby bridge tower beckoned.

"Come on, baby!" Big Boy growled, and yanked Tess toward that door, which God or the Devil or somebody had left unlocked for him.

Big Boy dragged Tess into what proved to be the gearhouse of the massive bridge; the gangster stood on the steel-grating floor and looked around at what resembled gigantic, monstrous watchworks all around him. Eyes darting about, he spotted a supply area, where a coil of rope waited.

He smiled.

He felt as at home here as Quasimodo in a bell tower.

"What are you doing?" Tess demanded, as he dragged her toward a huge spoke that lay horizontally as it revolved ever so slowly into its vertical twin.

"You play Sleeping Beauty," Big Boy said, and pushed her down on her back on the gigantic spoke. He began to tie her down with the thick hemp. "And I'll wait for your prince to come. . . ."

Tracy had known at once, when Big Boy sent all of his partners in crime bursting out that garage into the waiting armed arms of the entire city police force, that the cunning crime boss had only been providing a diversion for his own escape. And hearing the rumbling of metal wheels below the pavement, and the sound of the foghorn coming from behind the movable wall in the wine cellar had told Tracy just exactly how Big Boy was making that escape.

Tracy knew the underground train system connected the club with the warehouse and the riverbank. But he had to choose between those two places as the most likely one for Big Boy to head to. . . .

He targeted the riverbank, figuring Big Boy would consider that warehouse of his too likely to be crawling with cops in the aftermath of the assault on the club. But just the same, Tracy called by two-way as he ran, to have somebody cover the warehouse.

"Will do, Tracy," Patton's voice said.

Tracy was glad to find that Pat had made it safely out of the attic, but he didn't discuss the matter. He was too busy running. He was nearing the waterfront area now.

He moved past the dock to the rather steep incline of the riverbank. Fog hugged the river, and as Tracy moved down the slope, the pea soup was thick enough to partly obscure the nearby municipal drawbridge. Below him somewhere was the viaduct-type opening of the tunnel— the riverfront drop point where, in bootleg days, crates of liquor from Canada had been shifted from boats off the lake, to the river, through the tunnel to the Manlis warehouse and various speakeasies beyond.

Then, as he came down the embankment, he saw them! Big Boy escorting Tess out of the tunnel; the grotesque, hunched gangster, in his black tux with white carnation, looked like the headwaiter in Hades.

Gun in hand, Tracy sprinted down the slope; he called out to them— "Let go of her, Big Boy!"—as the slouchy gangster pulled Tess up the cement stairway. The lights of a ship of some kind were shooting through the fog toward the bridge.

Tracy could see the gangster looking around desperately; saw the evil gnome-king pull Tess into the tower of the bridge.

He kept running.

The wet riverbank slowed his steps, but he kept running, and then he was up the stone stairs, standing hesitantly by the door he'd seen Big Boy go in.

He knew that when he went through that door, odds were he'd be fired upon.

His hand settled on the knob. He turned it, pushed the door open, and could hear nothing but the inexorable grinding of giant gears. *I love you, Tess*, he thought, and he went in, slowly, sidestepping into darkness, for cover, putting his back to the cement wall, searching the room with his eyes.

The room was a large, dim, musty concrete chamber dominated by massive automated apparatus—gears, levers, giant wheels, interconnected like some meaningless mechanical puzzle. But the puzzle's meaning was actually quite clear: outside, the leaves of the drawbridge were raising to admit passage to that ship, and the gears were grinding, groaning, accordingly. The immense machinery extended well below the elaborate network of steel-grating catwalk that was the floor.

Then he saw her.

His breath caught in his throat.

Tied on her back on a giant spoke, roped down like an animal about to be slaughtered, hands and arms bound to her breast. The spoke was moving. Slowly, its great teeth were grinding together as the upright wheel meshed with the prone one.

Like the evil troll that he was, Big Boy peered up from behind machinery, near Tess, and called out, gloatingly.

"Drop the gun, copper," Big Boy said, "and maybe I'll let your sweetheart climb offa that merry-go-round."

"Don't do it, Dick!" Tess cried out. Her eyes were filled with as much anger as fear.

The spoke rotated a notch.

"Got yourself a feisty one, flatfoot," Big Boy said. "Pretty, too. But she ain't gonna be so pretty when that wheel turns her into toothpaste."

"Don't do it, Dick! Don't give up your gun!"

"Okay, Big Boy," Tracy said.

"Step into the light first. Let me see you."

"Don't, Dick! He'll shoot you!"

The spoke rotated a notch.

Tracy took a deep breath and stepped into the light; but the gun was still tight in his hand.

"You win, Big Boy," Tracy said, and threw his gun down.

But he threw it hard. Down past the machinery, down to the hard cement below the catwalk. When the gun hit cement, it fired spontaneously—just as Tracy figured it would. Only somebody who didn't really understand guns told you to *drop* 'em. . . .

As Tracy hoped, Big Boy didn't realize it was the detective's dropped gun going off, and thought he was being fired on from some new direction; the gangster turned and shot toward the sound, and the bullet whizzed and ricocheted, as Tracy—hoping these bouncing bullets wouldn't accidentally find Tess—dropped to his knees, and slipped back into the darkness.

The spoke rotated a notch.

On all fours Tracy crawled, weaving around through machinery, hands gripping the mesh of the catwalk, listening to Big Boy's heavy breathing. That was his compass.

He came up behind the gangster, but Big Boy sensed it or heard it or something, and pivoted, and Tracy drove a hard shoulder into the man's soft belly, sending him down to the steel-grating floor, Big Boy's own gun tumbling out of his hand, clattering on the steel but not, thankfully, firing on impact as Tracy's had, nor dropping down to the cement below.

They rolled on the wire-mesh floor, locked in each other's arms, like schoolboys wrestling at recess. Big Boy wound up on top, his girth pressed down on Tracy, his big hands closing around Tracy's throat. They were powerful hands and Tracy's world began to turn red; but before it could turn black, Tracy rocked Big Boy with a right to the jaw, and then rocked him again. On the third time Big Boy's eyes got cloudy and his fingers loosened and Tracy pushed him off, getting out from under him.

The spoke rotated a notch.

As Tracy got to his feet, wanting to get over to Tess, he realized the choking had taken its toll; he was dizzy, off-balance, and suddenly Big Boy was charging him like a bear. It knocked Tracy backward, hard, steel teeth digging into his back.

And now Tracy was between the giant spokes of moving gears, and Big Boy was on him, hands on Tracy's chest, pushing him, his head, his neck, into the path of the grinding gears.

Tracy slammed both his fists into both of Big Boy's ears, as if Big Boy's head were between cymbals he was clashing.

The gangster yowled in pain, fell forward on Tracy, almost shoving him into those hungry sprockets; but Tracy slipped out from under him and now Big Boy was face down, his neck on the gears, the cloth of his black tuxedo jacket caught there.

The gears were pulling Caprice in and the gangster was wriggling helplessly, like a fish on the deck of a boat, his screams finding their way above the grating of the gears.

For a moment that lasted a lifetime, Tracy stood, panting, looking at him.

Considering whether to just stand here and watch this

monster die. The monster responsible for Emil Trueheart's death. The monster who would kill Tess. Who had killed Manlis and Officer Moriarty and so very many others. A vicious beast with no respect for human life . . .

Tracy sighed, said, "Damnit," and yanked the big man out of the gears.

The spoke rotated a notch.

Big Boy paid the detective thanks by pushing Tracy aside, and scurrying for the gun he'd dropped; but Tracy threw a flying tackle into him, spilling him to the grating.

As the men stumbled to their feet, Tracy began hammering him with punches, and then put all his strength into a roundhouse right that staggered Big Boy to his toenails.

"I've had it," Big Boy said. He was out of breath; sweaty; dirty; bleeding from the ears, mouth, and nose. His tuxedo was grease-stained and torn.

He collapsed.

Tracy ran to Tess, began to untie her.

"Don't move, Tracy," a hoarse voice said.

Tracy froze. Tess looked up at him beseechingly.

The spoke turned another notch. Her head was only a few notches away from eternity. . . .

"Don't you move either, Big Boy. Don't even blink."

Tracy turned slowly.

On the catwalk with them now was a faceless figure. A faceless figure in a black floppy hat and a loose-fitting black topcoat. In a black-gloved hand was a .45 automatic.

While Tracy and Big Boy had struggled, the faceless one had slipped in, unnoticed by either of them.

"The Blank!" Big Boy was looking up from the crosshatch floor incredulously. "Who are you, anyway? *Redrum?*"

"No," Tracy said. "Redrum's dead."

"What . . . ?" Big Boy said. He was up on his hands.

The spoke rotated a notch.

"Let me untie the girl," Tracy said.

"No," the Blank said.

Big Boy struggled to his feet.

"I said, don't move, Big Boy!" The hoarse, theatrical voice echoed in the chamber. "And don't even *think* about trying for that gun. You'll never make it; too much lard."

"Who *are* you?" Big Boy demanded.

"Let me untie the girl," Tracy said tightly.

The Blank ignored him, speaking instead to Caprice: "I outsmarted you. All the crimes you've committed, and I brought you down with one you *didn't* commit. I knew you'd panic. . . ."

The spoke rotated a notch.

"Whoever you are," Big Boy said, "we can make a deal."

"No deal. I'm taking it all. With Big Boy Caprice and Dick Tracy *both* out of the way, I'll own this town."

Tracy said, "I'm untying her."

"Don't move!"

Tracy turned toward Tess and began untying her.

"I said, don't move!"

Tracy turned back and stepped toward the Blank. "I know what you've done. Give me the gun."

"Stay back! I'll shoot!"

"You won't," Tracy said, and moved toward the Blank.

Whose gun hand lowered momentarily, then raised again, until the .45 was trained on Tracy, a finger tightening on the trigger as the detective kept moving forward. . . .

Tracy didn't see where the boy came from, or how long he'd been there, or even how he got in; but that kid was there, all right, tackling the Blank from behind. The

Blank pitched forward, knocking against a guardrail, tossing the Kid off effortlessly, but losing the gun, too; the .45 fumbling from the gloved fingers, falling down past the grating to the cement with a *clunk*.

Tracy took the opportunity to run back to Tess, but Big Boy had taken his own opportunity, finally getting his hands on his own gun, and as the Blank began to rise, Big Boy fired two rounds into the figure, who flopped onto the grating again, faceless face up this time.

The spoke rotated a notch.

Big Boy whirled toward Tracy and Tess, but Tracy was already rushing him, and Big Boy seemed stunned that an unarmed man would so boldly charge a man with a gun; but that was exactly what Tracy did, and as Big Boy raised the gun to fire, Tracy fired a punch, a punch that rocked Big Boy back against the guardrail.

The gangster toppled over the side and into the center of the enormous, grinding impersonal gears, which caught him, pulled him in and possessed him and he screamed until they had crushed him like a walnut shell.

Tracy didn't see that happen: with the help of the Kid, he was yanking the ropes from Tess's feet and her hands, and pulling her free from the giant gear—which was a single tooth away from giving her the same fate as Big Boy.

"Big Boy thought he was a big wheel," the Kid said, "but compared to them things, I guess he *wasn't* so big." The boy was looking down past the guardrail into the machinery.

Tracy took Tess in his arms; she looked at him out of a dirt-smudged face devoid of makeup, her hair a tangle, her features twisted with countless emotions, and he'd never seen anyone or anything more beautiful in his life.

"I knew you'd come for me," she said.

"Don't ever leave me, Tess," he said.

"Never. Never . . ."

They kissed and the Kid took it in with eyes bigger than the mammoth gears.

With a tight smile, Tracy pressed Tess's hand, then gestured for her to stay put as he moved quickly to where the Blank lay dead, or dying, on the catwalk.

"Still alive," Tracy said, touching the pulse in the white neck. "Tess, my two-way got smashed up in the struggle. Go call for an ambulance, will you? See if you can find a beat cop. . . ."

Tess stared at Tracy for a long moment, then—with the boy in tow—hurried out of the gearhouse, into the night.

"It was an audacious plan," Tracy said, still kneeling over the slumped, bleeding form. "A plan you damn near pulled off. The city would have had a new ruler. . . ."

Tracy stayed with the troubled, misguided soul who had been the Blank—criminal or not, the Blank had spared Tracy's life more than once—waiting for the ambulance; but death came first.

The gears ground to a stop. Silence cloaked the musty chamber. The detective slowly rose. He looked down at the lifeless form with something not unlike sympathy.

Then his eyes hardened, and the gearhouse was just a place where an innocent woman had been saved from an unjust fate, and two criminals had met their due destiny.

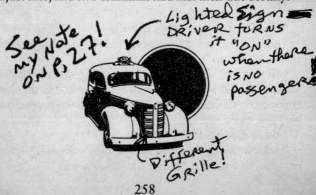

See my Note on P. 27!

Lighted Sign — DRIVER tURNs it "ON" when there is NO passengers

Different GRille!

— 30 —

Tracy, Tess, and the Kid shared one side of a booth at Mike's Diner. The proprietor plopped down bowls of chili in front of each of them.

"Doesn't taste as good as usual, Mike," Tracy told the counterman. "What'd you do—wash the bowls?" *EEK! HUMOUR??*

"Aw," Tess said, sampling hers, "don't listen to him, Mike. I think it's just marvelous."

"Except for the guy she goes out with," Mike said, "this lady has real taste." *WHAMMO!*

"Well, this stuff sure beats anything I ever ate in a hobo camp," the Kid told Mike, as if if paying him the supreme compliment of all time.

"Thanks a million, kid," Mike said, and smiled and shook his head as he headed back behind the counter. "Let me know when you're ready for your ice cream."

"Say, Mike," Tracy said, "you got to stop calling my friend here 'Kid.' It's not his name."

"It isn't?" the Kid asked.

"No, Junior, it isn't," Tracy said.

The Kid smirked. "Yeah, well 'Junior' isn't my name, either, ya know."

"Sure it is," Tracy said, and he withdrew a folded paper from his inside coat pocket; he unfolded the official-looking document. "I signed this, and some other papers this morning."

"What are they?"

"Adoption papers, son. I'm your old man now." Tracy returned to his chili. "Hope you don't mind."

ZANGO!!

The Kid studied the document; where is said "Name" were the words DICK TRACY, JUNIOR.

"Gosh," Junior said, looking at the piece of paper. "You mean, I'm gonna live with you, full-time? The orphanage is yesterday's news?"

"Last *year's* news," Tracy said. He smiled at the boy. "It's like I told you—you're on my team now."

The boy's chest swelled. "I'm gonna be the greatest detective who ever lived!"

"Well, then, you may be so smart you won't need this," Tracy said, "but here's a little present, anyway."

The detective took a small box from his pocket and handed it to the boy, who opened it and found a little two-way wrist radio.

"Wow! Does it really work?"

"Wait till my next call comes in and see."

"Mr. Tracy, I don't know what to say."

"Lose the 'Mister.' Make it 'Tracy.'"

"Well, uh . . . what about 'Dad' or 'Pop' or somethin'?"

"Those are fine, too."

"I guess I got everything a kid could ever want," Junior said, sighing, smiling, reflecting. "Except maybe a mother . . ."

Tracy and Tess traded significant glances. Then Tracy studied his chili. "Tess . . . I've been thinking."

"Yeah?" she said sassily. She dipped her spoon into her bowl. "What about?"

"Well . . . about you living alone."

She shrugged. "We both live alone. We have that in common."

Tracy cleared his throat; he searched for the words, but they were like clues eluding him. "Well, when two people have a lot in common, they ought to do something about it."

"Yes . . . ?"

"Well, I was thinking that you and I could . . . well, what do you think?"

She looked him right in the eye. "Dick Tracy, are you asking me to . . ."

"Do it," Junior said, and elbowed him. "Go on and give it to her."

Tracy smiled one-sidedly. "Maybe this isn't the right moment."

"What?" Tess asked.

"Aw, go on," Junior said. "Don't be a dumb dick."

Tracy laughed and fished the small jewelry box out of his suitcoat pocket—the same pocket where he kept his handcuffs. He hoped the contents of the box would be at least that binding.

"It isn't very big," Tracy said, "and it's taken a bite out of our nest egg, but . . ."

He handed her the box over Junior's mostly empty bowl.

She took it, opened it and the small diamond winked at her from its little velvet bed. She slid the ring on her finger and admired the view.

"Dick Tracy," she said, "that's the most beautiful diamond ring I ever saw."

"It looks better under this," he said, and offered her a big Sherlock Holmes-style magnifying glass.

She began to laugh, and so did Tracy, and so did Junior.

Then the boy got out of the way while the detective and the beautiful girl kissed; then the detective ruffled the boy's hair, and the beautiful girl hugged them both, and they all three ate ice cream, and lived happily ever after.

Except, of course, for the times when the detective's two-way wrist radio interrupted and sent him off on some wild adventure.

Which was when Dick Tracy was at his happiest anyway.

261

ABOUT THE AUTHOR

MAX ALLAN COLLINS has written the internationally syndicated comic strip DICK TRACY since its creator, the late Chester Gould, retired in 1977.

He is the author of some thirty novels in the suspense field, including three contemporary mystery series—Nolan, Quarry and Mallory (a thief, hitman, and mystery writer, respectively); and has written several historical thrillers about Eliot Ness, upon whom Tracy was partially patterned.

His acclaimed historical novel *True Detective*, introducing Chicago P.I. Nate Heller, won the Private Eye Writers of America "Shamus" award for best novel of 1983; its sequels *True Crime*, *The Million-Dollar Wound*, and *Neon Mirage* were also Shamus-nominated. A fifth Heller, *The Child on Scharter Street*, exploring the Lindbergh kidnap case, is due soon from Bantam Books.

Collins is also (with artist Terry Beatty) co-creator of the comics features "Ms. Tree" and "Wild Dog," and has scripted the "Batman" comic book and newspaper strip. He has coauthored critical studies on Mickey Spillane (with James Traylor) and TV detectives (with John Javna). A rock musician since the midsixties, he is currently performing and recording with two bands, "Crusin'" and "Seduction of the Innocent."

He lives in Muscatine, Iowa, with his wife Barbara and their seven-year-old son Nathan.